DESCENDANT

DESCENDANT

Graham Masterton

This first world edition published in Great Britain 2006 by
SEVERN HOUSE PUBLISHERS LTD of
9–15 High Street, Sutton, Surrey SM1 1DF.
This first world edition published in the USA 2006 by
SEVERN HOUSE PUBLISHERS INC of
595 Madison Avenue, New York, N.Y. 10022.

British Library Cataloguing in Publication Data

Masterton, Graham
    Descendant
    1.   Vampires - Fiction
    2.   Horror tales
    I.   Title
    823.9'14 [F]

ISBN-13: 978-0-7278-6380-5 (cased)
ISBN-10: 0-7278-6380-0   (cased)
ISBN-13: 978-0-7278-9171-6 (paper)
ISBN-10: 0-7278-9171-5   (paper)

Except where actual historical events and characters are being
described for the storyline of this novel, all situations in this
publication are fictitious and any resemblance to living persons
is purely coincidental.

All Severn House titles are printed on acid-free paper.

Typeset by Palimpsest Book Production Ltd.,
Polmont, Stirlingshire, Scotland.
Printed and bound in Great Britain by
MPG Books Ltd., Bodmin, Cornwall.

Diana

It was a sweltering Thursday afternoon and I was caught in the usual southbound traffic jam on the Kennedy Bridge when WRKA played 'Diana', and I felt as if my entire skin-surface was shrinking.

'Diana', by Paul Anka. That song has haunted me for the past fifty years, and I guess it always will. Whenever I hear it, I can't stop myself from turning my head around, just to make sure that I'm not being followed, or that somebody isn't watching me from some shadowy doorway on the opposite side of the street.

'*I'm so young and you're so old.*' It brings everything back. The glassy heat of the South London suburbs in the middle of summer, the large 1930s houses with their red-tiled roofs and their tennis courts, the flat sweet smell of British pubs, the shabby clothes and the tiny little cars.

And those things that ran through the streets, dark and voracious and utterly cruel. Clinging to ceilings, rushing up walls. You think that you know what it's like to be frightened? You don't have any idea.

When I finally arrived back home in Kenwood Hill, I closed the front door and stood for a long time with my back pressed against it, and my heart was beating like a jack-hammer. Two semicircles of crimson light shone on the wall from the stained-glass window at the top of the stairs, like blood-shot eyes. It was then that I thought, dammit, whatever the government might do to me, it's high time that you knew the truth. That's why I'm going to tell you what really happened during that summer of August 1957, and what hideous carnage we had to face. I'm going to tell you what happened afterward, too, and for me that was even more of a nightmare. All I did was put off the evil day. Sooner or

1

later, the decision that I could never bring myself to make is going to be yours.

I was officially warned never to talk about it. Two days after I was relocated to Louisville, a pimply young man came round to my house in a shiny grey suit and warned me not to say anything, ever, not even to my wife Louise. Even after all these years, I guess the government could still have me arrested for breaching national security, or lock me up in a nuthouse, but they can't terrify me the way that I've been terrified every single day for the past fifty years.

Because vampires never, ever forgive you for anything.

Antwerp, 1944

Captain Kosherick led me up the uncarpeted stairs of this narrow, unlit building on Markgravestraat, in the north-west part of the city. Two small children with grubby faces were standing in a doorway on the second landing, a girl and a boy, and Captain Kosherick said to them, 'You're going to be OK, you understand? We're going to arrange for some-body to take care of you.'

Behind them, in the gloom of her sitting room, an old woman was sitting in a sagging brocade armchair. Underneath her black lace widow's cap, her hair was white and wild, and her face looked like a shrivelled cooking apple.

'Somebody from the children's services will be calling around later!' Captain Kosherick shouted at her. Then he turned to me and said, 'Deaf as a fucking doorpost.'

'*Mevrouw!*' I called out. '*Iemand zal binnenkort de kinderen komen halen!*'

The woman flapped her hand dismissively. '*Hoe vroeger hoe beter! Deze familie is verloekt! Niet verbazend dat hij de mensen van de nacht heft gestuurd om het mee te brengen!*'

'What did she say?' asked Captain Kosherick.

'Something about the family being cursed.'

'Well, I think she was right on the money about that. Come take a look for yourself.'

He led me along the corridor and up another flight of stairs. I could smell boiled cabbage and another smell much stronger and more distinctive: the smell of blood. Although it was mid-October, it was unseasonably warm; the stairwell was alive with glittering green blowflies.

At the top of the stairs there was a much smaller landing, and then a door with two frosted-glass panels in it. The door was half ajar and even before we opened it I could see a woman's leg lying on the floor with a worn-out brown brogue lying close by.

Captain Kosherick pushed the door wide so that I could take in a full view of the room. It was a one-room apartment, with a large iron-framed bed in one corner, a fraying beige couch and a wooden wheel-back chair. There was a small high window over the sink, which had a view of a light grey sky and the dark thirteenth-century spires of the Vrouwekathedrall. Beside the sink there was a small home-made shelf with a red-and-white packet of tea, a blue pottery flour jar, a glass dish with a tiny square of butter in it and three potatoes that were already starting to sprout.

A picture of the Virgin Mary hung on the wall beside the shelf. Both of her eyes had been burned out with lighted cigarettes.

I looked down at the young woman lying face-down on the streaky green linoleum. She must have been twenty-seven or twenty-eight, with wavy brown hair which she had obviously tried to colour with henna. She was wearing nothing except a reddish wool skirt which had been dragged halfway down her thighs. Her skin was very white and dotted with moles.

There were spots and sprays of blood all around her, and several footprints, some whole and some partial, including some smaller bare footprints which must have been those of her children. But considering what had been done to her, there was remarkably little blood.

'Want me to turn her over for you?' asked Captain Kosherick.

I nodded. I was sweating, and the air was clogged with the brown stench of blood, but I had to make sure.

3

Captain Kosherick hunkered down beside the young woman and gently rolled her on to her back. She was quite pretty, in a puffy Flemish way, with bright blue eyes. Her breasts were small, with pale nipples. She had been split wide open with some very sharp implement from her breastbone to her navel. Her heart had been forcibly pulled out from under her ribcage and her aorta cut about three inches from her left ventricle. It looked like a pale, saggy hosepipe.

'You seen this kind of thing before?' said Captain Kosherick. 'The MPs told me to call you in as soon as they found her.'

I lifted my khaki canvas bag off my shoulder, unbuckled it, and took out my Kodak. I took about fifteen or sixteen pictures from different angles, while Captain Kosherick went out on to the landing for a smoke.

After I had finished taking pictures I searched the young woman's room.

Captain Kosherick came back in again. 'What are you looking for, if you don't mind my asking?'

'Oh, you know. Evidence.'

He was very young, even though he had a streak of grey hair and a bristly little moustache. But I guess we were all very young in those days, even me.

I lifted up the thin threadbare mat beside the bed. There were signs that one of the floorboards had been lifted, so I went to the sink and took out a knife to pry them up. Underneath, in the floor space, I found a rusty can of cooked ham, two cans of Altmecklenburg sausages, three cans of condensed milk, a box of cocoa powder and a box of powdered eggs, as well as three packs of Jasmatzi cigarettes.

'Quite a hoard,' said Captain Kosherick, peering over my shoulder. 'All German, too. Where do you suppose she got these from? Fraternizing with the enemy?'

'Something like that.'

'So somebody found from the resistance found out and they punished her?'

'That's one possibility.'

'Listen . . . I know this is all supposed to be top secret and like that, but who do you think might have done this?'

I looked down at the young woman lying on the floor. A blowfly was jerkily walking across her slightly parted lips.

'Oh, I know who did it. What I don't know yet is why.'

4

The Night People

I went downstairs again and knocked on the old widow's door. The two children were kneeling on the window seat looking down at the street below. A ray of sunlight was shining through the boy's ears, so that they glowed scarlet.

The old widow lifted her head to see me through the lower half of her bifocals, and made a kind of silent snarl as she did so.

'Did you see anything?' I asked her, in Flemish.

'No. But I heard it. Bumping, and loud talking, and footsteps. They were Germans.'

'The Germans aren't here any more. The Germans have been driven back to the other side of the Albert Canal.'

'These were Germans. No question.'

I looked at the children. I guessed that the girl was about six and the boy wasn't much older than four. In those days, though, European children were much smaller and thinner than American children, after years of rationing.

'Do you think they saw anything?'

'I pray to God that they didn't. It was three o'clock in the morning and it was very dark.'

'You want a cigarette?' I asked her.

She sniffed and nodded. I shook out a Camel for her, and lit it. She breathed in so deeply that I thought that she was never going to breathe out again. While I waited, I lit a cigarette for myself, too.

'You mentioned the night people,' I told her. *Mensen van de nacht*. I hadn't told Captain Kosherick about that.

'That's what they were, weren't they? You know that. That's why you're here.'

I blew out smoke and pointed to the ceiling. 'What was her name? Had she been living here long?'

'Ann. Ann De Wouters. She came here last April, I think

5

it was. She was very quiet, and her children were very quiet, too. But I saw her once talking to Leo Coopman and I know they weren't discussing the price of sausages.'

'Leo Coopman?'

'From the White Brigade.'

The White Brigade were the Belgian resistance. Even now they were helping the British and the Canadians to keep their hold on the Antwerp docks. Antwerp was a weird place in the fall of '44. The whole city was filled with liberation fever, almost a hysteria, even though the Germans were still occupying many of the northern suburbs. Some Belgians were even cycling from the Allied part of the city into the German part of the city to go to work, and then cycling back again in the evening.

I gave the old woman my last five cigarettes. 'Do you mind if I talk to the children?'

'Do what you like. You can't make things any worse for them than they already are.'

I went over to the window seat. The boy was peering down at three Canadian Jeeps in the street below, while the girl was picking the thread from one of the old brown seat cushions. The boy glanced at me, but said nothing, while the girl didn't look up at all.

'What's your name?' I asked the girl. My cigarette smoke drifted across the window and the boy furiously waved it away.

'Agnes,' the girl told me, in a whisper.

'And your brother?'

'Martin.'

'Mrs Toeput says that Mommy was sick so she's gone to Hummel,' Martin announced, brightly. The Flemish word for 'heaven' is 'hemel' so he must have misunderstood what the old woman had told him. The girl looked up at me then, and the appeal in her eyes was almost physically painful. He doesn't know his mommy's been killed. Don't tell him, please.

'Our uncle Pieter lives in Hummel,' she whispered.

I nodded, and turned my head so that I wouldn't blow smoke in her face.

'Did you see anything?' I asked her.

She shook her head. 'It was dark. But they came into the

6

room and pulled Mommy out of bed. I heard her say, "Please don't – what's going to happen to my children?" Then I heard lots of horrible noises and Mommy was kicking on the floor.'

Her eyes filled up with tears. 'I was too frightened to help her.'

'It's good for you that you didn't try. They would have done the same to you. How many of them were there?'

'I think three.'

Three. That would figure. They always came in threes.

The little girl wiped her eyes with the sleeve of her frayed red cardigan. 'I saw something shining. It was like a necklace thing.'

'A necklace?'

'Like a cross only it wasn't a cross.'

'Those are the *good* men,' interrupted the little boy, pointing down at the Canadians. 'They came and chased all the Germans away.'

'You're right, hombre,' I told him. Then I turned back to the little girl and said, 'This cross thing. Do you think you could draw it?'

She thought for a moment and then she nodded. I took a pencil out of my jacket pocket and handed her my notebook. Very carefully, she drew a symbol that looked like a wheel with four spokes. She gave it back to me with a very serious look on her face. 'It was shining, like silver.'

I gave her a roll of fruit-flavoured Life Savers, and touched the top of her dry, unwashed hair. Not much compensation for losing her mother, but there was nothing else I could offer her. I still think about them, even now, those two little children, and wonder what happened to them. They'd be in their sixties now.

The old widow said, 'You see? I was right, wasn't I? It was the night people.'

I didn't say anything. I wasn't allowed to tell anybody what my specific duties were, not even my fellow officers in the 101 Counterintelligence Detachment.

Captain Kosherick came back in. 'You done here?' he asked me. 'I got two corpsmen downstairs ready to take the body away.'

The little boy frowned at him. You don't know how glad I was that he couldn't understand English.

Frank Takes A Drink

Frank was sitting on the cobbles when I came out of the house, his purple tongue lolling out of the side of his mouth. Frank was a four-year-old black-and-tan bloodhound who had been specially trained for me in Tangipahoa parish, Louisiana, by the man-trailing expert Roger Du Croix. Actually Frank's saddle spread so far over his body that he was almost entirely black, but Roger had explained to me that he was still officially a black-and-tan.

In Belgium, they called him a 'St Hubert hound', after the monk who had first trained bloodhounds in the seventh century, the patron saint of hunters. Frank's real name was Pride of Ponchatoula but I had re-christened him in honour of Frank Sinatra, who happened to be my hero at the time. When I walked along De Keyserlei, with my greatcoat collar turned up, I liked to think that I looked as cool and edgy as Frank Sinatra did.

'How's it going, Frank?' I asked him. 'Hope you've been conducting yourself with decorum.'

Frank was a pretty obedient dog but now and again he had a fit of the loonies, which Roger Du Croix said was brought on by him picking up the smell of dead rats.

Corporal Little said, 'He's been fine, sir. I fed him those marrowbones and then he took a dump around the corner.'

'Well, thanks so much for the update,' I said. 'Listen – we'll be going out tonight, soon as it gets dark.'

Corporal Little looked up at the flat, narrow front of No. 5 Markgravestraat and said, 'Screechers?'

'No question about it. They split her open like a herring.'

'Holy Christ. Did you find out who she was?'

'Ann De Wouters, aged twenty-eight or thereabouts. I don't know why they specifically came looking for *her*, but her landlady seemed to think that she might have had some connec-

8

tion to the White Brigade. Could have been a revenge killing, who knows? Maybe they were just thirsty.'

Corporal Little looked around, his eyes narrowed against the bright grey October light. 'Think they've gotten far?'

'I don't think so. By the time they finished with her it must have been nearly daylight, and this whole area was heaving with Canucks by oh-four-thirty. My guess is that they've gone to ground someplace close by.'

Corporal Little reached down and tugged Frank's ears. 'Hear that, boy? We're going to go Screecher-hunting!'

Corporal Henry Little was an amiable, wide-shouldered young man with a red crew cut and a face covered in mustard-coloured freckles. He had a snub nose and bright blue eyes that looked permanently surprised, although I had never yet known him to be surprised by anything. Even when it was first explained to him what his duties would be, he did nothing but nod and say, 'OK, sure,' as if hunting vampires through the shattered cities of France and Belgium was no more unusual than chasing rabbits through the underbrush. Corporal Little's family had bred pedigree tracking dogs in Oak Ridge, Tennessee, which was why the detachment had enlisted him to help me. If Bloodhoundese had been a language, Corporal Little would have been word-perfect. Frank had only to lift up his head and stare at Corporal Little with those mournful, hung-over eyes, and Corporal Little would know exactly what he wanted. 'Cookie, Frank?' Frank had a thing for *speculoos*, those ginger-and-spice cookies they bake in Belgium, preferably dipped into Corporal Little's coffee to make them soft.

We climbed into my Jeep and Corporal Little drove us back through the narrow sewage-smelling streets, jolting over the cobbles until I felt that my teeth were going to shatter. We passed a dead horse lying on the sidewalk. A German shell had landed in the square two days ago and torn open a big triangular flap in its stomach, so a passer-by had killed it with a hammer.

Somewhere off to the north-west, from the direction of the Walcheren peninsula, I could hear artillery fire, like somebody banging encyclopaedias shut.

We turned into Keizerstraat and stopped outside De Witte Lelie Hotel. It was a small, old-style building with a sixteenth-century facade. The lobby had oak-panelled walls and a brown marble floor and it was milling with officers from the British 11th Armoured Division, as well as an argumentative crowd of Belgian politicians, waving their arms and pushing each other and shouting in French. The British officers looked too tired to care. One of them was sleeping in an armchair with his mouth wide open.

I went to the desk where the deputy manager was trying to rub soup from the front of his shirt with spit.

'I need to talk to Leo Coopman.'

He stopped rubbing his shirt and looked at me with bulging brown eyes.

'It's important,' I said. 'I need to talk to him about Ann De Wouters. Do you think you can get in touch with him?'

The deputy manager pulled a face that could have meant 'yes' or 'possibly' or 'why on earth are you asking me?'

'I'll be in my room until eight,' I told him. I tapped my wristwatch and said, '*Acht uur*, understand?'

Corporal Little and I went up in the rickety elevator to the fourth floor. Frank sat staring up at us and panting.

'Ann De Wouter's children were in the room when they killed her,' I said. 'Lucky for the boy he didn't wake up, but the girl did.' I could see myself in the mirror. I hadn't realized I looked so haggard. My hair was greasy and flopping over my forehead, and the mottled glass made it appear as if I had some kind of skin disease.

'She give you any idea what they looked like?'

'No. Too dark. But she was pretty sure that there were three of them, and she saw that one of them was wearing the wheel.'

We walked along the long blue-carpeted corridor until we reached 413. Considering there was a war on, my room was surprisingly sumptuous, with a huge four-poster bed covered in a gold-and-cream bedspread, and gilded armchairs upholstered to match. On the walls hung several sombre landscapes of Ghent and Louvain, with clouds and canals. A pair of grey riding britches hung from the hook on the back of the door, with dangling suspenders still attached. These had belonged to the German officer who had occupied this room only days before we had arrived. Corporal Little unclipped Frank's leash

10

and let him trot into the bathroom to lap water out of the toilet.

I went to the windows and closed them. The maid had opened them every morning since we had arrived here last week, even though there was no heat. I opened a fresh pack of cigarettes, lit one, and blew smoke out of my nose. Then I unfolded my street map of Antwerp and spread it out over the glass-topped table.

'Here's Markgravestraat, where Ann De Wouters was killed, and this is the way the Canadian division was coming in, so it's pretty unlikely that the Screechers would have tried to escape along Martenstraat. I reckon they left the building by the back entrance, which would have taken them out *here*, onto Kipdorp. That means they had only two options. Either turn left, and head north-west toward the Scheldt; or turn right, and make their way across Kipdorpbrug toward the Centraal Station.'

Corporal Little studied the map carefully. 'I don't reckon they would have headed for the river, sir. Where would they go from there?'

I agreed with him. They couldn't have escaped north because the Germans had blown all the bridges over the Albert Canal. Besides, the Brits were holding the waterfront area and most of the Brits were untrained conscripts – waiters and bank clerks and greengrocers – and they were even more trigger-happy than the Poles. They would let loose a wild fusillade of poorly aimed rifle-fire and then shout ''Oo goes there?' afterward.

I circled a five-block area with my pencil. 'We'll start in this streets around Kipdorp and work our way eastward along Sant Jacobs Markt.'

Corporal Little massaged the back of his prickly neck. 'That's going to be one hell of a job, sir, with respect. Think of all them hundreds of cellars they could be lying low in. Think of all of them hundreds of attics, and all of them hundreds of closets and linen chests and steamer-trunks. It could easy take us *days* before Frank picks up a sniff of them, and by that time they could be halfway back to wherever they're headed.'

'We'll find them, Henry, I promise you. I have a hunch about these particular Screechers.'

'With respect, sir, you had a hunch about those Screechers

in Rouen; and you had another hunch about those Screechers in Brionne.'

'I know. But those Screechers we caught in France, they were like cornered rats, weren't they? They were running and hiding and it took everything we could do to catch up with them.'

'Well, sure. But what makes these guys any different?'

'Think about it. They must have been keeping themselves holed up someplace in the city centre for the past five weeks. Either that, or they've had the brass cojones to make their way back in. They wanted to have their revenge on Ann De Wouters, and they obviously didn't care what chances they took. They were German-speaking, right? But they walked through a city crowded with British and Canadian troops, and they cut a woman open in front of her children, and they stayed there long enough to drink ninety per cent of her blood.'

Corporal Little looked impressed but still slightly mystified. 'So what does this specifically lead you to conclude, sir?'

'Don't you get it, Henry? *They're not scared of us.* They're not frightened to come out in the open. That's why I think that we'll find them. The only trouble is, when we *do* find them, they're not going to go down without one hell of a fight.'

Corporal Little gave me a smile of growing understanding. 'In that case, sir – we'd better double the watch on our rear ends, wouldn't you say?'

'Go get the kit, will you?' I told him. Most of the time I couldn't work out if he was a genius or an idiot savant.

The Kit

The Kit was contained in a khaki tin box about the size of a briefcase. It was scratched and dented, but then we had been carrying it with us ever since we had landed in Normandy in June, and we had used it five times since then.

Corporal Little opened it up and together we inspected the contents. A large Bible, with a polished cover carved out of ash-wood and a silver crucifix mounted on the front. A large glass flask of holy oil, from St Basil's Romanian Orthodox church in New York. A pair of silver thumbscrews and a pair of silver toescrews. A silver compass, about five inches across, with a base that was filled with the dried petals of wild roses. A thirty-foot whip made of braided silver wire. A surgical saw. A small silver pot filled with black mustard seeds. Two small pots of paint, one white and one black.

I lifted out a roll of greasy chamois leather and unwrapped it. Inside were three iron nails, about nine inches long. They were black and corroded and each had been fashioned by hand. I had no proof that they were genuine, but if the price that the detachment had paid for them was anything to go by, they should have been. These were supposed to be the nails that had been pulled out of Christ's wrists and ankles when he was taken down from the cross.

At the bottom of the tin box there was a circular mirror, made of highly polished silver, a large pair of dental forceps and a sculptor's mallet. Hunting Screechers was always a combination of science, religion, common sense and magic, so you needed the apparatus that went with each. You also needed a willingness to believe that a human being can defy gravity.

'Running kind of low on garlic,' said Corporal Little, lifting up a bunch of papery-covered cloves. Frank came sniffing around, his pendulous jowls swaying. 'See?' said Corporal Little. 'Frank knows that we're going out tonight, don't you, boy?'

Frank gave one of those barks that can deafen you in one ear.

An Oblique Conversation

Just after six o'clock the deputy manager rang up to my room to say that Leo Coopman had been 'unavoidably detained' on the north-east side of the city. However somebody in the lobby called Paul Hankar would be privileged to talk to me. I went down in the elevator alone and met him in the small dark bar at the back of the hotel.

Paul Hankar was a short, thickset man with a lumpy face like one of the peasants in a Brueghel painting, and rimless spectacles. He was wearing a black roll-neck sweater and a black suit with shiny elbows. I would have guessed that he was a schoolmaster in another life.

He stood up and shook hands. '*Aangename kennismaking*, Colonel. Pleased to meet you.'

'Actually it's captain. Captain James Falcon Junior, 101 Counterintelligence Detachment.'

We sat down and I offered him a cigarette. He took one and tapped it on his thumbnail. 'I heard you were looking for some special information,' he said. His English was flat but barely accented.

'You think you can help me?' I asked him.

'It's something we've been trying to keep quiet. Mainly because we didn't want the Germans to know that we knew. And because we didn't want to cause any panic. And because we didn't want to look like fools, in case we were wrong.'

'Do you know a young woman called Ann De Wouters? She rents an apartment on Markgravestraat.'

Paul Hankar looked at me acutely. 'I know the name, yes.'

'You can't do her any harm by telling me about her. She was murdered last night.'

He flinched, as if I had reached across the table and tried to slap his cheek. But then he recovered himself and said, 'I'm very shocked to hear that.'

'Her landlady said it was *mensen van de nacht*. Do you have any idea what she was talking about?'

A young boy in a long white apron came over to us and asked us what we wanted to drink. 'What do you have?' asked Paul Hankar.

'Apple schnapps.'

'Anything else?'

The boy shook his head.

'In that case, we'll have two apple schnapps.'

'One schnapps, one lemonade,' I corrected him. 'I need to keep a clear head tonight, and I know what that goddamned schnapps is like. My corporal calls it "nuts-water".'

Paul Hankar lit his cigarette and I noticed that his hand was

14

trembling. '*Mensen van de nacht?*' he said, wryly. 'That's one explanation, if you believe in such things.'

'But you don't?'

'I keep an open mind, Captain.'

'So tell me what's been happening.'

He coughed and wiped his mouth with a paper napkin. 'It started in August last year. We were having many successes against the Germans. We had infiltrated many of their administrative offices and also the power company and the water company. In July we were able to sink five barges on the Albert Canal which took them weeks to clear away.

'But then everything seemed to turn around. The Germans began to raid our hiding places and arrest our people by the dozen. Every time we planned to sabotage the docks, they would catch us before we had the chance to plant any explosives. They found our weapons and our wireless sets and our safe houses. It became clear to us that some of our own people must be betraying us.'

I didn't say anything. Behind him, there was an oval window with crimson glass in it, and the branch of a tree was tapping against it as if some beggar were trying to catch our attention.

Paul Hankar said, 'We noticed that some of our people were acting differently. They started to look ill, and to keep themselves to themselves. Also, they *smelled*. It's very hard to describe. Not altogether unpleasant, but *musty*, like the inside of a closet in which a dead man's clothes have been hanging.

'Gradually it became clear to us that every operation which was betrayed to the Germans was connected with one or more of these sick people.'

'What did you do about it?'

'Of course, we immediately isolated any of our people who showed any signs of illness or behaving in a strange way, and allowed them no contact with the rest of us. But even this didn't stop the infection from spreading amongst us, and we couldn't understand how this could happen. We have doctors who help us, but even they were mystified.

'It was Ann De Wouters who first discovered what the Germans had done. She had spent many months becoming close friends with a young German officer from the 136th Special Employment Division, who administered Antwerp

15

during the occupation. When I say "close friends", you understand what I am saying to you.'

He paused, and took a deep breath, as if he were trying to stop himself from sounding too emotional.

'She is, she *was*, a very moral young woman. But her husband Jan was arrested and shot by the Germans in 1942, and I think she believed that this was the best way she could take her revenge.

'Anyway – one night this young German officer invited Ann to a party at Major General Stolberg-Stolberg's house – he was the commanding officer of the 136th Special Employment Division. Some of the German officers got drunk and started boasting that they would soon exterminate all of the resistance in Antwerp.'

He turned around in his seat to make sure that nobody else was listening, and then he leaned forward and said, 'They claimed they had brought in some kind of infection from Eastern Europe which would spread amongst the White Brigade and within six weeks it would kill us all.'

Still I didn't reply. And still the branch kept tapping at the window. It sounded as if the wind was rising, and I prayed that it wouldn't start to rain. The scent of Screechers was so much harder to follow in the wet.

Paul Hankar said, 'They didn't seem to know exactly what this infection was, but they were very excited about it. Apparently they had used it against the resistance in Poland and also in France. They said that it had come from Romania.'

'I see. Any mention of *mensen van de nacht*?'

'The night people? As far as I'm concerned, that was only an hysterical rumour. It started to spread when people were discovered around the city with all of the blood drained out of them. Sometimes a whole family would be found in their apartment, grandparents, mothers and fathers, even babies . . . cut open, and their hearts pulled out. But in many cases their doors were locked on the inside and nobody could work out how anybody could have gotten in or out.'

'How do *you* think they were killed?'

'I don't know. I don't believe in anything supernatural. Once or twice, some of our people who had gotten sick were seen by witnesses in the vicinity of these tragedies, but we never found any conclusive evidence that they were responsible.'

I said, quietly, 'Ann was killed like that.'

'What?'

'They opened her up. Then they took out her heart and drained all the blood out of her.'

Paul Hankar's mouth tightened, but he didn't say anything. I watched him, and smoked, and eventually I said, 'Is there anything else you can tell me? It doesn't matter how trivial you think it is, it might help me to find out who killed her.'

'And then what, after you've found out who killed her? That won't bring her back.'

'I know. But it might stop it from happening again.'

He blew out smoke, and shrugged. 'I know very little, really. Ann kept her ears open whenever she was in the company of German officers, and once or twice she heard them discussing the killings, especially the one on Minderbroeder Straat, when twenty-three people died, including two nuns.

'The Germans never said anything to connect these massacres directly with their Romanian infection, but Ann told me more than once that she had a feeling that they might be associated. One of the SS officers said something like, "At last the Romanians are being of some use to us." And, "The sicker they are, the more blood they want." Also, one of our wireless operators managed to intercept some coded messages which were sent to Antwerp from the Sixth Army in Bucharest.'

'Really?'

'We could only pick up bits and pieces. But they kept referring to "carriers", in the sense of people who carry an infection.'

'These messages . . . did they contain any names?'

'What do you mean?'

'Romanian names. It could help us to find out what this infection actually is, and where it came from.'

'As I remember, only one Romanian name . . . Dorin Duca. It came up several times. It was not completely clear, because the messages were so fragmentary, but it appeared that somebody called Duca was supposed to be assisting the operation in Antwerp. However we never came across any Duca, so I doubt if he actually came here. We keep a very close check on who comes into Antwerp, believe me, and who leaves.'

The boy arrived with a bottle of apple schnapps and a bottle of lemonade, and two very small glasses. Paul Hankar immediately filled up his glass, knocked it back and filled it up again. 'If the Allies hadn't taken the city, there would have been no resistance left by Christmas.'

'What did you do when your people became infected?'

'I told you. We isolated them, broke off all contact. We couldn't jeopardize any of our operations.'

'So I could talk to some of them, if I needed to?'

Paul Hankar shrugged. 'I think many of them got very sick indeed, so maybe not.'

'How sick?'

Paul Hankar looked from left to right, avoiding my eyes. 'Well, they are dead now,' he said at last. 'You understand for our own protection that we had to dispose of them.'

'How many?'

'Altogether? Maybe thirty-five, thirty-six.'

'Do you want to tell me how you did it?'

'I don't understand.'

'Do you want to tell me how you disposed of them?'

'Does it matter?'

'Actually, yes, it matters a great deal.'

He lifted his hand with his finger pointing like a pistol. 'We shot them in the back of the head. Then we threw their bodies into the Scheldt.'

'OK. I was afraid of that.'

'We did something wrong?'

I shook my head. 'You did what you thought was right. I can't blame you for that.'

'You think this was possibly *easy*? All through the darkest times of the occupation, we had trusted these same people with our very lives, and they in their turn had implicitly trusted us. They were not only friends but relatives, some of them – fathers and mothers, brothers and sisters.'

'Sure.' I didn't like to tell him that shooting a Screecher could only make things a thousand times worse. The only saving grace was that they had thrown their bodies into the river.

We sat in silence for a while. Eventually Paul Hankar picked up another paper napkin and blew his nose on it. 'I am very sad about Ann,' he said. 'She was always so careful not to compromise herself. I always thought that she and I would both survive.'

'I'm sorry,' I said. I didn't think that I was old enough to tell him how obvious it was that he had loved her.

He finished his drink and stood up. 'I have to go now. I hope I have assisted you. If you find the people who murdered her—'

'We will. But you won't find out about it. Besides, what's the point of telling an art-nouveau jewellery designer who died in 1901?'

He nearly managed to smile. 'You know the name Paul Hankar?'

I nodded.

'I'm impressed. I didn't know Americans had such culture.'

Man-trailing

We left the hotel just as the pregnant-looking long-case clock in the lobby chimed eight. Frank was straining so hard on his leash that he sounded like a Cajun squeezebox. It hadn't rained hard, but a fine wet mist had descended over the city, and the cobbles were all slippery and shiny. I could hear heavy bombers somewhere in the distance, but they were very far away. *Drone, drone, drone.* Then that *crumpity-bump-crackle* sound of anti-aircraft fire.

Corporal Little said, 'Thirty-six of them, sir . . . Jesus. Do you know how far this could have spread? Half the city could be Screechers by now.'

'I don't want to think about it. Let's just concentrate on picking up the scent from Markgravestraat.'

We jolted our way back to Ann De Wouters' apartment building. Somebody had taken the dead horse away. We were flagged down three times on the way by Canadian troops who wanted to check our papers, so it took us almost twenty minutes

19

before we arrived there. 'US Counterintelligence?' they asked, half respectfully and half disdainfully. Some of them were so young that their cheeks were still pink.

We were admitted to No. 5 by an old man in a saggy beige cardigan with a face the colour of liver sausage. Frank snapped furiously at the old man's worn-out slippers so that he almost had to dance upstairs to get away from him.

'He won't hurt you,' I reassured him. 'I promise you, he's a friend to everyone.'

'I don't have any friends who try to bite my feet,' the old man retorted.

'It's not your feet, sir, it's your slippers. He thinks they're dead rats.'

We allowed Frank to have a good snuffle around Ann De Wouters' room. We said nothing while he crossed from one side of the linoleum to the other, thrusting his head underneath the bed and into the curtained-off space where Ann De Wouters had hung her clothes. He spent a long time licking the dried blood that was spattered over the floor. Bloodhounds don't identify scents with their noses, but with their tongues. I was hoping that the Screechers had left plenty of traces of saliva for him to pick up on.

When he was finished, Frank sat up straight and made a whining sound in the back of his throat.

'You ready, Frank?' Corporal Little asked him.

'*Urf*,' said Frank.

We went back down the narrow staircase. There was a light shining under Vrouw Toeput's door but I didn't want to disturb her. The old man with the dead-rat slippers was nowhere to be seen. When he reached the bottom of the stairs, Frank ignored the front door and turned sharp right, heading toward the back of the building. He led us past an alcove crammed with mops and brooms and strong-smelling bleaches, and up to a heavy oak door. I pulled back the bolts and unlocked it, and we stepped out into the fairy-fine mist.

'Told you,' I said. 'Out the back of the building, and on to Kipdorp.'

Frank hurried through a low archway on the opposite side of the yard, where six or seven bicycles were propped up, and then he hurried into the street, his claws clattering softly on the cobbles.

20

He hesitated for only a moment, and then he turned right, toward Sant Jacobs Markt, and Kipdorpbrug. Every now and then he paused and looked around, to make sure that we were following him. I seriously believe that he thought we were like two stupid children, and it was his responsibility to take care of us.

Although the sidewalk was wet, the scent of Screechers must have been very strong, because Frank went straight along the north side of Kipdorp and there was none of his usual circling and sniffing and whuffling around.

'I think we've got these jokers, sir,' said Corporal Little, triumphantly.

But when we reached Kipdorpbrug, Frank galloped straight up to the sandstone wall of the Maritime Bank and stopped. He looked upward, and barked, and then he turned back to us, whining in frustration.

We looked upward, too. The bank building was seventeenth century, five storeys high, with a flat Flemish-style facade. Apart from the window ledges, there wasn't a single hand-hold between the sidewalk and the roof.

I looked at Corporal Little and Corporal Little looked at me. We were both deeply impressed, and frightened, too. 'They went straight up,' I said. 'At least one of them, anyhow.'

We had known Screechers to run up twenty-foot walls, and jump from one sloping roof to another. We had seen one run across a ceiling. But we had never known one to climb up a sheer hundred-foot building.

Frank kept returning to the wall and jumping up and barking. 'Good boy,' Corporal Little told him, pulling his ears. 'Good boy, it's not your fault you can't climb walls.' It was difficult to know what to do next. We could have located the manager of the Maritime Bank and have him open up for us, so that we could follow the Screecher's trail across the roof, but that could take us hours, and in any case the Screecher had probably climbed down the front of some other building and come back down to ground level.

'My guess is, this was a dead one,' I said.

Corporal Little nodded. 'He must of left a real strong trail behind him, the way Frank's getting himself so excited. And if he could shimmy straight up a wall like that . . . '

'It's worth checking, though. Maybe he only climbed up part of the way, and then jumped back down again.'

I hunkered down and opened up the Kit. I took out the compass and opened up its silver filigree lid. The needle immediately swung around and pointed to the front of the bank building. When I held it up vertically, it pointed directly upward. There was no question about it. Our Screecher had gone all the way up to the roof, with no deviation.

'Like a rat up a drainpipe,' said Corporal Little, and Frank let out another expectant bark. I swear that dog would have talked if he'd had the larynx for it.

As I was fitting the compass back into the Kit, however, the needle started to creep back the other way, in the direction of Kipdorpbrug. It wasn't an urgent swing, but the needle was trembling a little, the way it always did when Screechers weren't too far away.

'Look at this,' I told Corporal Little, shining my flashlight on it. 'I don't think all three of them went up the wall. Maybe only one of them. I'm definitely picking up another trail in this direction.'

Corporal Little took hold of Frank's collar and tugged him away from the bank. 'Hear that, boy? More Screechers! Go get 'em, boy!'

In the Elephant House

Frank was much less certain about this secondary trail, and he kept stopping and snorting and going back on himself. Now and then he got distracted and started to investigate a lamp post, and Corporal Little had to drag him away.

I kept the compass in my hand, and even though the needle was just as hesitant as Frank, and kept swinging from side to side, there was no question that it was pointing in the general direction of Centraal Station, and the Antwerpse Zoo.

'Maybe they thought they could get away by train,' Corporal Little suggested.

I shook my head. 'There's no civilian trains running. And even if they managed to ride a military train, where would they go? Mechelen? Brussels? There'd be a very strong risk of them being caught, if they tried to go south.'

All of a sudden, as he snuffled his way across the wide cobbled expanse of Koning Astridplein, Frank must have picked up a much more definite scent, because he started to run ahead of us with a curious lope, his head down and his ears swinging. By the time he had reached the steps of the Centraal Station, he was galloping so fast that Corporal Little and I could hardly keep up with him.

The Centraal Station was an extraordinary building, like a richly decorated Renaissance palace, with a high glass dome which covered the platforms, and six elaborate spires. The square in front of it was jam-packed with Canadian and British trucks, as trainloads of troops were unloaded from Brussels. I can remember that night as if it were a dream: trying to follow Frank through all of those jostling soldiers and diesel-smelling trucks, all the lights and the shouting and the revving of engines. Some of the soldiers whistled at Frank and clapped their hands and called out, 'Here, boy!' but Frank was man-trailing and he wasn't going to be diverted by anything, not even lonely young Canadian soldiers who were missing their dogs from home.

He didn't run into the station. Instead, he skirted around it, and headed toward the entrance to the Antwerpse Zoo. We left the noise of the Centraal Station behind us, and followed Frank to the Zoo's main entrance. It was much quieter here, although I could still hear the distant grumbling of artillery fire. The Zoo was in darkness, but Frank ran straight through the turnstiles and disappeared.

'Frank!' shouted Corporal Little. 'Frank, you'd better come to heel, boy, or else there's no more marrow bones for you!'

We heard him bark, but he didn't come back. Then we heard him bark again, even further away.

'He's found one, for sure,' said Corporal Little.

'We'd better get after him, then.'

I opened the stud of my holster and tugged out my Colt

.45 automatic. This was only the third time since we had landed in Normandy that I had taken it out, and I had never fired it at anyone. It was loaded with bullets that had allegedly been cast from the pewter goblets from which the Disciples had drunk during the Last Supper, so it wasn't the kind of weapon that you would fire indiscriminately. But the Zoo grounds were impenetrably black and very extensive – nearly twenty-five acres of parkland and trees and animal houses, and if there were Screechers here I didn't want to be caught by surprise.

Corporal Little and I climbed awkwardly over the turnstiles and made our way along the path to the mock-Egyptian square where the elephant house stood. Our flashlights made shadows jump across the buildings like hopping hunchbacks, and a couple of times I was tempted to fire.

'*Frank!*' called Corporal Little, in a hoarse stage whisper. '*Frank – where the hell are you, you disobedient mutt?*'

We heard him bark again, and this time his bark echoed, like somebody shouting in a swimming pool.

'He's in there,' said Corporal Little, shining his flashlight on the elephant house.

There were no elephants in there, of course. When the Germans had first entered Antwerp, the zoo staff had shot all of the animals – elephants, tigers, gorillas, giraffes – in case they broke out of their cages and escaped. Apart from that, there was little enough food for the human population, let alone animals.

We entered the elephant house cautiously, with our weapons raised. It was like walking into Tutankhamen's tomb. The columns were gilded and decorated with acanthus leaves, and Egyptian hieroglyphs had been painted all over the walls. It was also dark and smelly and the tiled floor was gritty and wet, so that our boots made a scrunching noise.

'Frank?' called Corporal Little.

Frank turned around, and we saw his yellow eyes reflected in our flashlights, like some kind of hound from hell.

'*There,*' said Corporal Little.

Cowering in the corner, one hand clinging on to the bars of an elephant pen, the other hand raised to shield his face from my flashlight, sat a Screecher. He was tall and emaciated, with thinning brown hair, and a pallid, bony face. He was wearing a dirty grey overcoat with a deluge of brown stains down the front of it, and a cheap brown business suit, and his shoes had holes in the soles. Most people would have passed him on the street without a second glance, but Corporal Little and I had seen enough Screechers to recognize him immediately for what he was. It was the way he couldn't look directly at the light, and the way that his eyeballs kept darting from side to side, like cockroaches. He looked anxious and scheming, rather than terrified. Like most of the Screechers we'd encountered, he obviously believed that humans couldn't kill him, no matter what we did to him, but he did know that we could hurt him. What he was looking for with his shifty little eyes was a way to escape.

'Well, well,' I said, walking right up to him. I sniffed, and I could smell the unmistakable odour of rotting poultry and dried dill. 'Where are your friends, then?'

He said nothing, so I holstered my .45, knelt down on the floor and opened up the Kit. I took out the shiny silver mirror and held it up at an angle so that I could see his face in it. Contrary to what you've seen in the movies or read about in *Dracula*, Screechers are clearly visible in mirrors. The only difference is that pure silver doesn't reflect evil, so the mirror showed me the Screecher as he used to be, before he was infected.

Sometimes, of course, you can make a mistake, and a smelly, homely-looking character that you suspected of being a Screecher looks just as homely in the mirror. In that case you apologize and let him go on his way without banging nails into his eyes. But what I saw in the mirror that night at the Antwerpse Zoo was a good-looking young man in his mid-thirties with wide-apart eyes and a heavy jaw. He looked German, or Austrian, or maybe Swiss.

'*Wo sind deinen Freunden?*' I repeated, waving my flashlight from side to side to dazzle him. 'If you tell me where your friends are, I might be able to save your life. If you don't, then I won't have any choice. I'll have to kill you, here and now.'

The Screecher kept his hands held up in front of his face, and didn't answer me. Frank barked at him, but even Frank was sensible enough not to go too close. The Screecher may have looked like a down-and-out, but I knew from experience that he was quite capable of ripping Frank's head off with his bare hands.

'I'm giving you one last chance,' I said, in German. I took out my pistol again, and pointed it directly at his heart. 'We can save you . . . give you back the life you used to have before. Think of it, your family, your sweetheart. All you have to do is tell us where your friends are.'

I was lying, of course. I didn't know if it was possible to return a Screecher to normality, even if we were to give him a massive blood transfusion. We had never tried. Every Screecher by his very nature had committed mass murder, so we had never had much incentive.

'OK, then,' I told him. I cocked my pistol and gripped it with both hands. Even if I hit him directly in the heart it wouldn't kill him, but it would stop him long enough for us to put the thumbscrews on him, and prevent him from escaping.

I was just about to fire when the Screecher suddenly performed a backward somersault. Then he performed another, and another, right up the bars of the elephant cage, until he reached the ceiling, over thirty feet above our heads.

I fired two deafening shots, but the ceiling was vaulted and I was terrified of ricochets. The Screecher crawled quickly across it, clambering over the vaulting like a huge brown spider, heading for the entrance. Frank started barking again, and Corporal Little took out his pistol, too, but I shouted at him, '*No!*'

As the Screecher scuttled upside-down across the ceiling, I took the silver-wire whip out of the Kit and flicked it so that it unravelled. The whip was heavy and springy and jumped around with a tensile life of its own. I swung it back and lashed out with it, catching the Screecher just as he reached the architrave around the door. There was a small barbed grappling hook on the end of the whip, and it snatched at his coat. I yanked the whip hard, but his coat tore and the hook came free.

Frank was hurling himself up and down, barking insanely. Corporal Little manoeuvred himself until he was right beneath the doorway, his pistol raised. I lashed out again, and this time the grappling hook caught the Screecher in the back of the head, burying itself in his scalp. He cried out in pain, and reached around with one hand, trying to pull the hook loose. It was then that I gave another yank, and he lost his grip on the ceiling and slammed on to the floor on his back.

Immediately, while the Screecher was still concussed, Corporal Little and I seized his arms and wrenched off his overcoat. We pulled off his coat, his shirt, and his pants. I hated this part of the job. Live Screechers always stank of decay, like that chicken you should have cooked the day before yesterday, and their skin had a chilly greasiness about it which took carbolic soap and very hot water to wash off. Like all Screechers, this one was dead white, with a slightly bruised look across his abdomen and his inner thighs, the tell-tale sign of internal putrefaction.

Even before we had finished stripping him, he started to come to. His head lolled from side to side, and he coughed, and said something that sounded like German, although I couldn't understand what it was. Then he twisted his back, and tried to flap at Corporal Little with his right arm.

Without hesitation, I took the thumbscrews out of the Kit and fastened them tightly, so that his hands were forcibly held up in front of his bony chest. Then I pinioned his big toes together with the toescrews.

In English, he said, 'What – what are you doing? *What are you doing?* I will kill you!'

'I gave you an eighteen-carat golden opportunity, didn't I?' I retorted. 'All you had to do was tell us where your friends are hiding.'

'Go to hell. My friends will hunt you down and they will cut you open like pigs!'

'Oink! Oink!' Corporal Little taunted him.

Between us, we dragged him across to one of the Egyptian-style pillars. He was wriggling and struggling and trying to bite us, and he was unnaturally strong, considering how wasted he looked. It took a whole lot of grunting and shoving to press him up against the pillar, but while Corporal Little held him in position, I wound the whip around him six or seven times and made it fast. The silver wire cut into his skin as if it were candle wax.

'All right, then,' I panted, 'I'm going to ask you again. Where are your friends hiding?'

27

'You think that I will tell you anything?' he said, speaking in German again. He spat at me, although I was too far away, and the thick saliva ended up swinging from his chin.

'Listen,' I warned him, 'I don't want to hurt you, fellow, but if you won't cooperate . . . '

'Go to hell.'

I went over to the Kit and took out the dental forceps. Then I came straight back to the Screecher and gripped his nose tightly in my left hand, so that he couldn't breathe. He tried to waggle his head from side to side but I held him fast. 'Mmmmmhhff!' he protested, trying to keep his mouth closed. '*Mmmmmhhff!*'

But he couldn't keep his lips together for longer than a minute and a half. When he opened them, gasping for breath, I immediately forced my thumb under his upper lip. Then I gripped his left front incisor with the dental forceps, and wrenched it, hard. His gum made a sharp cracking noise, and welled up with blood, but the tooth was reluctant to come out. I had to jerk the forceps backward and forward three or four more times before I managed to extract it altogether. Immediately I gripped his right front incisor, and started to tug that, too.

'*Aaaaggghhhh!*' he choked, as I pulled the tooth out by its roots. Without hesitating, I moved the forceps across to his canines.

'You want me to stop?' I asked him.

He said nothing, but coughed, so that a fine spray of blood covered his chest.

'OK . . . maybe you need something more persuasive. What do you think, Corporal, something more persuasive?'

'Sounds good to me. Think of all the innocent people he must of killed.'

'That's right. Like Ann De Wouters. Now, why did you and your friends want to murder Ann De Wouters?'

'I told you to go to hell,' the Screecher spluttered.

'Well, yes, you did. But you and I have to talk first, and you have to tell me what I need to know.'

'You can't kill me.'

'What? Is that what they told you?'

'You can hurt me as much as you like but you can never kill me. When you have been lying in the cemetery for a hundred years, I will still be alive to piss on your grave.'

'Sorry, pal,' I told him. 'I hate to be the one to break this to you, but somebody's been shooting you a line. Not only can I kill you, but I can kill you in such a way that you will wish you had never been born.'

The Screecher spat out more blood. 'You're lying.'

'I'll prove it to you. That's unless you tell me where your friends are.'

The Screecher struggled against the silver wire, but he succeeded only in cutting himself, so that blood ran down his skinny white thighs. When I thought back on it after the war, I sometimes found it hard to believe that I could have treated anybody with such cruelty, even a Screecher. But then I remembered all the times we broke into houses in France and Belgium and the Netherlands and found heaps of men, women and children, massacred so that the Screechers could feed on them. When I remembered that – the smell and the flies and the tangles of pitiful bodies – what *I* was doing, by comparison, seemed almost restrained.

I took the bottle of holy oil from the Kit, unstopped it, and held it up in front of the Screecher's face. 'With this oil, I thee anoint,' I told him.

'You think that scares me, you shitbag?'

'No, I don't. In fact I don't think your or your friends are scared of anything, which makes you very dangerous. And because you're so dangerous, that makes me all the more determined to kill you.'

I poured about a tablespoonful of oil over the Screecher's head, so that it ran down his face and dripped from the end of his nose. He shuddered, and took a deep snorting breath. To him, in his state of utter unholiness, consecrated oil would have felt scalding.

I took hold of his oily hair and twisted it up into a point, like the wick of a candle. Then Corporal Little stepped forward, and handed me his Zippo.

'Last chance,' I said, flipping back the lid. 'You could save yourself a whole lot of pain here, believe me.'

The Screecher said nothing, so I snapped the lighter into flame. The Screecher stared at me with such venomous hatred that I wished that I had blindfolded him.

'I'm going to count to three,' I told him. 'Then you're going to burn like a church candle.'

'I'll do the counting for you,' he said. '*Eins – zwei – drei – now* do whatever you have to do!'

I lit his hair, and immediately the whole of his scalp caught fire. His hair shrivelled and his skin blistered and even his ears were alight. He managed to bear it for nearly five seconds without moving and without crying out, and he even managed to keep his eyes open. But then the oil on his face burst into flame and he closed his eyes tight shut and screamed. I had never heard a man scream like that before. It sounded just like a French woman in Normandy whose legs had been crushed by a Sherman tank. Three soldiers had pulled her out but her legs had stayed where they were.

The Screecher tossed his head wildly from side to side, which only had the effect of fanning the flames and making them burn more fiercely. He screamed and screamed for nearly half a minute but then he stopped screaming, and let his head fall back against the pillar. The flames died down and he was left smouldering, his whole head blackened and raw, his lips enormously swollen and his nostrils clogged with blood.

I used the Zippo to light a cigarette. I waited for a while, smoking, and then the Screecher slowly opened his eyes.

'Now that *smarts*, doesn't it?' I asked him.

'You can't kill me,' he said, his voice thick with pain.

'Oh yes I can. Do you want to know how?'

'You can't kill me, whatever you do.'

I reached into the Kit and produced the nails. 'You see these? Do you know what these are? These are the same nails that the Romans used to nail Christ to the cross. And do you know what I'm going to do with them? I'm going to hammer them into your eyes, and right into your brain. That won't kill you, I admit, but it will have the effect of paralysing you, so that you won't be able to stop me from doing what I'm going to do next.

'I'm going to cut your head off with this saw, and I'm going to take your body to the Calvary Garden of Sint Paulus Kirk, and I'm going to bury it there, because I have special dispensation from the Dominican monks to do that. Then I'm going to take your head and I'm going to boil it until the flesh falls off and your brains turn into broth. And that is how I kill people like you.'

'Whatever you do, we will have our revenge on you. I can promise you that.'

I smoked my cigarette right down to the very last eighth of an inch, and then I stepped on it. 'Corporal Little,' I said, 'how about passing me that holy oil again?'

Corporal Little did what I asked him. I took the stopper off the oil and said, 'This is what we call burning the candle at both ends. Just our little joke.'

With that, I poured oil between his legs, all over his scraggy pubic hair and his penis, and relit Corporal Little's Zippo.

The Screecher stared at the flame out of his swollen, half-closed eyes.

'I want you to know that I am doing this simply for the pleasure of it,' I told him. 'I don't care whether you tell me where your friends are, or not. I'm going to kill you whatever. I just want to hurt you as much as I possibly can before I do.'

Corporal Little was holding his collar but Frank made a strangled whining noise and scrabbled his claws on the floor, as if he wanted to get away. I don't know if that was what convinced the Screecher that I was serious, but he suddenly said, 'Seventy-one Schildersstraat, on the corner of Karel Rogierstraat. They're hiding in the attic.'

'How many of them?'

'Two. A German called Pelz and a Romanian called Duca.'

'Is Duca the dead one?'

'Dead? What do you mean? He's not dead.'

'What I'm asking you is – is Duca *strigoi vii* or *strigoi mort*?'

'I still don't understand what you mean.'

Corporal Little said, 'Sounds like this guy doesn't even know half of what he was getting himself into.'

'Oh, I think he has the general idea. It's just that they didn't fill him in on all the gory details. They promised you that you'd live for ever, didn't they? That's what they said. They said you were going to be a hero, and turn back the tide of the war. I'll bet they offered to pay your family a fortune, too. Take care of your folks and your girlfriend.'

'What are you going to do now?' asked the Screecher.

'What do you think I'm going to do now?'

'You said you could give me back the life I had before.'

31

'Did I? Did I really say that?'

'You promised me that if I told you where my friends were, you would let me go.'

'Well, that was very stupid of me, wouldn't you say? Because I have no way of checking if your friends are really where you say they are, or not.'

'I swear that I am telling you the truth. Seventy-one Schilderstraat. Fourth floor, in the attic.'

'What's your name?' I asked him.

'Ernst . . . Ernst . . . *Hauser*,' he said, almost as if he could barely remember.

'Where do you come from?'

'Drensteinfürt. It's a village near Münster, in Westfalen. Why?'

'After the war, I want to write your family, and tell them where you died. I think they deserve that much. Not *how* you died, of course. They wouldn't want to know that. But where.'

'You're really going to kill me, aren't you?'

I nodded. 'It's what I do, Ernst. It's what I came here for.'

Corporal Little handed me the mallet and one of the nails. I positioned the nail so that the point was only a half-inch away from the Screecher's eyeball.

'I can't tell you that I regret doing this,' I told him. 'The plain truth is that I don't.'

The Stations of the Cross

Father Antonius opened the small garden door at the side of Sint Paulus Kirk, on the corner of Veemarkt and Zwartzusterstraat, and the hinges shuddered as if they were in pain. Father Antonius was bald and almost comically ugly, with enormous ears and drooping jowls, so that he looked as if he were distantly related to Frank.

'I didn't expect you so soon, Captain,' he told me, in a

thick, phlegmy voice. 'In fact, to be truthful, I didn't expect you at all.'

'Well, God was on our side and we caught up with one of them at the Zoo.'

'You've—?' asked Father Antonius, making a cut-throat gesture with his finger.

'We have his body in the back of the Jeep. Is it OK to bring it in?'

Father Antonius didn't look at all happy, but he said, 'Yes, we agreed. So, yes. I will make sure that we bury it right away.'

Corporal Little and I went back to the Jeep. Between us, we lifted the rough hessian sack off the back seat and carried it through the gates and into the Calvary Garden. At this time of the night, the garden was a deeply unsettling place to visit, not only because of its Gothic arches and its dark shadowy corners, but because it was crowded with sixty-three life-sized statues depicting Christ's journey to the cross, culminating in a crucifixion on top of a stone mound. The figures stared at us blindly as we shuffled between them like a pair of grave-robbers. The sack in which we had tied up the Screecher's body swung heavily between us, and my end of it was soaked in blood.

Up above us, searchlights flicked nervously across the sky, although the night was unusually quiet, and there was no sound of bomber engines or artillery fire.

'Here,' said Father Antonius, pointing to an open area of grass. 'If you leave him here, we will do the rest.'

'Thank you, Father.' I lowered my end of the sack and wiped my hands on my handkerchief. 'There may be two more. We've been given an address but we're not yet sure if it's genuine.'

Father Antonius crossed himself. 'I wish you God's protection in your work. I don't pretend to understand what you are doing. I don't even know if I believe in such things. But these have been terrible days, and anything which can help to bring them to an end . . . '

A bitter wind was blowing across the Calvary Garden as we walked back between the silent stone figures, and dead leaves rattled against the walls. Corporal Little said, 'When are we going after the other two, sir?'

'Not until it gets light. If they're hiding where Ernst said they were hiding, I don't think that they'll have tried to make a break for it yet. They're probably still waiting for poor old Ernst to come back.'

We closed the garden gate behind us and climbed in the Jeep. On the floor in front of the back seats was a cardboard box which had originally contained cans of condensed milk. One corner of the box was stained dark brown.

'Let's just make sure that he never *can* come back, shall we?'

Frank barked and shook his head so that his ears made a flapping noise.

Ground Zero

I slept until well past oh-seven-hundred hours, which I hadn't done for months. Most nights I had terrifying dreams about shadows chasing after me, and I woke up with a jolt while it was still dark. One of the hotel maids tapped on my door and came in with a pot of coffee and two bread rolls with red plum preserve. She was a shy young girl, plump, with a pattern of moles on her cheek.

'What's your name?' I asked her. I could see myself in the closet mirror and my hair was sticking up like a cockatoo.

'Hilda,' she whispered.

'Well, Hilda, maybe you could open the drapes for me so that I can see what kind of a day it is.'

'It's raining, sir. It's a bad-luck day.'

'A bad-luck day? What makes you say that?'

'It's Friday the thirteenth.'

'You're not superstitious, are you?'

She shook her head, but then she said, 'One of the girls downstairs thinks that you're a *tovenaar*.'

Tovenaar is Flemish for a black magician. The girl must

34

have seen my Bibles and my crucifixes and all the paraphernalia of Screecher-hunting.

'No, I'm not a *tovenaar*. Tell her I'm a *goochelaar*.' A *goochelaar* is a conjuror, the kind who pulls rabbits out of opera hats and strings of coloured bunting out of his ears.

'Yes, sir.' She tugged back the heavy velvet curtains and she was right. The sky was gloomy and the window was speckled with raindrops. 'You should be careful today, sir.'

'I'm always careful. Here.' I reached over to the ashtray on my night-table and fished out a couple of francs to give her a tip.

I met up with Corporal Little and Frank in the lobby downstairs. The hotel was bustling with activity because some of the British were leaving. Outside, Keizerstraat was crowded with Jeeps and trucks and British Tommies wearing raincapes.

'You had something to eat, Henry?' I asked Corporal Little.

'Sure thing. Frank and I shared some sausage.'

'You know what the Belgians put in those sausages?'

'Hate to think, sir.'

'Reconstituted Nazis, with additional cereal.'

Corporal Little had parked around the corner. We climbed into the Jeep and manoeuvred our way toward Schildersstraat. Frank took the rain as a personal insult and kept shaking himself impatiently.

No. 71 was a tall grey building right on the corner of Karel Rogierstraat. The downstairs windows were covered with grimy lace curtains and all of the upstairs windows were shuttered. Corporal Little parked halfway up the kerb and we went to the brown-painted front door and knocked. The knocker was cast in bronze, in the shape of a snarling wolf. A knocker like that was supposed to keep demons out of the house, but if Ernst Hauser had been telling us the truth, it certainly hadn't worked here.

We knocked three times before the door was opened. A plain young woman in a white muslin cap and a plain brown dress stood in front of us, holding a mop. From inside the house, I could smell bleach and fish boiling.

'We're looking for three men,' I told her, holding out my identity card. 'Do you have anybody staying here?'

'Nobody now. Only my grandfather.'

'How about before?'

'Before? Yes. We had five Germans here before the Allies came, and another man, but they're all gone now.'

'Another man?'

'I don't know what he was. He didn't speak German. I don't know what language it was. He used to talk to us sometimes and I think he was asking us questions but we didn't understand.'

'Maybe he said something like *buna dimineatza*? Or *noapte buna*? Or *multzumesc*?'

'Yes, that word *multzumesc*. He was always saying that.'

'Can you tell me what he looked like, this man?'

The girl looked embarrassed. 'He was tall, taller than you. With dark hair combed straight back.'

'What else you can tell me about him? I mean, if I were to see him in the street, how would I recognize him?'

She lowered her eyes. 'He was very handsome. My mother's friends used to come round for tea in the hope that he would be here.'

'Really?'

'If he passed them in the hallway they would start to giggle.'

'What kind of handsome, would you say? Did he remind you of anybody? A movie star, maybe?'

'Well, I know it sounds funny, but if you can imagine Marlene Dietrich as a man instead of a woman. High cheeks, very proud-looking. Also, he spoke very warm, if you understand me, always looking you right in your eyes, so you didn't mind if you didn't know what he was saying. His eyes were green like the sea and he had a scar on the side of his forehead . . . like a V-shape.'

I gave Corporal Little a brief translation of what the girl had said, and the corporal grinned and shook his head. 'Sounds like this young lady didn't exactly fail to be swept off her feet, either. She didn't happen to notice his sock size, by any chance?'

I turned back to the girl. 'Did this man ever tell you his name?'

'No. But I heard one of the Germans call him Herr Doktor.'

'What were the Germans like?'

'Horrible. I hated both of them. They kept coughing, as if they were ill, and they always smelled bad.'

'Frank picking up anything?' I asked Corporal Little.

'Not so far, sir. But it's been raining all night.'

'Do you think there's any possibility that these men may still be here?' I asked the girl.

'What do you mean?'

'Could they still be hiding in the house? In the attic, maybe?'

'Their rooms are empty. I had to clean them after they left.'

'Do you think we could possibly take a look around?'

'I don't know. My mother isn't here. She won't be back for an hour.'

'We wouldn't disturb anything, I promise you.'

'She doesn't even like me to answer the door. It was only because you wouldn't stop knocking.'

'OK, then . . . we wouldn't like to get you into any trouble. We'll go find ourselves a cup of coffee and come back later.'

She smiled, and said, '*Dank U.*' And I can still see that smile now, and her white linen cap, and her hand holding the mop.

We drove to a cafe at the far end of Karel Rogierstraat. There were chairs and tables set out on the sidewalk but because it was raining there was nobody sitting there except for one old man. He was sheltering under the dark green awning, smoking a meerschaum pipe.

Corporal Little tied Frank to the cast-iron umbrella stand and we went inside. The interior was very gloomy, even though there were decorative mirrors on every wall. Behind the bar an old Marconi wireless was playing 'I'll Be Seeing You'. We sat down in the corner, lit up cigarettes, and asked for two filter coffees. The proprietor was a fat middle-aged man in a floor-length apron. Every time he turned toward the window the grey morning light reflected from his glasses, so that he looked as if he had pennies on his eyes.

'Do you know what today is?' I asked Corporal Little, breathing smoke.

At that instant there was a deafening bang, louder than a thunderclap, instantly followed by another one. The cafe windows cracked diagonally from side to side, and everything in the whole place rattled and shook. We both stood up, just as a huge billow of brown smoke came rolling along Karel Rogierstraat, immediately followed by a shower of bricks, chairs, torn fragments of sheet metal, window frames, curtains, roof tiles, and even more bricks.

We hurried to the doorway. Frank was cowering behind a plant pot, his eyes wide, trembling. Debris was still falling from the sky, including a huge metal cylinder that looked like an old-fashioned kitchen stove. It bounced and bounded over the cobbles and slammed into an office doorway across the street.

'Jesus,' said Corporal Little, who never blasphemed. 'What the hell was that?'

I looked down toward Schildersstraat. Through the gradually clearing smoke, I could see that No. 71 had been completely demolished, along with three or four houses on other side. The whole intersection had been reduced to mountains of rubble, and bodies were lying everywhere – a young woman in a black coat, with an overturned baby carriage – an elderly couple whose heads had both been blown off – six or seven nuns who must have been walking on the opposite side of the street, lying on top of each other like dead pigeons. The cobbles were strewn with body parts and blown-apart sofas and a black Citroën taxi that looked like some surrealistic panther standing on its hind legs. All of the windows within a hundred-yard radius had been blown out, and in some houses, fires were blazing.

I walked slowly down the street and stood on the edge of the crater that had been No. 71. The crater was almost twenty feet deep, as if the house had been hit by a meteor. I was still deaf from the double-blast, so it was like walking through a silent movie, with the rain falling, and people running in all directions.

I turned around. Corporal Little had been following me, with Frank. He said something, but I couldn't hear what it was, and then he shrugged. I knew what he was trying to tell me, though. If there had been Screechers hiding in the attic, they had been obliterated, along with the rest of the house, and the young girl's grandfather, and the young girl herself, with her white linen cap and her mop.

For the first time since we had landed in Normandy, I felt that I wasn't the sole representative of the Angel of Death.

I'll Be Seeing You

'So what's the plan now, sir?' asked Corporal Little.
'God knows,' I told him. I was still half-deaf.

We were sitting in one of the dank stone alcoves in De Cluyse cafe on Oude Koornmarkt, eating chicken *waterzooi* and potatoes. The cafe was converted from a thirteenth-century cellar, and it was lit only by candles in small glass jelly-jars. It was so cold that we were both wearing our over-coats and mittens, and our breath was smoking. Frank was lying under the table, making disgusting noises with a pork knuckle.

'I mean, supposing those other two Screechers weren't hiding in that building at all? We only have that Hauser guy's word for it, after all.'

'Well, you're absolutely right, Henry, but it's going to take days to clear all that rubble, and even then we may not know for sure.'

'What do you reckon it was? Gas main?'

I shrugged and said nothing. But I had guessed what it was, the instant I had heard that distinctive double-bang. The house in Schildersstraat had been hit by the first German V-2 to strike the centre of Antwerp. The first bang was a sonic boom, as the rocket came out of the sky at over three times the speed of sound. The second was over a ton of high explosive.

Six days before a V-2 had hit the village of Brasschaat, about eight kilometres to the north-east of Antwerp, and all of us officers in 101 Counterintelligence Detachment had been briefed that this was probably a 'range-finding' shot, with more V-2s to follow.

The stove-like object that had bounced along the street had confirmed it for me. It was the rocket's combustion chamber, which weighed over six hundred kilos and almost always survived the explosion.

I lifted up a scraggy piece of chicken leg on the end of my fork, with a shred of wet leek hanging off it. 'What do you think they fed this on? Newspaper?'

A second V-2 landed on the city in the middle of the afternoon, when Corporal Little and I were walking along Keizerstraat. Frank did a four-legged jump and cowered against the nearest wall.

'It's OK, boy,' Corporal Little reassured him, but Frank never did get used to the seismic shock of V-2 explosions, which made the cobblestones knock together like pebbles on the beach. If bloodhounds are capable of having nervous breakdowns, poor old Frank got pretty close to it.

That Sunday, October 15, a rocket destroyed twenty-five houses on Kroonstraat at Borgerhout, killing four people and injuring a hundred more. Over the next few days, more and more V-2s hit the city centre. There was a total news blackout – nothing on the wireless, and nothing in the newspapers except vague warnings about 'flying bombs' – so nobody knew what was really happening. The city authorities were desperate to avoid any panic, and, just as importantly, they didn't want the Germans to find out whether their rockets were hitting their targets or not.

After the Schildersstraat attack, Corporal Little and Frank and I spent three more weeks in Antwerp, searching for any trace of the Romanian Screecher and his German companion, just in case Ernst Hauser had been lying to us, or they had been hiding in some other house when the V-2 struck. But after we had dragged Frank up and down every rubble-strewn street and every smelly alley between Prinsstraat and Lange Nieuwstraat, and talked to more than two hundred people, including police officers and hospital orderlies and priests, we finally had to conclude that they had either left Antwerp and returned to Germany, or else that first V-2 had simply atomized them.

As the winter grew colder and colder, and the Germans retreated, we were sent into Holland. We visited houses in Eindhoven and Breda and Tilburg, and found the grisly evidence that Screechers had been there – men, women and children, with their hearts cut out and all of the blood drained out of them. But the Screechers themselves had long gone, and they had left no trail that Frank could usefully follow.

Whenever I think of that winter, I think of finger-numbing cold, and skies as dark as lead. I think of desperate tiredness, and boredom – driving miles and miles between avenues of poplar trees, and seeing nobody for hours. It felt as if the war had passed us by and we were completely alone in the world.

On the morning of January 16, 1945, a message came through Brussels that my mother had died, and that I should return home immediately. Operation Screecher was over – as far as I was concerned, anyway – because I was never sent back to Europe. Corporal Little was ordered to take Frank back to Antwerp, where he could help the Belgian rescue services to locate buried bodies. The city was still under daily attack from V-2 rockets, and already more than three and a half thousand people had been killed.

The last time I saw Corporal Little and Frank was on the long stone mole at Zeebrugge harbour, where I was due to board a British troopship. It was the middle of the afternoon and it was snowing hard. The lighthouse on the end of the mole was back in action, and every now and then the snow was illuminated by a bright sweeping light.

'Well, Henry, it's been an experience.'

'Yes, sir, it has.' He hesitated for a moment, and then he said, 'Think we did any good, sir?'

'I don't know. I guess we never will. I can't see us going into the history books, can you?'

'No, sir. But we'll remember it. You and me, and Frank.'

Frank made that whining noise in his throat and irritably shook the snowflakes from his back.

I shook Corporal Little's hand and walked back along the mole to the dockside. Somewhere, in some alternative existence, I think that I'm still walking along it now, with the lighthouse flashing on and off, and the snow falling all around me, and the bang and clatter of cranes still echoes in my ears.

I didn't yet know how my mother had died, but I was already feeling a devastating loneliness, as if had lost not only the woman who had given birth to me, but part of my ancestry, too.

Mill Valley, 1943

I was swinging in the hammock in my parents' backyard when my father came walking through the overgrown grass and said, 'There's two military guys want to talk to you.'

I sat up a little and shaded my eyes with my hand. Two middle-aged men in sharply pressed army uniforms were standing by the kitchen steps with their hats tucked under their arms. One had a silvery-grey crewcut and the other had horn-rim glasses and a heavy black moustache.

'They wouldn't tell me what they wanted,' said my father. 'If you'd prefer me to say that you're not at home, well, I'm more than happy to. You know my views on the military.'

My father was what you might call a professional noncon-formist. He always reminded me of Groucho Marx in *Horse Feathers* when he sang 'Whatever it is, I'm against it'. He looked a little like Groucho Marx, too, in his slopy-shouldered cardigans and his baggy corduroy pants, with his pipe always sticking out of the side of his mouth. He was Professor of Slavic Languages and Literature at Berkeley, but he was also a writer and a fly-fisherman and when he played the piano on summer evenings with the parlour windows open his music was so sentimental that he could make you choke up.

The officer with the silvery-grey crew cut raised one hand and called out, 'James Falcon Junior? Need to talk to you, sir!'

I looked at my father and my father shrugged. I clambered out of the hammock, catching my foot so that I staggered on one leg for the first couple of paces, but I managed to hold on to the apple I'd been eating.

The officers approached me. 'I'm Lieutenant Colonel Kenneth Bulsover and this is Major Leonard Harvey.'

They stood with their backs like ramrods and they almost had *me* standing up straight. Not long ago, I found some photographs of myself that my brother took around that time, and you've never seen such a skinny, lanky, twenty-five-year-old streak in your life, in a baggy pair of jeans and a striped shirt that was five times too big for me.

'We need to talk in private,' said Lieutenant Colonel Bulsover. He didn't look at my father and at first my father didn't understand what he was saying.

'This is just about as private as you can get,' he said, taking his pipe out of his mouth. 'There isn't another house for half a mile. Hey – we could beat a pig to death with baseball bats and nobody would hear us.'

Lieutenant Colonel Bulsover looked at him as if were mentally deficient. 'When I say private, sir, I mean that I need to talk to your son confidentially. On his own.'

'Oh? *Oh.* What for? This family doesn't have secrets.'

'That's as maybe, sir. But this is wartime, and this country has secrets.'

'Oh.'

My father hesitated for a moment and then he put his pipe back in his mouth and walked away across the grass, jerkily turning around now and again as if half expecting us to call him back. Eventually he climbed the steps and disappeared into the kitchen. The screen door banged.

Lieutenant Colonel Bulsover placed his hand in the small of my back and gently steered me down toward the far end of the yard, where the tangled raspberry canes grew. It was very hot and still that day, and I remember that everything looked magnified, as I were seeing it through a lens.

'Major Harvey and I, we're attached to the Office of the Co-ordinator of Information in Washington, DC. About three weeks ago we received some information from a resistance agent in Belgium. He confirmed something that our intelligence agents have been suspecting since the early days of the war in Europe.'

'Oh, yes?'

Major Harvey cleared his throat with a single sharp bark. 'Mr Falcon – what Lieutenant Colonel Bulsover is about to tell you now is absolutely top secret. That means you are prohibited from divulging any of this information to anybody. Your father, your mother, your best friend, even your family cat. If we discover that you have been giving anybody else even the faintest hint of what we are going to discuss with you, you may discover that your life is forfeit.'

'What?'

'You'll be shot,' said Major Harvey.

I stared at him in disbelief. 'I'll be *shot*? Are you *serious*? In that case, excuse me, I don't want to hear it.'

'You *have* to hear it, James,' said Lieutenant Colonel Bulsover, firmly. Then, in a quieter tone, 'You have to. You're the only person we've been able to find who seems to have a comprehensive knowledge of the particular problem we're faced with. The only person of an appropriate age, anyhow.'

'I don't understand. I don't know anything about any military stuff.'

'I know that. But you know all about these.' With that, Lieutenant Colonel Bulsover reached inside his coat and produced a sharply folded sheaf of papers.

I didn't have to open them to recognize what they were. They were tear sheets of my paper 'The Strigoi: myth versus reality in popular Romanian folk-culture'. I had written it for my anthropology exam in the summer, and Professor Ewan had been so impressed with it that he had submitted it to the *North American Journal of Ethnography*. Admittedly, the *Journal*'s circulation was only a little over 2,500 copies, so it wasn't exactly like being published in *Life* magazine, but it was first article I had ever gotten into print, and I was seriously proud of it. I even had some cards printed, *James R. Falcon Jr, Author and Anthropologist*, and handed them out to all of my friends, until my father told me to stop acting so swell-headed.

'The *strigoi*?' I said, cautiously. I was strongly beginning to suspect this was a practical joke, set up by some of my friends at Berkeley. 'What do the *strigoi* have to do with the war in Europe?'

'More than you'd think. In August of 1940, under the terms of the Vienna Diktat, Germany forced Romania to give up the territory of Northern Transylvania to Hungary, which Hungary had been claiming for centuries was theirs.'

44

'Well, sure, I know that.'

'What you may *not* know is that the Romanians would have had to surrender Southern Transylvania, too, but they made some kind of offer to the Germans, which the Germans accepted, and allowed them to keep it.'

Major Harvey said, 'We've been trying for three years to find out exactly what this offer was. It was codenamed *Umarmung*, which didn't mean anything to us, at the beginning.'

'*Umarmung*,' I repeated. 'Embrace.'

'That's right. And how many times does the word "Embrace" appear in your article, James? Forty-seven, to be exact. And according to what you've written here, the Embrace is the way in which the *strigoi* initiate humans into becoming one of them.'

I shrugged. 'Could be a coincidence. I mean, "embrace", that's a pretty common word, wouldn't you say? You can embrace all kinds of things, you know – like a religion, or a philosophy. Or your next-door-neighbour's wife.'

'True. And the Romanians embraced Nazism. They still chose to fight on the German side, even though the Germans made them surrender all of that territory. But after we received this report from Belgium, we're pretty sure now that "Embrace" means something very specific. We think it's the kind of embrace that *you* were writing about.'

I kept a straight face for about ten seconds longer, and then I burst out laughing. 'God, you guys are good! You even sound like you know what you're talking about! Who set this up? I'll bet it was Stradlater, wasn't it? Tell me it was Stradlater!'

'James—' said Lieutenant Colonel Bulsover, but I interrupted him.

'"How many times does the word 'Embrace' appear in your article, James?"' I mimicked him. '"Forty-seven, to be exact." You're excellent! Look at you standing there, like you both have pool cues stuck up your asses!'

Lieutenant Colonel Bulsover waited until I had finished. Then, as if I hadn't said anything at all, he continued.

'Since February last year, James, we've been receiving reports of some very unusual killings. They started in Romania. More than sixty members of the Red Knights resistance group were murdered, all within the space of a week.

That immediately deprived us of vital intelligence and it drastically reduced our ability to sabotage the Nazi war effort from within.'

I looked at him with my eyes narrowed. 'Come on, now. This *is* a joke, isn't it?'

'Not for the victims. And not for the Allies, if this continues.'

'Come on, admit it. If it wasn't Stradlater, who was it? Not Dungan! Dungan wouldn't have the brains!'

'James,' said Major Harvey. 'It wasn't any of your friends and it isn't a joke.'

'All right,' I said, although I still believed that they were bullshitting me. 'What does any of this have to do with me?'

'Since the Red Knights were all murdered, we've been receiving more and more intelligence which suggests that the Nazis have been infiltrating local resistance groups and literally wiping them out. It happened all across the Eastern Front, especially after they took Bessarabia and Bukovina back from the Russians. Now it's happening in Holland and Belgium and France.

'The reason why this has everything to do with you is that all of the victims had their chests cut open, their main arteries severed and the blood drained out of their bodies.'

Dinner with the Falcons

That evening, my mother made *bors cu perisoare*, sour meatball soup, which was one of the specialities of her village in north-eastern Romania. We sat and ate it in the kitchen, with the windows open, so that the last of the sun shone across the table.

My mother Maricica was beautiful in a dark-haired, white-skinned way, like a Madonna in a church painting. She did everything gently and gracefully. She could even peel apples gracefully, their skins unwinding in spirals. She always spoke softly, too, although the quietness of her voice belied a very strong character.

Dad was fuming. He didn't like secrets and he didn't like anything to do with authority. His father had been a biochemist and a violin player and had knitted his own sweaters, mostly green with orange zigzags. He had brought Dad up to believe that a man was answerable only to his own intellect, and God, in that order.

'You can't even give us a hint what they want you to do? Your own family?'

I shook my head. 'They said if I told anybody – even you – they'd shoot me.'

'Oh my God,' said my mother. 'They *threatened* you? They come here, uninvited, into my house, and threaten to shoot you, my son, in my yard?'

'Hey, it's my house, too,' my father protested. 'And my son. And my yard, come to that.'

'We should complain to the army,' said my mother.

'They said I have to go to Washington next week,' I told her. 'They're going to pay my fare and everything.'

'They can't coerce you,' said my father. 'Is this why we pay taxes? Tell them you don't want to go to Washington.'

I spooned a meatball out of my soup. 'But I *do* want to go to Washington. I think this is going to be really, really interesting.'

'I see. It's so interesting you can't tell us what it is?'

'Dad – not only will they shoot me, they'll probably shoot you, too.'

'Pah!' said my father, pushing his chair back in disgust, the same way he did when I beat him at chess.

But my mother was staring at me across the table and there was a look in her eyes which told me that she had guessed why the army had come looking for me. After all, what was the one thing that made me different from all of the rest of my college friends? I had a Romanian mother, who had told me all kinds of scary Romanian folk tales when I was little. None of my friends had been brought up on stories of *strigoi* and *strigoaica*, the creatures of the night, and none of my friends had researched Romanian legends as thoroughly as I had, and published a paper on them.

I have to admit that I decided to write a paper on *strigoi* out of perversity, almost as a joke. Everybody in my class thought that I was a clown, including my professors, and I guess I decided to live up to their expectations. It's difficult to grow up normal when your father expects you to recite Edward Arlington Robinson to amuse his lunch guests when you're only four years old, and your mother sings you Romanian lullabies about what will happen to you if you betray love. 'If you betray love, you will squirm like a snake, walk like a beetle, and you will own nothing but the dust of the land.'

The Strigoi

Even though she told me so many stories about them, my mother never gave me the impression that she actually believed in the *strigoi* – and she was brought up in Tanacu, where they still cross themselves if a crow flies down their chimney, or a black dog urinates against their gatepost. As recently as the summer of 2005, a priest from the Holy Trinity monastery in Tanacu strangled and crucified a nun because he thought she was possessed by demons.

To begin with, I didn't believe in the *strigoi*, either – but like I say, I thought it would be a terrific wheeze to write a paper that discussed them as if they *were* real. Only two or three weeks after I had started work on it, however, I began to come across credible documentary evidence that the *strigoi* might be more than imaginary – letters, newspaper reports, even some blurry old photographs. I couldn't help asking myself: what if they *did* exist? Even more intriguing: *what if they still do*?

I studied the *strigoi* for nearly two years. I made scores of phone calls and talked in person to more than two hundred Romanian immigrants of all ages. I searched through private libraries and smelly old collections of rare books. Without realizing it, day by day, I was becoming one of the world's greatest experts on *strigoi*.

One of the elderly Romanian immigrants I interviewed for my college paper talked to me about his cousin, who became a *strigoi mort*. 'He was the handsomest man you ever met. Tall, witty and irresistible to women. But he could be very melancholy, too. Once when he came to visit us I saw him standing by the window and there were tears in his eyes. I asked him what was wrong and he said, "Look." He reached out his hand and it passed straight through the glass of the window pane without breaking it. I could actually see his hand outside the window, still with his gold wedding band on it. Then he drew his hand back in again, and the glass was completely intact. I felt a chill like nothing I had ever felt before. He said, "I am dead, Daniel, and I can never go home again, ever."'

It was this man who first drew me a picture of the wheel which the *strigoi mortii* wear around their necks – a diagonal cross to symbolize a kiss, with a circle around it to represent endlessness. Usually, the *strigoi mortii* fashion the wheels themselves. They use gold from any rings they wore when they were still human, with copper to enhance its electrical conductivity. The wheel is much more than symbolic: it gives the *strigoi mortii* exceptional night vision, and it contains the protective power of absolute evil. Several respected academics suggest that J. R. R. Tolkien was inspired by the wheel when he wrote *The Lord of the Rings*, and that the physical and spiritual degeneration of Gollum is a close parallel to what happens to people when they become infected by *strigoi*. You'll remember that Gollum's eyes lit up, so that he could see better in the dark, just like the *strigoi mortii* when they wear the wheel.

By the time I had finished writing my paper, I still hadn't conclusively proved that the *strigoi* did exist (like, I had never knowingly *met* one) but I had a wealth of anecdotal evidence that they *might*. I ended up my paper by saying 'on balance, it appears highly likely that the *strigoi* did once haunt the remoter regions of Transylvania and Wallachia, and a few may do so even today'.

And I was right. Which was why Lieutenant Colonel Bulsover and Major Harvey came knocking at my door to tell me that the joke was on me.

My Training

I flew to Washington, DC, on August 11th, 1943. It was the first time I had ever flown, and I saw mountains with scatterings of snow on them and fields of wheat that seemed to stretch forever, with cloud shadows moving over them slow and lazy, as if whales were swimming through the sky. Somewhere I still have the blue American Airways timetable with 'Buy More War Bonds!' printed on the front.

I was met at Washington National Airport by a skeletally thin man in a flappy grey double-breasted suit and tiny dark glasses. He raised his hat to me and asked me to call him Mr Corogeanu. He drove me to a large ivy-covered house on the outskirts of Rockville and it was there, during the next three months, that I was given my basic training in *strigoi* hunting.

Since I already knew a whole lot more about the *strigoi* than almost anybody else, what they were really giving me was military training. I was taught to fire a gun, and to read a map, and to climb over a ten-foot wall. I was also introduced to a laconic animal-trainer with no front teeth who had been specially recruited from Barnum & Bailey's Circus. He gave me daily instruction in wielding a bullwhip, which is a darn sight more difficult than it looks. I spent whole afternoons lashing my own calves until they looked like corned beef.

Meantime, the *strigoi*-hunting Kit was gradually being assembled, mostly according to the details I had provided in my college paper, although it was Mr Corogeanu who suggested the black and white paint. According to him, *strigoi* are repelled by the sight of a dog with an extra pair of eyes painted above its real eyes.

It was during my training sessions that we started calling the *strigoi* 'Screechers'. The word *strigoi* comes from the

Romanian word *striga* meaning 'witch', and this in turn comes from the Latin cognate *strega*, which has its origins in *strix*, the word for a screech owl. Besides that, my side-arms instructor always used to say, 'If you want to immobilize those creatures, you have to hit 'em dead centre,' and the way he slurred his words always made it sound like 'tho' Screechers'.

I wish I knew where they acquired the nails from the crucifixion. I asked Lieutenant Colonel Bulsover several times but he always refused to tell me. All he said was, 'It was a case of you scratch my back and I'll scratch yours.' I always wondered if this meant that – in return for these priceless relics – the United States had agreed to support the creation of an independent State of Israel, but maybe I was reading too much into it.

Six weeks before D-Day, I was introduced to Corporal Little and Frank, so that Frank could get used to my smell and Corporal Little could be briefed on what he was supposed to be doing. Three weeks before D-Day, we were embarked from New York on the USS *New Hampshire* to sail to England. We were taken over to Normandy a week after the first landings on Omaha Beach. We were all seasick, even Frank. The rest I've already told you.

Except that it didn't end there. Nothing ends, when you get yourself involved with the *strigoi*. The *strigoi* are immortal, and their sense of grievance is immortal. That's why, when two US Army officers drew up outside my house in New Milford, Connecticut, in July 1957, I almost felt a sense of relief, because I had always known in my heart of hearts that this was coming.

New Milford, 1957

My wife Louise answered the door. The two officers stood on the veranda with their caps tucked under their arms, just as Lieutenant Colonel Bulsover and Major Harvey had done fourteen years before. It was a hot, bright day, and they were both in shirtsleeves.

'Captain Falcon?'

I came out of my study and put my arm around Louise's shoulders. 'Help you?' I asked them. I didn't like the sound of 'Captain'.

'Like to have a few words with you, Captain, if that's OK.'

'Sure. What's it about?'

'Maybe we could come inside?'

I invited them into the living room. The dark oak floor was highly polished and the sun was shining on it, so that when they sat on the couch opposite me it was difficult for me to make out their faces. They were both young, though. One was sandy-haired and the other was wearing black-rimmed eyeglasses like Clark Kent.

'We're from counterintelligence at Fort Holabird, sir. We need to speak to you in confidence.'

I turned to Louise and said, 'How about some coffee, honey?'

'OK,' she agreed, although she wasn't especially happy about it. Louise was very petite, with bouncy brunette hair and an Audrey Hepburn look about her, but she had her own opinions about almost everything, which were usually the exact opposite of mine, and she never allowed me to treat her as if she were a 'little woman'.

She went into the kitchen and started a percussion solo for spoons and cups and coffee percolator. The officer in the black-rimmed eyeglasses leaned forward and said, sotto voce, 'We've had a communication from British intelligence, Captain – MI6. It concerns a series of incidents in the suburbs south of London, England.'

'Incidents? What kind of incidents?'

The sandy-haired officer said, 'Homicides. Well, I say they're homicides, but they're practically massacres, to be honest with you. Thirteen people killed at a business conference; six children killed at an orphanage; nine women killed at a social club. Altogether, seventy-three people dead in the space of five weeks.'

I slowly sat back. I didn't say anything. I had already guessed what was coming.

'MI6 have kept all of these killings out of the news.

They've been telling relatives that there's some kind of bug going around – Korean Flu, something like that. In fact they're actually calling their investigation "Operation Korean Flu".'

The officer in the eyeglasses said, 'It's not a bug, though, Captain. All of the victims were cut open and the blood drained out of them. Exact same scenario as Operation Screecher, during the war.'

Louise came in with a tray of coffee and gingersnaps, which she passed around with a tight, shiny smile. 'Gingersnap? They're home-made. Not by me, I'm afraid, my mother.' While she did so, none of us said anything, except, 'Thank you.'

When she had finished pouring coffee, Louise waited for a while, and all three of us looked at each other in uncomfortable silence. At last she said, 'Maybe I'll go outside and cut some roses.'

'Sure, good idea,' I told her. She hesitated a moment longer, but the officer in the eyeglasses raised his eyebrows at her expectantly, and she left. I could see her through the French windows, snipping away at the rose bushes as if she were giving all three of us vasectomies.

'Before we tell you any more, Captain, we have to remind you that you are still bound by the same rules of confidentiality that you were during Operation Screecher.'

'Maybe I'd prefer it if you didn't tell me any more. We're not at war now, are we?'

'Well, yes, Captain. I'm afraid we are. It may not be an all-out fighting war, but it's still a war, and your country needs your help.'

'What if I decline to give it?'

'We don't actually think that you will, Captain.'

'I see,' I told him. I wasn't stupid. However callow these officers looked, they worked for one of the most secret and highly specialized counterintelligence units in the Western world, and I could tell when I was being seriously threatened.

The officer in the eyeglasses said, 'According to our records, you were in Antwerp, Belgium, in the winter of 1944, searching for a Romanian national by the name of Dorin Duca.'

'That's right. I never found him, though. Or *it*, I should say. I always assumed that he was killed by a V-2.'

'In actual fact, sir, Duca escaped to the Netherlands. He

was located by another operative from Operation Screecher and detained.'

I frowned at him. 'I didn't know there *were* any other operatives in Operation Screecher. I thought that I was the only one.'

'No, Captain, not exactly. Other operatives were occasionally brought in as and when the situation called for it.'

'Well, that's news to me. Besides, what do you mean by "detained"? You can't "detain" Screechers. All you can do is eliminate them. Knock nails into their eyes and cut their heads off.'

'This particular operative had special abilities which allowed her to take Duca into detention.'

'This was a *woman*?'

The officer nodded. 'She confined Duca to a casket and the plan was to fly him to England and then ship him back here to the United States to see if we could learn anything useful from him as regards counterintelligence operations.'

I shook my head. 'I can't believe this. We were going to bring a Screecher to America? *Deliberately?* Didn't anybody have the first idea how dangerous those creatures can be?'

'Oh, I think so, sir. After all, Screechers wiped out practically the entire resistance movements in Bessarabia and Bulgaria during the war, and they did some major damage to the French and Dutch underground movements. The Nazis even used them in Warsaw, during the Uprising – sent them down the sewers to hunt down members of the Home Army.'

'But what possible use could a Screecher be to *us*, once the war was over?'

The officer took off his eyeglasses. 'The opinion was that we needed to maintain our edge over the Russkies, Captain. It was all part of Operation Paperclip.'

'I don't know what Operation Paperclip was.'

'That was the codename we used for bringing Nazi scientists and intelligence experts to the United States after the war. Not even the State Department knew about it, to begin with. None of them had visas, and most of them had their files altered to conceal the fact that they were hundred per cent Nazi sympathizers, or worse.'

'You're talking about people like Wernher von Braun?'

'Exactly. Von Braun developed the V-2 for Hitler, and now he's developing rockets for the Army Ballistic Missile Agency. Then there's Hans von Ohain, who used to design jet engines for Heinkel – he's Director of the US Air Force Aeronautical Laboratory – and Alexander Lippisch, who did the same for Messerschmitt – he's in Cedar Rapids, designing jet fighters for Convair. Reinhard Gehlen used to be in charge of intelligence for the Wehrmacht, and he's set us up with the most effective counter-espionage network that we've ever had. Kurt Blome – he used to test plague vaccines on concentration-camp victims. Now he works for the US Army Chemical Corps.'

'There were seven hundred sixty of them altogether,' put in the sandy-haired officer.

'But *Duca*? Duca isn't even human!'

'We're aware of that, Captain, but it made good military sense to bring him over here, too. If the Russkies got hold of him, think of the damage that they could do to our intelligence-gathering.'

Louise was standing in the sunshine, not clipping roses any more, but raising her face to the sky, with her eyes closed, as if she were enjoying the warmth of the sun, or praying. I had a terrible sinking feeling that I was about to let her down, and very badly, but not through any fault of my own. I stood up and walked to the French windows and lifted my hand up, pressing it against the glass. But her eyes were still closed and she didn't see me.

'You'd better tell me what happened,' I said.

Lost and Found

'Duca was sealed into a casket and flown out of Holland on the night of December 17, 1944, along with two marines, a lieutenant from the counterintelligence detachment and the operative who had managed to detain him.'

'Do you know how Duca was caught?' I asked him. 'We looked all over northern Belgium and Holland for him, for weeks, and we didn't even get a sniff of him.' I called Duca 'him' because these officers did, but I always thought of any *strigoi* as an 'it', especially a *strigoi mort*. They weren't people. They weren't even ghosts of people. They were things. They could be deeply sentimental, but they only looked like people.

The sandy-haired officer unbuckled his briefcase. 'From all the reports I've read, Captain, they caught him mostly by sheer chance. He was hiding in the cellar of a house in Breda when it was shelled by British artillery, and he was trapped. The Dutch resistance had been looking for him, and they had the good sense not to let him out of that cellar but to give his location to US counterintelligence.'

'So why the hell didn't they tell me? I was the one who was hunting for Duca.'

'They didn't tell you, Captain, because they knew what you would do to him, and they wanted him – well, *alive* isn't quite the word for it, is it? But they didn't want him destroyed.'

'So this female operative somehow managed to seal Duca up in a box? I can't imagine how she did it but I'm very impressed. What happened to him after we flew him to England?'

'That's the problem, Captain. When they took off from Holland it was snowing very hard – blizzard conditions. They were supposed to fly to Biggin Hill airfield in Kent but their plane never arrived. The Royal Navy sent out air-sea rescue boats to search for it, but they couldn't find any trace at all, nothing.'

He took a photograph out of his briefcase and passed it over to me. It showed the muddy fuselage of a DC3 on the back of a trailer.

'Last May, though, a dredger was clearing the Thames Estuary near a place called Leigh-on-Sea, and it struck one of the plane's propellers. The aircraft must have hit the water at full speed and buried itself in the mud. That British air ace – what was her name, Amy Johnson – she disappeared in almost the same place in 1941, and they still haven't found *her* plane, either.'

'So they dug the plane up and found Duca's casket?' I asked him.

'That's right.'

'And nobody realized what was in the casket, so they opened it?'

'Right again.'

'Jesus,' I said.

'MI6 are very, very anxious to get this situation under control as quick as possible,' said the officer.

'I'll bet they are.'

'It's not just a question of innocent lives being lost, Captain. It's a question of national security. Think of what could happen if the Russkies get wind of this and track Duca down before we do. British intelligence has more holes in it than a Swiss cheese, so it's a distinct possibility. If we lose Duca to the communist bloc – well, to put it bluntly, we're in very deep doo-doo.'

'Oh, you bet we are,' I told him. 'And if the press find out that US counterintelligence were covertly trying to smuggle a *strigoi* into the country at the end of the war, without the knowledge or approval of the State Department, and in complete disregard of the very obvious dangers to public safety, some pretty important heads are going to be rolling, don't you think?'

'You can't tell anybody about this,' said the officer. 'Not even your wife. Nobody.'

'So what do you want me to do?'

'You're booked already on a TWA Starliner from Idlewild to London. You leave tomorrow evening at nineteen-forty-five.'

'What about a man-trailer?'

'A dog? British quarantine laws won't allow you to take a dog with you. You'll be met in London by somebody from MI6 who will brief you more fully and provide you with a tracker dog and a trained handler.'

I sat down again and I didn't say anything for a long time. The two officers watched me tensely, almost as if they expected me to make a run for the door.

At length, I said, 'Supposing I say no?'

'Saying "no" is not actually one of your options,' said the sandy-haired officer.

'What am I going to tell my company? I can't just disappear without telling them where I'm going, or how long I'm going to be away.'

'We'll take care of that, Captain.'

'OK – but I'll have to get some stuff together. Silver mirror, compass, Bible, all that kind of thing. And I need the nails they used to crucify Christ. Where am I going to find those?'

'We have your Kit already, Captain,' said the officer with the eyeglasses. 'Everything's in there, just the way it was when you handed it in, including the nails. All you need is some fresh garlic.'

'You think this is funny?'

'No, Captain. Not in the slightest.'

'So you want me to eliminate Duca, if I can find it. You don't want me to bring it back here to the States?'

'I'm afraid you don't have the expertise to detain him, Captain. Nobody does. Nobody that we can find, anyhow.'

'So – this female operative who *did* detain it? Do you have any idea who she was?'

The sandy-haired officer said, 'Yes, Captain, actually we do. That was one of the things I was instructed to tell you about. You were bound to find out, sooner or later.'

I looked from one officer to the other. Both of them looked highly embarrassed.

'It was your mother, Captain. Maricica Falcon, née Loveinescu.'

'My *mother*? What the hell are you talking about? My mother died of a heart attack at home in California.'

'I'm sorry, Captain, no she didn't. When you were being trained to hunt *strigoi*, you told your instructors that you learned most of your basic information about vampires from your mother. The counterintelligence detachment sent some people to talk to her, and they found out that she knew almost as much about the *strigoi* as you did. Not only that, she had some practical knowledge, too. Like, how to seal *strigoi mortii* into lead caskets, in such a way that they couldn't escape.'

I was stunned. My *mother* had been sent to capture Duca? I had never thought that she believed in the *strigoi*. In fact, she had always said that they were only stories, to frighten naughty children into behaving themselves.

I thought of my father, sitting on the veranda, his eyes glistening with tears. 'She had a problem with her heart,' he had told me, hoarsely. 'And now I have a problem with mine.' He must have known what had happened to her, and yet he had never said a word. He had even emptied her ashes into the sea at Bodega Bay, which used to be one of her favourite places. Except that they couldn't have been *her* ashes at all.

London, 1957

They had reserved me a sleeping berth on the TWA flight to London so that I would be rested and ready to start work as soon as I arrived, but shortly after I dozed off I started having terrifying nightmares. The droning of the airliner's turboprop engines gradually turned into the noise of a huge, dark factory crammed with strange machines for crushing people's bones, and I found myself running past dripping pipes and greasy electric cables, with a dark figure running just ahead of me. I knew that I was supposed to catch up with this figure, but I was frightened to run too fast, in case I did.

After less than four hours, however, it began to grow light, and the flight attendant brought me a cup of coffee. 'Are you all right, sir?' she smiled. 'You were shouting in your sleep.' She had very blue eyes and freckles across the bridge of her nose.

'Oh, yes? What was I shouting?'

'I don't know. Something about teachers, I think. You were telling them to get off you.'

'*Teachers*? If only.'

It was surprisingly hot when we landed in England, well over eighty degrees, and the sky was cloudless. As I came down the steps of the plane, I was greeted by a young man with wavy Brylcreemed hair and sunglasses. The only concession he had made to the heat was to take off his tweed coat and hang it over his arm, and roll up his shirtsleeves.

'Captain Falcon? How do you do, I'm Terence Mitchell.'

'How are you?' I asked him, and shook his hand, which was soft and sweaty.

'Hope you had a comfortable flight, sir?'

'Well, it was certainly a darn sight faster than the last time I did it.'

'They'll be bringing in jets next year, and that'll make it even quicker. Six hours to New York, or so I believe. Amazing when you think it takes six days by boat. This way, sir. I've got a car waiting outside.'

I hadn't been back to England since the end of the war, but it hadn't changed much. The same flat smell of English cigarettes, and body odour. The same dinky little cars, and red double-decker buses. The same clipped accents, as if everybody had been to elocution school.

'Don't worry about your things,' said Terence. 'I've arranged to have them sent straight round to your hotel.'

A beige Humber Hawk was parked by the kerb outside the terminal, with a uniformed bobby standing beside it. The bobby gave Terence a nod as we approached, and strolled off. Terence opened the door for me and then climbed in himself. 'Gasper?' he said, taking out a box of Player's cigarettes.

'No thanks. I gave up two years ago. Had a cough I couldn't get rid of.'

'You won't mind if I do?'

We drove out of the terminal and along the Great West Road toward the centre of the city.

'Good book?' asked Terence, nodding at the blue-bound volume I had brought to read on the flight.

'*Comparative Folk Mythologies of Dobrudja,*' I told him, holding it up.

'Oh. I'm more of a Nevile Shute man myself.'

It always surprised me how green London was. The narrow streets were bursting with trees, and every little front yard had its bushes and its neatly trimmed hedge. Among the rows of houses stood the tranquil spires of Victorian churches, which gave the suburbs the appearance of order and respectability and enduring faith.

'Very nasty business this, sir,' said Terence, with his cigarette waggling between his lips. 'Seven more fatalities yesterday morning, in Croydon.'

'You don't have to call me "sir" all the time, really. Jim will be fine.'

'Right-oh. Jim it is.' He pronounced it as though it had inverted commas. He looked ridiculously young to be an SIS operative, but he was probably the same age as I was when I was hunting the *strigoi* during the war. He was pale and round-shouldered, and he reminded me of one of those young English pilots you see clustered around Spitfires in wartime photographs, all smiling and most of them doomed to be incinerated alive before their twenty-first birthdays.

'How are you managing to keep this out of the news?' I asked him.

'It's been jolly difficult, to tell you the truth. Fortunately there's been some Korean influenza going around, so most of the time we can blame it on that.'

'These seven . . . in *where* did you say?'

'Croydon. It's a borough, about ten miles south of London. Not the most attractive spot on earth. Pretty grotty, as a matter of fact.'

'Were they all in the same room when they were killed?'

'Yes, apart from one lad. They found his body upstairs. Only eleven years old. Very nasty business. They all belonged to the same family, except for one of them, an elderly lady who was a friend of theirs. It was a birthday party. Shocking. There was blood all over the food.'

'You haven't touched anything?'

'The bodies have been taken away, but that's all. Everything else is just as we found it.'

'OK . . . but I'll need to take a look at the bodies, later.'

We were coming into West Kensington now, past the Natural History Museum and the Brompton Oratory, and the traffic was beginning to build up. As we reached Harrods store in Knightsbridge, Terence tossed his cigarette out of the window and took out a fresh one, tapping it on the steering wheel to tamp down the loose tobacco. 'The first murders were on the 23rd of May, at the Selsdon Park Hotel. Eleven men and two women at a business conference.'

'I read the police reports. I saw the photographs, too. Property developers, weren't they?'

'Estate agents. It was a total fluke that we found out who might have killed them.'

'Oh, yes?'

'One of our senior chaps just happened to be round at Scotland Yard for some security powwow when the news about the murders first came in. Look at that bloody cyclist! He must have a death wish!' He leaned out of the window and shouted, 'Nutcase!'

'Go on,' I told him.

'Oh, yes. As luck would have it, our chap used to liaise with US counterintelligence during the war, and he remembered that your people always wanted to be urgently notified of any mass killings, especially if the victims had their hearts cut out, or the blood drained out of them. At the time, your people never actually told him why they wanted to be notified, or what it was all about, and our chap *still* had no idea what it was all about, but he thought, "Hallo! Mass killing – people with all the blood drained out of them," and he got on to your people anyway. Your people came back to us in less than twenty-four hours, and they came round to HQ and gave us the full SP. I must say I find it really fascinating, in a grisly sort of way. But it isn't exactly easy to believe, is it? You know – *vampires*.' He bared his teeth and gave a bad imitation of a Bela Lugosi '*ho-ho-ho!*'.

'Let me tell you, Terence,' I said, 'you need to believe.' I probably sounded too serious and pontificating, but I was very tired. 'If you think that Russian spies are dangerous, you don't know what dangerous is. The *strigoi* are the most vicious creatures you are ever going to meet in your entire life.'

We drove around Hyde Park Corner, with its massive stone arch and its triumphant statue of Winged Victory. Then we made our way down the Mall and past Buckingham Palace. A troop of Horse Guards jingled their way down the centre of the road, their helmets sparkling in the sunlight. The last time I had been in London it had been grim and grey and badly bombed, but this was like driving through a brightly coloured picture-postcard.

After another fifteen minutes of sitting in traffic around Trafalgar Square and up Ludgate Hill, we arrived at MI6 headquarters in the City. It was a large ugly office building with a soot-streaked facade and plastic Venetian blinds in a nasty shade of olive green. Terence parked his Humber around the back, and led the way in.

'You're fully cleared, right up to level one,' said Terence, clipping an identity tag on to my shirt pocket. I peered down at it. I don't know where my photograph had come from, but my eyes were half-closed and I looked as if my mouth was stuffed with cheeseburger.

The building was very warm and stuffy and smelled of floor-polish. Three or four plain-looking women passed us in the corridor and they all said 'Hillo!' with that funny little English yelp.

We went up to the top floor. Terence said, 'It's supposed to stay warm until Sunday, but I can't see it myself. You know what they say about the English summer – three hot days followed by a thunderstorm.'

He knocked at the walnut-panelled door marked Director of Operations (SIS), and we walked into a large office with a panoramic view of the City and the River Thames. I could see Tower Bridge, and London Bridge, and the dome of St Paul's Cathedral. Everything was hazy with summer heat, so that it looked like an impressionist painting, except for the constant sparkling of traffic.

As we entered, a tall, heavily built man in a grey suit rose up from behind an enormous desk, like a whale coming up for air. He had a large elaborately chiselled nose and deep-set eyes, and short shiny chestnut-coloured hair, which I could imagine him polishing every morning with a matching pair of brushes.

'Aha! You're the, ah, Screecher fellow,' he said. He spoke in a hesitant drawl, with the sides of his mouth turned down as if he found the whole business of talking to be rather a damn bore. He reached across his desk and gave me a crushing handshake. 'Charles Frith. So gratified that you could get here so promptly. Good flight?'

'Great, thanks. I never flew over the Pole before.'

'Really?' he said, as if I had admitted that I had never ridden to hounds. 'This is all turning out to be very unpleasant indeed, so we're ah. Glad of any help that you can give us.'

'How many have been killed altogether?'

Charles Frith blinked at me. 'Perhaps you'd like a cup of

tea? I usually have one around now. Or coffee? I think we can run to some instant.'

'Tea's fine.' During the war, the British seemed to spend more time brewing up tea than they did fighting the Germans. It was usually strong and astringent and tooth-achingly sweet, but I had developed a taste for it myself.

'Ninety-seven fatalities so far,' said Terence. 'That's including yesterday's figure.'

'Any eyewitness statements?'

'One or two people have said that they heard things. At the Selsdon Park Hotel, there were several reports of screaming in the middle of the night. But the screaming didn't last very long, apparently, and the witnesses thought it was somebody throwing a party. Well, I mean, it could have been, for all we know.'

Charles Frith said, 'I talked to the Metropolitan Police Commissioner yesterday evening, and unfortunately he can give us very little to go on. The police found footprints made by some very narrow shoes, but no identifiable fingerprints, and no fibres to speak of. In several cases there was no obvious means of entry and ah. The premises were secured from the inside, making access virtually impossible. To a *human* assailant, in any case.'

We all sat down around Charles Frith's desk. All he had in front of him was a leather blotter, three telephones – one black, one green and one red – and a framed photograph of a grinning blonde woman with a gap between her front teeth.

'I expect CIC told you that the *strigoi* are capable of entering a room through the thinnest of apertures,' I told him. 'They rarely leave much in the way of fingerprints or footprints, but they *do* leave a very distinctive smell, which is why we use dogs to hunt them down.'

'We've arranged for a tracker dog. And ah. Somebody to handle him.'

'OK, that's excellent. The sooner I meet him the better.'

'*Her*, as matter of fact,' Terence corrected me.

The Full SP

We sat in Charles Frith's for the next three and a half hours, so that we could study all of the case files together – all the forensic evidence, all of the photographs, all of the witness statements. I wanted to see maps and reconstructions and transcripts of coroners' court proceedings.

I insisted that we go right back to the very beginning, from the moment that a Thames dredger called the *Mary Ellen* had struck the propeller of that buried DC3. I didn't tell Charles Frith or Terence that I knew who had died in it. I was afraid that I might catch myself unawares, and fill up with tears.

The wreckage had been discovered on April 11th. It had been raised out of the mud on May 15th by a combined team from the Air Ministry and the British Aeronautical Archeological Committee. It had been taken on a flatbed truck to the Royal Aircraft Establishment at Farnborough for cleaning, research and possible restoration.

Because of the total secrecy that had surrounded Operation Paperclip, the disappearance of this plane and its cargo had never been officially reported. After the war it had mostly been forgotten, since the counterintelligence agents involved had gone back to civilian life, or retired, or died. Even when the plane's excavation was widely shown on television, radio and newsreels – even a two-page spread in *Life* magazine – nobody in the CIC put two and two together and realized which plane it was, and what it had been carrying. That only happened when the pilots and their marine escort were formally identified – and by that time it was too late.

For me, the most poignant paragraphs came from HM Coroner Sir Philip Platt-Dickinson, at Southend-on-Sea. 'The remains of five adult individuals were discovered in the wreckage. There was no soft tissue remaining, only bones, but judging from the positions in which they were found, all of them were instantly killed when the aeroplane struck the water at a speed that must have been well in excess of 200 mph, and was almost completely buried in the estuary mud.

'The pilot and his co-pilot were identified by their dog-tags as officers in the United States Army Air Forces. The remains of two further individuals, both male, were identified as officers in the United States Marine Corps. The remains of the fifth individual, who was female, carried nothing at all that allowed me to make a positive identification, although the recovery team found a gold wedding ring and a rectangular gold wristwatch from Shreve and Company, which I am given to understand is a respected jewellery shop in San Francisco, California. Her dress and shoes were also of American origin.

'Animal remains were found close to the female individual and these were identified as being those of a bloodhound, probably six or seven years old.

'The American Embassy in London was notified of the exhumation of these individuals and their remains were duly removed for repatriation to the United States, where they could be formally identified, and given appropriate funeral rites.'

I sat in that MI6 office in London and in my mind's eye I could see that rectangular gold wristwatch. I could even remember the day that my father had given it to my mother – their twenty-fifth wedding anniversary in April 1941. We had drunk sweet white wine in the yard while cherry blossoms blew all around us like snow and my mother had sung Romanian *doina*.

> '*Who made doina?*
> *The small mouth of a baby*
> *Left asleep by his mother*
> *Who found him singing the doina.*'

The casket had been examined by an Air Ministry crash-investigation team led by Professor Roger Braithwaite, who was renowned worldwide for his expertise on unusual air accidents. Apparently it had been secured to the floor of the

DC3 with webbing straps, but these had snapped on impact when the aircraft crashed. The casket had slid forward, smashing into the co-pilot's seat and breaking his back.

Terence passed me a selection of black-and-white photographs. These showed the casket from four different angles, resting on a trestle in a large empty hangar, with several bespectacled men in laboratory coats standing around it. It appeared to be fashioned out of a thick lead alloy, beaten and welded by hand. It measured approximately nine feet long, three feet wide and two feet six inches deep. It weighed over 750 pounds.

When it was lifted out of the aircraft, the casket was tightly fastened with two lengths of braided silver wire, which formed a cross over the lid. At 6:45 on the evening of May 17th, Professor Braithwaite jotted in his notebook that he had decided to cut this wire and take the lid off the casket to see what was inside.

The next morning, May 18th, when RAE technicians opened up the hangar, they noticed that the casket appeared to be intact, but the silver wire had been neatly cut and was lying on the floor. There was no sign of Professor Braithwaite or his two assistants.

By 6:00 pm that day, Professor Braithwaite and his assistants had still failed to put in an appearance, and none of them were answering their home phone numbers. The security services were immediately notified, and a major search initiated. Watches were kept on all British ports and airports, and roadblocks set up in Hampshire and Surrey. Several houses were searched, including Professor Braithwaite's holiday cottage in the Lake District.

Some days later, when the press made polite enquiries about Professor Braithwaite's whereabouts, they were told that he had flown to the United States to undertake several weeks of 'background research'. It's hard to remember how trusting the press used to be in those days.

To date, though, neither Professor Braithwaite nor his assistants had been sighted anywhere, dead or alive, and there was no evidence to explain what might have happened to them.

Except, of course, the empty casket. The lid of the casket was still in place on the morning of May 18th, but investigators were able to lift it open without difficulty. Inside they found it to be lined with whitethorn wood, and thickly bedded with dried garlic flowers and wild roses. On one side lay an empty sack made of thin brown linen, like a torn-open shroud. There was a deep impression in the petals, as if somebody had been lying there, motionless, for a very long time.

'Didn't anybody suspect what had happened, even then?' I asked Charles Frith. 'Didn't anybody think to ask what kind of creature could have been lying in a sealed casket for nearly thirteen years, without air, or food, or water?'

'Afraid not, old man. Security services are never very good at communicating with each other, at the best of times.'

'Somebody could have used their imagination.'

'Imagination?' Charles Frith blinked at me as if I had used a four-letter word. 'Not a requirement for MI6, I'm sorry to say.'

The police reports on all of the recent killings were depressingly similar, and all of the photographs, too. Heaps of bodies with their clothes torn open, their abdomens sliced apart and their hearts pulled out from underneath their ribcages. Men, women and children – even toddlers, in little white socks. In the background, cheap floral wallpaper, decorated with loops and spatters of blood. Nobody had ever seen anybody entering the crime scenes. Nobody had ever seen anybody leave.

'We're um – we're quite certain that this is the work of – you know – *strigoi*?'

'No doubt about it. One *strigoi mort* and at least two *strigoi vii*, and they're going to multiply fast.'

'More tea?'

'No thanks. I think I'll go to my hotel, if that's all right with you, and take a shower. I need to call my wife, too. Then I want to go to this house in Croydon and take a look at this birthday party. Terence, do you think you can arrange for our dog handler to meet us there? Say about three-thirty?'

'I don't anticipate any problem with that, "Jim". I'll give her a tinkle.'

I stood up and Charles Frith stood up, too. 'Tremendously pleased to have you on board, Captain Falcon.'

'Well, me too, sir. I have a very personal interest in catching this particular Screecher.'

'Really?'

'It's a long story, sir. I'll report back to you later.'

'Ears. Good. Oh – but there's one more thing. You've been issued with a side arm. Colt .45 automatic, I gather. It's all been approved but I have to ask you to be very discreet with it. This *is* England, you know, not the Wild West.'

'Of course,' I told him.

'Ears,' he repeated.

On the way back along the corridor, I said to Terence, 'He kept saying "ears". What did he mean by that?'

'Oh . . . that's English upper-class for "yes".'

House of Flies

For my first night in England, the SIS had booked me a room at the Strand Palace Hotel. It was comfortable in a well-worn, shabby way, although the traffic was so noisy that I had to close my window, and the furniture reeked of cigarettes. I booked a transatlantic call to Louise, and tried to take a shower. The shower-head gurgled, and sneezed, and then dribbled. I took a shallow bath instead.

I was lucky. It could take hours before a call to the States came through, but the operator rang me back after only twenty minutes. Louise answered, and although she sounded quite close, I kept hearing an echo, so that she said everything twice.

'I'm going to the Marriotts' this evening. They're having a cookout they're having a cookout.'

'That's great,' I said. 'Are you going to see your sister this weekend?'

'I don't know, it depends if Dick's coming home if Dick's coming home.'

'Listen, I have to go, but I love you.'

'Be careful, Jimmy, won't you please won't you please?'

'I'll be careful.' I hadn't been allowed to tell her what I was doing here in England – only that it was connected with my work for the intelligence services during the war. But Louise wasn't the kind of woman to be easily fooled. She had stood in the bedroom doorway watching me pack as intently as if she were making an 8mm home movie in her head – a home movie that she could play back later, in her mind's eye, if I never came back to her.

I had known Louise since college. We had dated once or twice, and had a good time together, but Louise was always much more serious than I was. She liked string quartets and art galleries and live theatre, while I preferred beer and swing music and W. C. Fields movies. Not that I wasn't academic. You couldn't help being academic, with a father like mine. But I wasn't a *sensitive* academic. I didn't carry a lily around, and I didn't lisp.

As it happened, though, Louise and I met up again in 1949, at a friend's party in North Beach, and I invited her to Mill Valley for the day. We were both different people by then. She had been through a violent marriage and lost a baby. I had been chasing *strigoi* in Europe. We saw qualities in each other that we hadn't been able to appreciate when we were younger. In Louise, I saw thoughtfulness, and a deep appreciation for the value of human life, but an unexpected willingness to have fun, too. I don't exactly know what she saw in me, but I always tried to be kind to her, and protective, and I even pretended to like her cheese and macaroni.

Terence called for me at 2:30 pm and we drove to Croydon. Terence was right, Croydon was 'pretty grotty' – a densely overcrowded suburb with mile after mile of Victorian and Edwardian shops and pubs, interspersed with sorry-looking semi-detached houses and filling stations and used-car lots. The sky was beginning to cloud over, although the heat was still unbearable. Terence was steadily perspiring in his coat and necktie, but he didn't make any attempt to take them off.

We reached an ugly red-brick pub called the Red Deer, where the main road divided. Terence took a right up a steep, narrow street lined with scabby-looking plane trees. We passed a huge Victorian church, faced with flint, and then pulled up outside a large three-storey house. There were two men standing around outside the front gate, smoking. Terence said, 'Couple of our chaps. Couldn't have the constabulary here, somebody might ask awkward questions.'

I climbed out of the car and looked up at the house. It was massive and clumsily proportioned, built of the same shiny red brick as the pub we had passed, with a gabled roof and window frames painted bright blue. The front garden sloped up from the street, and was crowded with laurel bushes. The soil was so chalky here that the flowerbeds were strewn with big white lumps of limestone.

Terence introduced me to his 'chaps'. Like Terence, they both seemed to be far too young to be MI6 operatives, like two schoolboys. One of them said, 'Don't know what the latest score is, by any chance?'

'Last I heard, Evans took four wickets for sixty-four.'

'Crikey. I thought he'd broken his finger.'

'Our dog handler not here yet?' I asked.

'Shouldn't be too long. Do you want to take a quick shufti inside?'

'Sure, why not?'

One of the chaps led the way up the steps to the front door, which was propped open with a dog-eared telephone directory. Six pint-bottles of lumpy-looking milk stood on the doorstep, the family's last delivery. I followed the chap into a high, airless hallway, which had a wide staircase on the left-hand side.

'House was shared, you see,' the chap told me. 'Mister and missus and three children lived on the ground floor, while the grandparents lived upstairs.'

Although the house was detached, it stood only six feet from the house next door and the windows were all glazed with yellow and green glass, so the hallway was deeply gloomy, like an aquarium. On the wall hung a damp-spotted print of a miserable-looking maiden, by Dante Gabriel Rossetti.

'Window cleaner looked in and saw the bodies,' said Terence. 'Otherwise, who knows, it might have been weeks.'

We went through to the dining room, which was thick with

71

the smell of decaying food and human blood, and noisy with the buzzing of hundreds of flies. Dark brown woollen drapes had been drawn across the bay window, but enough sunlight penetrated the room for me to be able to see what had happened here.

The dining chairs had been set back against the walls, presumably so that the family could stand around the dining table and help themselves to the buffet. Plates and cutlery were scattered on the mustard-yellow carpet, as well as trodden-in sandwiches and cakes. On the sideboard stood bottles of Scotch whisky and Gordon's gin and Emva Cream sweet sherry, as well as six or seven bottles of light ale and Mackeson's stout. I was reminded that the British liked their beer warm.

The words HAPPY BIRTHDAY JACKIE had been cut out of coloured paper and stuck on to the mirror.

'Difficult to tell how the buggers got in,' said Terence. 'Back door was locked, and all of the main windows were closed.'

I stepped carefully across the dining room and drew back the drapes. Three of the small upper windows were open. Even a child would have found it impossible to climb through them, but a *strigoi mort* could slide through the narrowest of gaps. Once inside, he would have opened the front door for any *strigoi vii* who might have accompanied him. It wasn't easy to tell how many *strigoi* had been here, because there was so much blood and so much mess, but they usually went out feeding in threes.

I looked back at the dining table. All the food had been splashed with dark brown blood – the birthday cake, the sausage rolls, the mashed-sardine sandwiches – and now flies were crawling all over it so that the whole table looked as if it were rippling.

I went to the door. There were bloodstained fingerprints on either side of the door jamb. 'You say that one of the bodies was found upstairs?'

'Eleven-year-old boy, yes.'

'See these fingerprints? My guess is, the kid was trying to escape, and somebody blocked the doorway to stop the Screechers from going after him. Unsuccessfully, of course. Because, look.'

I pointed to some smudges of blood on the wallpaper. They ran diagonally up the wall, each one higher than the next, until they reached the ceiling. I stepped back into the hallway and looked up. The smudges continued across the ceiling toward the staircase, and up the sloping ceiling above the stairs, too.

'Footprints,' I said. 'The boy tried to get away and one of the *strigoi* chased him.'

'On the *ceiling*?' said Terence. He looked at the chap and the chap raised his eyebrows and puffed out his cheeks, but didn't say anything.

'You have to understand what we're up against here,' I told him.

The other chap came in from outside. 'Your dog handler's here,' he told us. 'Bit of all right, as a matter of fact.'

Bullet

I went out on to the porch – not only to greet my dog handler but to breathe some fresh air. During the war I had grown pretty much inured to the ripe stench of cut-open human beings, but over the past twelve years I had forgotten how sickening it was, and how it seemed to cling to your clothes and your hair for hours afterward. You could even taste it in your mouth when you were eating.

The dog handler had parked her pale green Hillman Minx estate car next to Terence's Humber, and was opening the back doors so that her dog could jump out. The dog came up the path first, a glossy black Labrador with a crimson tongue, panting furiously in the heat. The dog handler followed, and the other chap hadn't been exaggerating – she was 'a bit of all right'.

She was very slim, with dark shiny hair cut into a bob. She looked as if she might have had some Burmese or Siamese blood in her, because she had high cheekbones and dark feline eyes. She was wearing a white short-sleeved blouse with the collar turned up, and she was very large-breasted. I don't know what it is about white blouses and big breasts that does it for me, but for a split second I felt a rush of blood to the head, as if I were fifteen years old again.

Her waist was cinched in with a large silver-buckled belt, and she wore a navy pencil skirt that came down just below the knee.

'Hallo,' she smiled. She had a clear, upper-middle-class accent, and she spoke as if she were reading the BBC news. 'You must be Captain – *Falco*, is it?'

'Falcon. With an "n". Like peregrine falcon. But call me Jim.'

'All right. I'm Jill Foxley, from the Metropolitan Police dog section at Keston.'

'Great to meet you, Jill Foxley. And your dog, too. What does he answer to?'

'His proper name is Willowyck Gruff but his working name is Bullet.'

'Bullet, I like that. Hey, Bullet! How are you doing, boy?'

Bullet turned to me and gave a single contemptuous bark.

'Hey! I think he likes me already.'

Jill said, 'I'm sorry. He's very loyal, once he gets to know people. But he's been trained to be suspicious of strangers.'

'Well, that's what we need, suspicious. In fact we need *very* suspicious. You've been briefed about this job, I hope? I mean, you know what you and me and Bullet here are supposed to be looking for.'

'Yes. They gave me a general idea. They said that if I needed to know anything more, I should ask you about it. Apparently you're the world's greatest expert.'

'And? What do you think?'

She pulled a face. 'I'm not at all sure. At first I thought they were having me on toast. But I've always liked unusual work. Bullet and I spent the last six months tracking down heroin smugglers in Limehouse. That was fascinating. You know, all that Chinese culture and everything.'

'You understand what these Screechers are, don't you?'

'Well, yes.' She seemed embarrassed. 'Vampires, sort of.'

'Exactly. We're not dealing with human beings here. They

74

don't have a soul and they don't have a conscience. They don't have any compunction about killing anybody of any age, with no warning at all.'

'Like wild animals, then, really?'

'Unh-hunh. They're not like animals. They're intelligent, and they're so damn quick you can't even see them, and they won't give you any second chances.'

'I understand.' She had an alluring way of tilting her head sideways and looking at me out of the corner of her eyes.

'Well,' I said, trying to sound brusque and professional, 'you'd better bring Bullet inside. You've visited a homicide scene before? It's not too salubrious in there.' The language I was using, I was starting to sound quite British. I would probably start saying 'constabulary' next, instead of 'cops'.

'Don't worry,' said Jill. 'I've been called to quite a few murders. The last one was a husband who beat his wife and their seven-year-old daughter to death with a hammer, and then cut his own throat with a bread knife. That was quite yucky.'

'Quite yucky? Yes, I guess it must have been.'

Out of her navy-blue pocketbook, Jill pulled a strip of brownish fabric about the length of a woman's scarf. She held it up against Bullet's snout so that he could sniff it and lick it. 'This is a piece of the linen shroud they found in the casket,' she explained. 'If the same Screecher has been here, then Bullet will be able to tell.'

'Good for Bullet. Let's take a look, shall we?'

I led her through the hallway into the dining room, with Bullet trotting obediently beside her. I think she was determined not to show that she was nauseated, but as soon as she entered the door she clamped her hand over her mouth and couldn't stop herself from letting out a high, cackling retch. 'Oh my God, it's disgusting.'

'Do you want to go back outside?'

She shook her head. 'I can manage, thanks. It's the flies, more than anything else. I can't stand flies.'

'Join the club. But this is fairly typical of a Screecher attack. The *strigoi mort* gains entry first – in this case I'm guessing that it came through one of the skylights here. It probably came in so fast that nobody saw it – or, if they did, it would have looked like nothing more than a dark blur, whizzing through the room. It would have opened the front door and let in its companions, and then the three of them would have come back in here and had themselves a feast.'

Bullet was snuffling around the carpet, occasionally licking it with his thick crimson tongue.

'How many victims were there?' asked Jill.

'Seven. The Screechers would have sliced their stomachs open first, and cut the Achilles tendons in their heels so that they couldn't get away. Then they would have gone from one to the other, cutting them open even wider, pulling out their hearts, and drinking their blood directly from their aortas.'

'That's so horrible.'

'Yes, it is. But if you and I don't stop them, the Screechers are going to multiply. I don't know how much they told you when they briefed you, but there are two kinds of Screechers – the infected ones who are still alive, the *strigoi vii* – and the dead ones, the *strigoi mortii*.'

'I didn't completely understand that when they briefed us. The *strigoi mortii* – they're really dead? I mean *dead* dead?'

'Dead in the sense that they're not human any more, and never will be. They can be *nostalgic*, for sure, in a very selfish way. They can shed tears for their lost humanity. They can even have relationships with humans. You'd never know if you passed a *strigoi mort* in the street, except that they usually look unnaturally flawless. Perfect skin, perfect teeth. It's just that they have no soul.'

'They said that the dead ones spread the infection.'

'That's right . . . by sharing their blood or other bodily fluids with human beings who attract them. They call it "the Embrace" or "the Witch's Kiss".'

'There must be a cure for it, surely?'

I shook my head. 'Once you've caught the infection, that's it. You have a raging thirst for blood and you can never get enough of it. It's like being a drug addict, only a thousand times worse.'

'So what happens to you?'

'In the end, you can't stand it any longer and you go looking for the *strigoi mort* who first infected you. You drink more of its blood, which poisons you, and so you in your turn become a *strigoi mort*. Very good-looking, an idealized version of yourself. But utterly dead, and unable to rest, for ever.'

Bullet came up to Jill and let out another bark. His tail was beating furiously against the table leg.

'He's picked up the scent. He wants to go after it.'

'In that case, we'll let him, shall we?'

'Of course. I hope you're fit.'

'Are you kidding me? I swim, I play tennis. I paint fences. Painting fences . . . you'd be surprised what good exercise that is.'

Bullet was already heading for the door. Jill looked at me and shrugged, and so we followed him.

I went to the car and heaved out the battered metal case containing my Kit. 'I think we have a trail,' I told Terence.

'Oh.' He didn't look very pleased about it. It was one thing to talk about *strigoi*. Hunting them was something else altogether.

Bullet made his way out of the house and up the street, with Jill and Terence and me trying to keep up with him. Unlike Frank, he didn't turn back once to see if we were following. At the top of the hill we reached a small public park called Haling Grove. There was a brick-and-concrete air-raid shelter by the front gates, which could have made a good hiding place for *strigoi*, but its doorway was sealed with corrugated iron, and its ventilation holes had all been bricked up.

We walked through the shadow of some horse-chestnut trees until we reached an open space. The park was strangely deserted, even though it was such a hot day, in the middle of the summer vacation period. In those days, the British didn't fly to Spain or France or Florida during the summer. They couldn't afford to. They went to the seaside for a week, and then they spent the rest of the time at home, tending their gardens or building shelves.

The park was probably no more than three or four acres, surrounded by mature oaks and beech trees. Bullet loped across the bright green grass ahead of us. On the other side of the grass stood a large stained-oak summer-house with a dark thatched roof, where an elderly woman sat, wearing a black dress and tiny green sunglasses. She was so white-faced that I could have believed she was dead.

'They would have been long gone by now, wouldn't they?' panted Terence. Perspiration was trickling down the sides of his cheeks.

'Oh for sure. This will probably come to nothing. But if we can pick up more than one trail, we can begin to work out where they're hiding themselves.'

'Triangulation,' said Jill. She must have been much fitter than Terence or me, because she wasn't out of breath at all, and she looked as cool as a Pimm's No. 1.

Bullet had passed the summer-house, and now he was standing beside a wide flowerbed planted with dahlias. Along the back of the flowerbed ran a brick wall, over eighteen feet high, which looked as if it marked the park's southern boundary. Bullet sniffed at the soil and barked three or four times.

'Go on, Bullet!' Jill told him. 'Follow up, boy!'

Bullet crossed the flowerbed and went up to the wall. He turned around for the first time and looked at us in frustration.

'Clever,' I said. 'I'll bet you ten bucks they climbed the wall and ran along the top of it.'

'There's a door further along,' said Terence. 'We could check the other side, couldn't we?'

The door was half-open, and led through to an overgrown area of old glasshouses and abandoned wheelbarrows and compost heaps. Jill guided Bullet along the length of the wall, sniffing at it, but it seemed as if I was right, and the *strigoi* had made their way along the top of it. Even if we could have lifted him up there, there was no way that Bullet could have balanced along the coping to follow their scent. About three hundred yards away, the wall passed under the branches of several large oak trees, and it was my guess that the *strigoi* had used them to climb down from the wall and escape into the street nearby.

We spent a half-hour crisscrossing the street and the park's pathways, but Bullet had lost the scent completely. Jill gave him a handful of black-and-red dog biscuits, patted him on the head and said, 'Well done, Bullet. Never mind.' Bullet ate his biscuits with a crackling sound like gunfire and I had never seen a dog look so furious. Jill said, 'He's very annoyed. He hardly ever loses a trail.'

'We'll get them,' I told her. 'Screechers have to come out and feed, and that's their greatest weakness.' I wiped my forehead with the back of my hand. 'Jesus, it's hot. Anybody feel like a drink?'

Terence looked at his watch. 'It isn't opening time for another two and a half hours. But there's a sweetshop on the corner, down at the bottom of the road. I could get you a bottle of Tizer.'

I hadn't realized that British pubs were closed all afternoon, until 6:00 pm. And so it was that I was driven back into central London, drinking this fizzy bright orange cordial out of a heavy glass bottle, feeling sweaty and tired and more than a little sick.

Death On A Double-Decker

I slept badly that night – as badly as I used to sleep during the war.

The Strand Palace had no air conditioning and the endless *knock-knock-knock* of taxi and bus engines seemed to penetrate right through my pillows. I had a nightmare in which I couldn't find my way out of Haling Grove Park and the old woman with the white face and the green sunglasses was sliding after me as if she were on wheels.

I took a tepid bath around 7:00 am and then I went down to the dining room for breakfast. I ordered a 'full English' – bacon, sausages, fried eggs, grilled tomatoes and mushrooms. Everything was cold and lying in congealed grease and I could only conclude that I must have been hungrier during the war, or younger and less discriminating. The coffee tasted like weak beef stock.

While I pushed my food around my plate, I read the *Daily Express*. Cairo radio had incited Arabs to rise up against the

British and sabotage the RAF Venom jets at Sharja airfield, where they were being used against rebel forces in Muscat and Oman. Pan Am had announced that they were beginning trans-Polar flights to London from the West Coast, flying time about eighteen hours. A British doctor had been killed by the polio epidemic in the British Midlands because he had vaccinated all of his patients but hadn't thought to vaccinate himself.

In spite of the warm weather, British roads were unusually empty because 'motorists feared bonnet-to-tail snarls in traffic'.

Not a word about mass killings in Croydon or Selsdon or anywhere else. Not a word about *strigoi*. On television that night were *Sir Lancelot*, *Criss Cross Quiz* and *Gun Law*.

The waiter came over and looked at my plate. 'Not to your liking, sir?'

'No, it was great. Just a little too much.'

'Perhaps you'd care for something else, sir? Porridge, perhaps?'

'No, thanks.' I had seen the porridge and it looked like badly poured concrete.

I was crossing the lobby on the way back to my room when the receptionist called me. 'Captain Falcon, sir – you have a telephone call!'

I went into the phone booth at the side of the lobby. It was Terence calling me. 'We've had another one, "Jim", really bad this time. I can't tell you anything over the blower but I'm coming to collect you in fifteen minutes. It's South London again.'

'OK.' I could see my eyes in the small mirror at the back of the telephone booth. They looked expressionless, as if they didn't belong to anybody at all.

We drove to Wallington, another suburb on the far side of Croydon Aerodrome, a wide grassy field which – up until the war – had been London's principal airport. Wallington was avenue after avenue of 1930s semi-detached houses, with white-painted pebbledash walls and monkey-puzzle trees in their front gardens. Bank-clerk land.

Terence was wearing the same shirt and green necktie that he had been wearing the day before. He smoked even more furiously than ever, and it was obvious that he was very nervous and upset. 'Seventeen killed, that's what they told me.'

'Seventeen? Jesus.'

This time, a whole avenue had been cordoned off by police. Two bobbies stopped us and made a meal of checking our identity cards. 'You're an *American*, sir?' asked one of them, peering at me as if he had never seen a real live American before, and was wondering why I wasn't wearing a Stetson hat and a bolo necktie.

Eventually, they let us through and we drove about a half-mile to the end of the avenue. Here we found more police, as well as two fire trucks and five ambulances. I could see Charles Frith, wearing an immaculate light-grey suit, talking to a senior police inspector. This must be really serious, if Charles Frith had actually ventured out of his office.

The avenue was crossed by a low, green-painted railroad bridge. A green double-decker bus was wedged under the bridge, so that the front half of its roof had been ripped back-ward. Six or seven policemen were erecting high canvas screens around the bus, while two firefighters were up on the bridge, lowering a tarpaulin over the top of it.

'Ah, Jim,' said Charles Frith, as I approached him. 'This is Inspector Ruddock, Metropolitan Police. Inspector, this is our American friend, Captain James Falcon.'

Inspector Ruddock was a stocky man with a scarlet face that looked as if it were just about to explode. He had pale blue eyes with colourless eyelashes, like a pig's. He eyed me up and down and said nothing at all.

'This happened at about six thirty this morning,' said Charles Frith. 'The bus comes down Demesne Road here but I'm told that it usually turns off at Chesterfield Avenue, which is ah – the *second* side road just back there. This morning it kept straight on and as you can see. Tremendous bang apparently. Residents came out to see if they could help but ah – no survivors, I'm sorry to say.'

'I'd better take a look,' I told him.

Inspector Ruddock said, 'I'm not happy about that, sir. Not until my men have finished their job. Don't want any evidence buggered up.'

'No need to worry about that, Inspector,' said Charles Frith, in his urbane drawl. 'Captain Falcon here is a very experienced investigator who specializes in this sort of business.'

'All the same, sir, I'd—'

Charles Frith gave him the coldest possible smile, and said, 'Carry on, Jim.'

Inside the bus, I breathed in a strong smell of blood and fat, like a butcher's shop, but it was far less nauseating than the house in Croydon, because the passengers were freshly killed. All the same, it was stifling in there, especially now that it was draped in a heavy tarpaulin, and the windows were speckled with flies.

Two forensic scientists in white lab coats and rubber gloves were dusting for fingerprints and taking photographs, watched over by a sweating detective in a badly fitting brown suit. The detective looked at me with deep suspicion when I climbed on to the platform. I held up my identity card and said, 'Captain James Falcon, from the CIC. I'm temporarily seconded to MI6.'

The detective frowned at my card and said, 'MI6?' He was sandy-haired and freckly and put me in mind of Spencer Tracy, if Spencer Tracy had been six inches taller. 'What's this got to do with MI6?'

'Can't answer that one, I'm afraid. What do you think happened here?'

'I'm not sure I'm supposed to tell you.'

'Believe me, you're supposed to tell me.'

Inspector Ruddock dragged aside the tarpaulin and said, irascibly, 'We're cooperating with the US intelligence services, Johnson. Whatever Captain Falcon wants to know, just tell him, will you?'

He disappeared, and Johnson blinked at me in dismay.

'Sorry,' I said. In the brief time that I had stayed in Britain during the war, I had learned that 'sorry' was the key word that would get you out of any kind of awkward situation. Somebody steps on your foot? You say 'sorry' and they say 'sorry' and you say 'sorry' again and that's the end of it, unless one of you feels it necessary to say 'sorry' a third time.

'Well, come on, then,' said Watkins. 'We've got eleven stabbing victims on the lower deck, five upstairs and then there's the driver.'

'The driver was stabbed too?'

'No, he died of chest injuries when the bus hit the bridge.'

He led the way down the aisle. Our shoes made sticky noises because the floor was varnished with blood. Most of the passengers were sitting upright, as if they were still waiting to be carried to their destinations. There were eight men, most of whom looked like factory workers on their way to start an early shift, and two women with their hair tied up in scarves. Office cleaners, more than likely.

The bus conductor was lying sideways on one of the bench seats at the back of the bus. His hands were covered in blood as if he had been struggling to defend himself against an assailant who was wielding a very sharp knife. In fact three fingers of his right hand were almost completely severed, and were dangling on thin shreds of skin.

Every one of the passengers had been stabbed in the lower part of the stomach, and then the knife pulled upward until it met the breastbone. Since they were all still sitting in their seats, it was clear that they had been attacked very rapidly, before they had time to react. That spelled *strigoi mort* to me. A *strigoi mort* could flicker through a busload of people like this and kill all of them in a matter of seconds. The passengers' pants and skirts were soaked in blood, and several of them had little heaps of glistening pink intestines in their laps.

'Can't think why the poor sods didn't put up any kind of a fight,' said Watkins.

I didn't say anything, but leaned forward and examined the stomach wound of one of the cleaners. Whatever had been used to slice her open, it must have been wickedly sharp, because it had cut clean through her thick white elasticated girdle. She was looking at me with a suspicious expression, as if she were just about to speak to me.

'Do you have any idea who might have done this?' Johnson asked me.

'Oh, yes,' I nodded.

'But you're not going to share it with me?'

'No.'

'Well, I must say that this is all bally frustrating.'

'Sorry. Maybe your boss will fill you in, later.'

I climbed up the steep curving stairs at the back of the

bus, on to the top deck. It was the same story here, except that two of the passengers sitting right at the front of the bus had been crushed under the railroad bridge. Their mutilated heads lay on the seat behind them, one of them still wearing a wiry brown toupee, like a ventriloquist's dummy.

I ducked down under the roof of the bus to check their bodies. Both had been gutted, like everybody else. One of them had been cut so wide open that his entire digestive system was hanging from the edge of his seat – bowels, stomach and liver, in a glutinous cascade that was crawling with flies.

On the other side of the bus, however, I saw the body of a young boy, no more than five or six years old. He was wearing school uniform – a blue blazer with a badge on the pocket, and grey flannel shorts, and grey woollen socks, and brown Clark's sandals. His head had been compressed against the side of the bus window, so that his eyes were bulging out and his skull was oval. But what interested me more than anything else was that – unlike everybody else on the bus – he hadn't been stabbed. He was dead, but his stomach was intact.

Johnson came up the stairs and said, 'Everything all right?'

'I don't know yet.'

'But you still can't tell me who did this? Or why? It really would help me an awful lot if you could give me an inkling.'

I knew who had done it. There wasn't any doubt. I knew *why* they had done it, too. An early-morning bus full of dozy shift-workers must have looked like a mobile feast to Duca and his *strigoi vii*. I guessed that they had planned to take it someplace secluded and drink the blood of everybody on board. At 5:30 in the morning, there would have been few people around to disturb them.

I went downstairs again and took another look around. Then I climbed off the bus and walked around to the driver's cab. The driver was a balding man in his early fifties, with a hand-rolled cigarette tucked behind his ear. He was slumped forward over his steering wheel with his eyes closed, as if he had simply nodded off. The sliding door to his cab was marked with seven or eight fresh scratches, some of which had gone right through the red paint to the bare aluminium underneath.

It looked as if a Screecher had tried to get into the cab, stabbing at the door in frustration.

I was still examining the cab when Jill arrived, with Bullet. Today she was wearing a yellow blouse and natural-coloured slacks, and no make-up. She had probably had to come down here at very short notice, as I had.

'Good morning,' she said, in a hushed voice, looking at the bus.

'Not for these folks.'

'They told me seventeen. It's dreadful.'

'Yes. But the Screechers didn't get the chance to do what they wanted to do.'

'What was that?'

'I'm pretty sure that they were trying to commandeer the bus so that they could take the passengers someplace and drink them dry. But it looks like the driver saw what was happening inside his bus and panicked.' I pointed up at the railroad bridge. 'I don't think he did this deliberately. He was probably trying to go for some help.'

'Wait a minute . . . they were trying to commandeer the bus? You mean Screechers can *drive*?'

'Of course they can. Screechers are no different than they were before they were infected. They can drive, they can use telephones, they can do anything. The *strigoi* virus affects people's bodies and it snuffs out their soul, but it doesn't affect their memory, or their intellect, or any of their practical skills.'

'I didn't realize. I mean, when you think of vampires you can't help thinking *medieval*, can you? You know, castles and horse-drawn carriages and things like that.'

'Why don't you let Bullet here take a sniff around the bus? There's some officious detective called Watkins in there, but don't let him bother you.'

'OK. I'll call for help if he starts being too bossy.'

One of the bobbies lifted the tarpaulin for her. Bullet jumped on to the bus and she followed him. 'Pretty girl,' the bobby remarked, as I walked past him. I didn't say anything. I was married to Louise, and I had always thought of myself as faithful. But I was surprised how pleased I had been when Jill had turned up.

* * *

I rejoined Charles Frith and Terence.

'Got everything you need?' said Charles Frith, peering at his wristwatch. 'I must get back to Town by twelve thirty. Lunch with the minister, for my sins.'

'Jill – Miss Foxley – she's seeing if she can pick up a trail.'

'Do we know exactly what went on here?'

'Attempted hijack, most likely.'

'"Hijack", eh?' Charles Frith seemed to like the American sound of that. '"Hijack". Mm. Well, keep me informed.'

Inspector Ruddock came over, looking hot and cross. 'There's some press boys wanting to know what's happened. And they say they'd like some pictures, too.'

'Tell them that somebody on the bus was infected with the Korean flu, and collapsed. The driver tried to take the bus to the nearest hospital and misjudged the low bridge. Everybody else on the bus has been quarantined, just to be on the safe side. You'll give them have a fuller statement later.'

'Oh, I will, will I?' said Inspector Ruddock, aggressively. 'And what will I tell them then?'

Charles Frith patted the silver pips on his shoulder. 'I'll let you know after lunch. Now I really must dash. Can't keep the minister waiting.'

Beneath the Trees

Bullet spent over fifteen minutes sniffing around the bus, downstairs and up. When Jill emerged from the tarpaulin she looked pale and upset.

'I've never seen anything like that before. That was too horrible for words.'

'Are you OK?' Her hair was damp with perspiration and I lifted a strand of it out of her eyes. 'Do you want a drink of water or anything?'

'No, I'm all right. It's the way that they're just sitting there.'

Bullet looked up at me and barked, twice.

'I really think he's getting to like me.'

'Actually he's warning you not to get too close.'

'Oh. Sorry. Sorry, boy. Do you think he'll *ever* get to like me?'

Jill smiled. 'Once he gets to know you better, I'm sure he will.'

'OK, then,' I said, 'does he have a trail for us to follow?'

'Yes, he does, and I think it's quite strong.'

I called out to Terence. 'Terence! We're going Screecher-hunting. You want to go get your car?'

'Oh! OK, then! Righty-ho!'

Jill and I walked along the crown of the road, trying to keep up with Bullet, while Terence crept along behind us in his Humber.

Although the sky was cloudless, we could hear distant collisions of thunder, and the lime trees along the avenue began to rustle uneasily. After only ten minutes we reached the entrance to a large public park, where there was a tarmacadam parking lot surrounded by giant elms.

'What's the betting the Screechers were planning on bringing the bus here?' I asked Jill. There was a bus stop close, only ten yards away, for numbers 403 and 403a, so the bus would normally have passed this way.

Bullet hesitated and lifted his head. He sniffed in several different directions, as if he couldn't make up his mind which way to go.

'I think they must have split up somewhere here,' said Jill. She took the scarf-like piece of linen out of her purse and held it in front of Bullet's nose to refresh his memory. Bullet immediately galloped through the entrance to the park and crossed the parking lot until he reached the trees on the far side. There he stopped again, and barked.

'He's confused,' said Jill. 'He can still smell something, but it's different.'

We led Bullet up and down the parking lot for over ten minutes. Every now and then he lifted his head and sniffed the air, but the strong scent that he had been following from the bus seemed to come to an end here, very abruptly.

'You know what this means?' I said. 'The *strigoi* have a car. Or even cars plural.'

'That's going to make things damned awkward,' said Terence, mopping his face with his handkerchief. 'How can we follow them if they're driving around in bloody cars?'

I got down on one knee and opened up my Kit. Bullet snuffled around me suspiciously while I took out my compass and opened up the silver-filigree cover.

'That's rather fancy,' said Jill. 'What is it?'

'*Strigoi* compass. For locating any nearby Screechers.'

'Really? It looks like an antique.'

'It is. It's nearly three hundred years old. The priests of the Romanian Orthodox Church designed it, in 1682, on the instructions of the Voivode of Wallachia, Serban Cantacuzino.'

'The who of where?'

I held the compass up higher, and slowly moved it right and left. 'Serban Cantacuzino was a great social and religious reformer. He had the Bible translated into Romanian, and it started a huge religious revival, like the King James Bible in the West.'

The compass needle spun around and around. 'He was determined to root out the *strigoi*, all of them, because they were so unholy.'

'Obviously he didn't have much luck.'

'No . . . the *strigoi* got him first. Some treacherous boyars allowed a *strigoi mort* to slip through the window of his palace one night, and the poor chap was sliced open and completely drained of blood.'

The compass needle suddenly stopped spinning, and started to see-saw in between north and north-east.

'I'm pretty sure the *strigoi mort* must have driven off,' I told Terence and Jill. 'But there are still some other Screechers not too far away. Bullet can smell them, can't you, boy?'

Bullet growled in the back of his throat.

'It's quite a thing, isn't it?' asked Terence, bending over and peering at my *strigoi*-compass. 'How does it actually work?'

'Look at the needle. It's made up of pearl, copper, and silver. Silver is highly sensitive to evil and moral impurity.

Copper is responsive to lies and deception – ask anybody who has ever taken a lie-detector test. And pearl goes dark when you expose it to hydrogen sulphide.'

'Hydrogen sulphide?'

'That's the principal gas given off when human beings start to decompose.'

'Golly,' said Terence. 'That makes it sound almost scientific, doesn't it?'

I stared at him. *Almost scientific*, my rear end. He was talking about a theological tracking device invented and constructed by some of the leading intellects of the seventeenth century. I didn't argue about it, though. I had a job to do, and very little time to do it in.

Gradually, nervily, the needle began to settle down, although it was still twitching from side to side. Whatever it had picked up, it was still quite a long way off, and the needle couldn't seem to make up its mind exactly which way it wanted to point. To me, that meant that it had probably picked up more than one Screecher, and was dithering between the two, as Bullet was. Distance: maybe a half-mile. Direction: diagonally north-east across the park, across an avenue of poplars, and then a bright green playing field.

'Go on, boy,' said Jill. Bullet circled around for a while, sniffing and snorting and sneezing as if he had a head cold. Then, without warning, he tore off across the playing field.

'Bullet, slow down, boy! Bullet!'

Jill ran after him and I jogged after Jill, my metal Kit banging painfully against my knees. Terence had gone back to his car and was slowly driving toward us up the avenue of poplars, even though motor vehicles weren't allowed inside the park. I could see two uniformed park-keepers in the distance, staring at him, although they were too far away to make out the expressions on their faces.

'Bullet!' shouted Jill.

Bullet crossed the playing field to the other side, and ran into a copse of horse-chestnut trees. At this time of the year the trees were dark green and heavy with pink blossom, and the ground beneath them was deeply shadowed. Jill disappeared into the gloom and I followed her. Bullet started barking again and this time he wouldn't stop.

I had almost caught up with Jill now. Together, we burst into a clearing amongst the trees, and there was Bullet, barking and snarling and running from side to side.

'Oh God,' said Jill.

Standing in the middle of the clearing were four people. A young man with short, scruffed-up hair and a pale, bruised-looking face, wearing a torn sport coat and badly stained grey-flannel pants. A girl with gingery curls, as pale and bruised as the boy. She was plump, about seventeen years old, and she was wearing a white summer dress with red-and-grey cats printed on it, like the Siamese cats in *Lady and the Tramp*, but the front of her dress was flooded with dark maroon blood.

The young man was standing behind a round-faced middle-aged woman with permanent-waved hair. The woman's flowerpot hat had been knocked askew and she was panting hysterically. Not surprising: the young man had one arm around her neck and he was holding a long wide-bladed kitchen knife right in front of her face.

The gingery-haired girl was holding the wrist of a skinny young boy, aged about eight or nine, who was so frightened that he had wet his khaki shorts and could barely stand up. The girl was holding a kitchen knife, too, and repeatedly prodded the boy in the chest and the shoulders with the point. The boy kept whining '*Ow! – Ow! – Ow! – Ow!*'

I reached behind my back and lifted my Colt .45 out of its holster. I held it up in both hands, cocked it, and took two steps closer.

'You don't need me to tell you what to do,' I announced. 'I'm going to give you till three and then I'm going to kill you.'

The young man looked at the gingery-haired girl and then he looked back at me. 'Bugger off,' he told me.

'Not a hope, pal. You heard what I said. I'm giving you a count of three and then I'm going to kill you. *One.*'

'I thought I said bugger off,' the young man challenged me.

'You did. But I think you were under the misapprehension that even if I shot you, I couldn't kill you. You're a Screecher, after all, a *strigoi vii*, and as such you think you're immortal.'

The young man frowned. 'What do *you* know about it, you tosser?'

'I know very much more than you do, pal, if my old friend Duca is running true to form.'

The young man lowered his arm so that the point of his kitchen knife was digging into the woman's blouse, just above her waistband. A small spot of bright scarlet blood appeared amongst the pattern of lime-green leaves. The woman whimpered and started to cry, and helplessly opened and closed her hands.

The young man said, 'I don't know who you are, mate, and to be honest with you I don't give a monkey's. But if you don't sling your hook right now I'm going to get the right hump and do this poor old bag right in front of you.'

'*Two,*' I told him. 'And for your information, the bullets in this gun were cast from the melted-down goblets that were used by Christ's disciples at the Last Supper. Not only that, they've been plated with pure silver and rubbed with garlic from the Pope's summer residence at Castel Gandolfo.'

'You're having a bubble, mate.'

'You want to try me?'

'Beryl!' said the young man, half-turning toward the girl.

I took another step forward. I had never been Roy Rogers, but at this distance I could have blown at least half of the young man's face off without too much risk of hitting the middle-aged woman.

'*One,*' I warned him.

At that moment, the girl swung her elbow back and stabbed the little boy in the middle of his stomach. The blow was so forceful that I could hear the *chop!* as the blade went in. Without any hesitation, the girl whipped the knife upward so that he was cut open from his belt to his chest. The little boy let out a horrible high-pitched scream like a run-over cat. Then he fell backward on to last autumn's leaves.

I fired once and hit the girl in the shoulder. The bang of a .45 is absolutely deafening, and disorienting, too. I fired again and hit her in the side. Lumps of red flesh flew off her hip, and she rolled over backward and sideways, just behind the boy. She tried to get up so I shot her again, blowing off her left kneecap.

'*Jim!*' screamed Jill.

I swung around, pointing my pistol at the young man. But

I was too late. He had already thrust his knife into the middle-aged woman's stomach, right up to the hilt, and her blood was running down his wrist and staining her skirt. She was staring at me in pain and shock and for some reason I couldn't help noticing the large brown mole on her upper lip, as if she had suffered that blemish all her life, only to die like this.

I aimed at the young man's head, but he ducked down behind her. I tried to dodge to the side, but he swung her around, as if he were dancing with her, with the knife still buried in her stomach. No matter which way I tried to get a clear shot at him, he kept her between us.

'Terence!' I yelled. I needed someone to outflank this young Screecher, and hit him from the side. '*Terence, where are you for Christ's sake!*'

It was then that I turned to Jill. She was standing under the trees, her eyes wide, holding on to Bullet's collar.

'Jill! Set Bullet on him! Jill, he's going to kill her!'

But it was too late. The Screecher yanked his knife upward and the woman's intestines piled out on to the ground, unravelling themselves like yards and yards of overcooked cannelloni. The Screecher turned and ran away through the woods, and he was running so fast that all I could see was a brief grey shadow and a flurry of leaves. There was no point in wasting a Last Supper bullet on him.

I turned around. The gingery-haired girl had gone as well.

'Did you see which way she went?' I asked Jill.

'We have to call for an ambulance,' she told me. Her voice was jerky and erratic and she was trembling uncontrollably.

I gripped her arms and shook her. 'Did you see which way she went? The red-head? Send Bullet after her!'

'They're going to die,' said Jill. She tried to turn around and stumble away but I wouldn't let her.

'Listen, Jill, they're probably dead already. Terence will call an ambulance. You and me, we have to go after the Screechers. That's what we're here for.'

She shook her head. 'I can't send Bullet after those people. I can't. I can't do this any more. I didn't realize.'

'Jill, for Christ's sake pull yourself together. We have to get after them now!'

'No,' she said. 'I can't do this any more. I thought I could but I can't.'

I let her go. There was nothing else I could do. I couldn't let Bullet run after the Screechers on his own, and he certainly wouldn't listen to me.

I walked over to the little boy. His arms and legs were sprawled as if he were jumping into the air, but he would never jump again. He was white-faced and dead. The woman moaned and I crossed over to see how she was. Her intestines were stuck all over with leaves and twigs and she was staring at them in despair.

'Pray for me,' she whispered.

I nodded. 'Every morning, from now on, until the day that I die. I promise you.'

'You're a strange bloke,' she said.

I didn't answer her. What can you answer, when a dying woman says that to you?

Hunt for the Dead

Charles Frith was furious. He paced around his office, throwing up his arms from time to time as if he were singing the finale to a grand opera.

'You don't know what it took to cover this up! Seventeen dead people in a 403 bus! A woman and a boy disembowelled in a public park! This is worse than the Buster Crabb business!'

The red phone rang and Charles Frith picked it up. '*What?*' he barked, even louder than Bullet. Then, 'Oh, sorry, Home Secretary.'

I leaned close to Terence and said, 'Buster Crabb business?' As far as I knew, Buster Crabb was a movie actor with big muscles. I think I'd seen him in some third-rate Western.

'Buster Crabb was a Royal Navy diver,' said Terence, hoarsely. It was obvious from the way he was talking out of the side of his mouth that 'the Buster Crabb business' had been a serious embarrassment. 'They found his body in Chichester harbour, early last year. No hands, and his head fell off when they tried to lift him out of the water.'

'Hey, yes,' I nodded. 'I think I read about that. It was that time that Khrushchev visited England, wasn't it, and they thought this guy had been secretly diving under Khrushchev's ship?'

'That's right,' said Terence, uncomfortably.

'That was MI6?'

'Perhaps. Possibly. But you certainly didn't hear it from me.'

Charles Frith banged the phone down. 'It's the *Daily Mail* again. They've got hold of this bloody idiotic idea that MI6 has been secretly running some kind of mad-scientist experiment, turning our agents into sociopathic assassins, and that some of them have escaped. "Human Killing Machines On The Loose". Sir David's frothing at the mouth.'

'Sir David's *always* frothing at the mouth,' said Terence.

'I just want to know what the devil we do now,' said Charles Frith. 'I mean, what's the plan, Jim? I thought we were going to track these buggers down and exterminate them before the press or the public got wind of what was going on. That's what I promised Sir David, anyway, and if we can't do it I need to know now.'

'It might be an idea to let the *Mail* run with their story about "killing machines",' Terence suggested. 'We can always prove them wrong later . . . and it's better than telling them that South London is infested with Screechers.'

'Forget about the press relations,' I told him. 'Press relations won't mean anything if we can't locate the *strigoi mort*.'

'You're talking about this fellow Duca?'

'It's not a *fellow*, sir,' I insisted. 'It's a *thing*. We have to find it, and destroy it, and we have to do it real quick. Duca's been infecting people much faster than I expected. You only have to do the math.'

I turned Charles Frith's blotter around and jotted on it with my mechanical pencil. 'Seventeen people contain one hundred seventy pints of blood, but the human stomach only has the capacity to swallow four pints at a time. Obviously Duca didn't know in advance how many passengers were going to be riding on that bus, and even if there were more than he and his fellow Screechers needed, it still would have been necessary for him to kill them all. But if they *did* need seventeen people, we could be talking about forty-two Screechers here.'

'Oh my God,' said Charles Frith. 'This is out of control already, isn't it?'

'If you have forty-two Screechers in the South London suburbs and all of them are looking for eight or nine pints of fresh human blood three times in every twenty-four hours . . . then, yes, this is out of control.'

The green phone rang. Charles Frith picked it up and bellowed, '*What?*'

He listened for a moment, and then he said, 'No, Commissioner. Absolutely not, Commissioner. I'm sorry, Commissioner, not a chance. No. And a very good day to you, too.'

He slammed the receiver down and said, 'Sir Kenneth Bloody McLean. They should demote that man back to constable. No – cloakroom attendant.'

He sat down in his big leather armchair and swung from side to side, breathing like a man who eaten a large lunch, smoked a cigar and then run up eight flights of stairs. Eventually, he said, 'What's it going to take to find this Duca fellow? *Thing*, I mean?'

I drew a few more lines on Charles Frith's blotter. 'When I was hunting down Screechers after D-Day, it was a totally different ballgame. We were attached to an advancing army, which was driving the Screechers ahead of us. But here – well, this is South London, in peacetime. We can't go from street to street, searching every house. We can't ask the Royal Engineers to blow up buildings for us if we suspect that a couple of Screechers are hiding in the attic.'

'So what can we do?'

'We'll have to use a combination of plain old-fashioned police-work, plus some inspired deduction, plus – well – something else.'

'Something else?' asked Charles Frith, suspiciously, raising one brambly eyebrow.

'I guess you'd probably call it sorcery; or the occult.'

'You mean Dennis Wheatley kind of stuff? *The Devil Rides*

Out? Dear God, I can just hear myself explaining this to Sir David.'

'I hope you won't have to, sir. But let's make a start. From what happened today, it's pretty clear that Duca has found himself an automobile. We need to check any reports of stolen vehicles in that part of South London over the past six weeks, but we also need to ask the public if they have seen a neighbour's automobile – not stolen but being regularly driven by somebody unfamiliar.'

'What are you getting at?'

'*Strigoi mortii* aren't half-rotten and sick-looking like *strigoi vii*. They look perfectly normal. In fact they usually look *better* than normal. But they're dead, and dead people find it difficult to rent or buy property, because – well, they're dead. So they have a habit of killing other people and taking over their lives – their homes, their property, even their clothes – and usually they're clever enough to do it without arousing suspicion.'

'So how do we get the public to help us?'

'I'm not really sure, to tell you the truth. Maybe some kind of announcement in the newspapers.'

'I've got it,' said Terence. 'We could tell the press that we've had an intelligence report from Washington. They suspect that a KGB spy has moved into a flat or a house in South London, and that he might be driving the car belonging to the previous occupier. We could give out a special telephone number for the public to call. We could even offer a reward.'

Charles Frith pulled a disapproving face. In his opinion, newspapers were only good for wrapping up cod and chips. But Terence's idea was actually a pretty good one. We were right in the depths of the Cold War, and every day the press was full of scaremongering stories about Soviet spies living amongst us, leading what appeared to be commonplace lives (and as we later discovered, they actually were).

'Very well,' Charles Frith told Terence, 'why don't you scribble something down on paper and see if you can have it on my desk by five o'clock? I'll talk to Sir Kenneth bloody McLean and see if he can get his beat chaps to start asking questions about people driving cars that they shouldn't be. What are you going to do, Jim?'

I looked at my watch, the gold Breitling that Louise had given me on our wedding day. 'I have some persuading to do.'

Tea for Two

Terence let me borrow his Humber and I drove back over Chelsea Bridge toward the south suburbs. The sky was deep blue and streaked with mares' tails, and it was so warm that I drove with all the windows open and my cow's lick blowing. The river Thames sparkled in the sunlight like smashed mirrors.

I drove through the built-up centre of Croydon at an over-heated crawl. I hadn't driven a manual shift for over ten years, so I kept stalling, and kangaroo-jumping, and it took me over an hour to get to Purley. By the time I turned into Combe Road, my shirt was sticking to the leather seat and I was so thirsty that I could have drunk blood.

Purley was a prosperous suburb with huge 1930s houses concealed behind high beech hedges. Shining new Rovers were parked in every gravelled driveway, and I could see tennis courts and gardeners clipping rose bushes and well-dressed children running around in Aertex shirts and white socks and sandals. There was a tranquil air of summer heat and confidence and money.

I found 'The Starlings' at the end of Combe Road, an enormous mock-Tudor house with glittering ivy all down one wall and pigeons warbling on the roof. I steered the Humber into the drive and parked outside the garages. A middle-aged man in a droopy cotton sun hat was clipping the edges of the front lawn, not that they looked as if they needed clipping. The lawn itself was so perfectly kept that it looked unreal, and striped like a pair of green silk pyjamas.

I climbed out of the car and walked up to him, shielding my eyes with my upraised arm.

'I'm looking for Jill,' I told him.

'Oh, yes?'

'My name's Jim Falcon. Captain James Falcon, actually. Jill and I have been working together.'

'Yes, I know about that. Well, as much as I'm allowed to. I'm her father.'

He climbed up over the herbaceous border on to the driveway. He had a squarish, pugnacious face, and a prickly grey moustache.

'Is Jill home?' I asked him. 'I really need to talk to her.'

'I don't know if that's a very good idea, Captain Falcon. Jill came home in a state of considerable distress and we had to call the family doctor to give her a sedative.'

'I'm sorry.'

'She hasn't told us what happened, and of course we haven't been pressing her to tell us, because we're aware that it's extremely hush-hush. But if it's going to have this kind of an effect on her . . . well, we're her family. We have to put her personal well-being first, before her work.'

'Yes, sir, I can understand how you feel. I know Jill's extremely shocked and I'm sorry about that. But this investigation we're working on is critical. We're talking about people's lives here, sir. Maybe hundreds of people's lives. Maybe even more.'

'Well, I'm really not sure.'

I paused for a moment, and then I said, 'Sir – you saw action during the war, I guess?'

'Yes, of course. I was out in Burma.'

'You saw plenty of things that shocked and distressed you, I'll bet. You saw people killed.'

He blinked at me. 'Captain Falcon – are you trying to tell me what I think you're trying to tell me?'

I nodded. 'What Jill and I have been doing together – it's just as important as what we did during the war. In some ways, even more so, because nobody's prepared for it.'

'Something to do with the bloody Russians, I suppose?'

'I'm sorry, I'm not allowed to tell you. But I need her, sir. I need her expertise. I need Bullet. The situation's getting more and more desperate by the day and she has to pull herself together.'

'I can't say I'm altogether happy about it.'

'Look at it this way, sir. Jill also has to realize that her entire career could be in jeopardy. I covered up for her this afternoon. I told my boss that she took Bullet to Croydon to follow up some new trails we found. But if she won't get back on the job they'll probably have to demote her, or even sack her.'

Her father lowered his head so that I couldn't see his face under the brim of his sun hat. 'All right,' he said. 'I'll see what I can do.'

Jill was lying on a flowery chintz sofa in the drawing room. Bullet was lying on the rug next to her, panting.

'I thought you'd come, sooner or later,' she said, wanly. 'Turned out to be sooner.'

Her eyes were swollen and there was a feverish pink flush on her cheeks. She had pulled her hair back with a pale blue Alice band, which made her look even younger, like a sixth-former from some upper-class English girls' school. She was wearing a white cotton robe, although her legs were covered by a silky throw with fringes.

I looked around the room. Traditional, yet expensive, with Staffordshire figures of shepherdesses on the mantelpiece, and oil paintings of galleons at sea. Through the French windows I could see a York-stone patio with cast-iron garden furniture, and beyond, to a tennis court, where a twentyish couple were shouting and laughing as they knocked the ball backward and forward over the net.

A clock discreetly chimed two.

'How are you feeling?' I asked.

'Better, thanks. A little woozy. The doctor gave me something to calm me down.'

'Are you going to be coming back? Or is this your way of saying you quit?'

She looked up at me and I could tell that she didn't really know what to say. 'I've seen dead bodies, of course. It's part of the job. But I've never seen anybody killed before. Not right in front of me.'

'So that's it. You quit.'

At that moment, the drawing-room door opened and a middle-aged woman appeared, wearing an orange silk dress. She had the flat, pretty face of a Burmese, and there was no question where Jill had inherited her exotic looks from. She came forward and held out her hand.

'Mya Foxley. I'm Jill's mother.'

'Jim Falcon. Good to meet you.'

'Is everything all right, Mr Falcon? We were very worried when Jill came home in such a state.'

I gave her a tight, noncommittal smile. 'I know. I'm sorry. I wouldn't have bothered you but Jill's doing some very important work for us.'

'And?'

'And I just came to remind her *how* important.'

'I see.' Mrs Foxley looked uneasy. I don't know if she was expecting me to explain myself any further, but when it was obvious that I wasn't going to, she said, 'Would you like some tea?'

Jill and I talked for nearly an hour. Her mother brought in a plateful of Scottish shortbread called petticoat tails and I ate about seven of them. I hadn't realized how hungry I was.

I tried not to push Jill too hard. Instead, I encouraged her to think about what she had seen, and why it had shocked her so much. From my own experience during the war, I knew that people can be much more distressed by tiny poignancies than by major tragedies. The baby's shoe, lying in the ruins.

Jill said, 'What I can't get out of my head – that *strigoi* who killed the little boy – she was a *girl*. It never occurred to me that you could have female Screechers, too.'

I put down my teacup. 'Sure you can. They're called *striogaica*. In some ways, they're supposed to be even more powerful than the male *strigoi*. According to the folk stories, they can turn your butter rancid, stop your cows from giving milk, ruin your harvest – even ruin your marriage.'

'They sound horrendous. That one we saw, *she* was horrendous.'

'Well, she was still alive and physically decomposing, which didn't make her very attractive. But once they're dead – or *un*dead, rather – the *striogaica* are supposed to be very alluring. Some of the stories even say that they can fall in love with

100

human men, and have children who are half human and half *strigoi*. They're still just as dangerous, of course – they still need fresh human blood, so you wouldn't want them living in your neighbourhood.'

Jill said, 'I couldn't help thinking – what if that happened to me? I think that was what I was afraid of, more than anything else.'

'First of all, that's not going to happen to you, because Duca is not going to catch you unawares, the way it did with those poor people. Second of all, if it did, I would immediately know what had happened to you, and I would hammer nails into your eyes, cut your head off and bury your body in consecrated ground. So you'd have nothing to worry about.'

For the first time that afternoon, Jill actually smiled. She reached out her hand to me and touched my shirtsleeve. 'I'm sorry,' she said. 'I've really let you down, haven't I?'

'Your stiff upper lip went a little floppy, that's all. I came around to starch it for you.'

'So what do we do now?'

'I think we need to take Bullet back to the park, and follow any trail that the Screechers left behind them. I very much doubt that they would have gone straight back to the place where Duca's hiding, but if we can find out where *they're* holed up – they're bound to make contact with him before too long.'

'All right, then. Just give me ten minutes to get dressed.'

She stood up. I hadn't realized how short she was, without her shoes. 'I'll wait for you,' I said, and nodded toward the tea tray. 'I'll – uh – take care of these cookies.'

As she left, her mother came back in, and gave me that look that only mothers can give you, when you're taking their daughters away.

Bynes Road

We drove Bullet back to Beddington Park. The woods where the middle-aged woman and the little boy had been killed were already screened off with ten-foot-high sacking, and signs saying *Metropolitan Police No Entry*. I took the Kit out of the trunk of the car, and then we showed our identity cards to three sweating bobbies in shirtsleeves, who allowed us in.

Inspector Ruddock was still there, looking even closer to detonation than before. 'Oh, it's you,' he said. 'What the devil do *you* want?'

'We're going to be following any trail that the perpetrators may have left behind them.'

'About bloody time. I wanted to get the dogs out hours ago, but believe it or not I was countermanded.' He pronounced 'countermanded' as if it were one of the most disgusting words in the English language, like 'mucus'.

'Yes, sir, I know,' I said, trying to calm him down, but that only made his eyes bulge and his nostrils flare even more widely. I have to say, though, that I loved apoplectic Englishmen like him, especially if they were on my side. They were like hand grenades with the pin out, morning till night.

Jill let Bullet off the leash and he scampered off through the woods. I gave Inspector Ruddock a half-hearted salute, and then I followed Bullet and Jill, carrying my Kit.

'Madness,' I heard Inspector Ruddock protesting. 'Bloody lunacy, the whole bloody thing.'

In the clearing, we found two forensic scientists from the Metropolitan Police Laboratory at Hendon, still raking through the leaves and taking photographs.

'OK if we play through?' I asked them.

One of them stood up and took out a pipe. 'Actually, old boy, we've just about finished here. No footprints, but plenty of blood samples. If you catch the blighters, we should be able to match them for you.'

He lit up his pipe, and he was sucking at it furiously when his companion came over, holding up his tweezers.

'George – have a dekko at this.' I thought he was showing us a leaf at first: a curled-up shred of something pale and wobbly, with turquoise-tinged edges.

George took out his pipe and peered at it. 'Human skin,' he said, almost at once. I suddenly thought of the shots that I had fired at the ginger-haired girl, and the lumps of flesh that had sprayed out of her arm.

'That's *green*,' said Jill.

'Of course, which tells us that the owner of this particular piece of skin must have been dead for at least twenty-four hours.'

I looked at Jill and gave her the slightest shake of my head. She looked back at me, wide-eyed. Don't say a word about Screechers.

'Odd,' said George. 'You haven't had any earlier reports of any missing persons in this area, have we?'

'Not that I know of,' I told him. 'But take that piece of skin back to your laboratory, would you, and preserve it? We might need it for evidence later.'

George said, 'What's going on here? I really get the feeling that we're being kept in the dark.'

'Yes, you are. And for a very good reason.'

George took out his pipe again. 'It's not very helpful, you know, when they keep us in the dark. Hard to know what we're supposed to be looking for.'

'You're looking for anything that doesn't seem to be natural. Like that piece of skin.'

'Hmm,' said George, frowning around the clearing as if he had lost something important.

Bullet picked up the Screechers' trail almost immediately, and began to trot ahead of us with his nose down. He led us to the edge of the park, and out into the suburban streets again, heading back in the direction of Croydon Aerodrome. Every now and then we found spots of blood on the sidewalk, which indicated that the ginger-headed girl must have been pretty seriously wounded.

Jill said, 'Another thing – I always thought that vampires could only come out at night.'

'You're thinking about the *nosferatu*, like Dracula, and all the vampires you see in the movies.'

'The *strigoi* are different?'

'They have some similarities, but they're more like distant cousins. The thing is, the *strigoi* were isolated for hundreds of years in the forests and mountains and small village communities in Romania, and because of that they became very inbred, and they developed different strengths and different weaknesses. They can walk around in sunlight, which the *nosferatu* can't do, and they can eat normal food. And, like I say, there's even a legend that female Screechers can even conceive.'

'How can a dead woman give birth to a live baby?'

'Search me. How can a dead woman walk around at all? But when a *strigoi vii* becomes a *strigoi mort*, there's a radical change in its body chemistry. It becomes – I don't know, like liquid mercury, and smoke. It can walk on ceilings and it can pass through a gap only an inch wide, which is why the people in Romania always close their windows at night, even in the summer.'

'Here, look,' said Jill. Bullet had reached a red mailbox at the corner of the street – what the British call a pillar box. The female Screecher must have leaned against it for a while, because there were splatters of blood on the asphalt pavement all around it, and a smear of blood on the white enamel plaque which gave the times of mail collections.

'I hope she hasn't gone too much further,' I said. We had already walked over a mile and a half, and we were close to the perimeter of the aerodrome.

But Bullet turned around and barked at us, and so we continued.

We climbed a grassy hill next to the main airfield, where young children were flying kites and kicking footballs. From here, we could see all the way across Croydon, with its Victorian town hall tower, and even as far as the City of London, and the dome of St Paul's. It could have been idyllic, 'Earth has not anything to show more fair', if we hadn't been following that dogged black Labrador on the trail of *strigoi*.

As we crossed the grass, Jill said to me, 'I was wondering how you started chasing Screechers. It's rather a funny choice of career, don't you think?'

'Hey – I'm not a professional Screecher-chaser. My real job is giving cultural advice to businessmen. You know, if American executives want to know how they should behave when they sell their products in Belgium, say, or Greece, or India, I tell them what the protocol is. In India, for instance, nobody ever says no. You want something they don't have, they always tell you tomorrow.'

'So why Screechers?'

'My mother's fault, most of all. She was Romanian. She told me all about the *strigoi* when I was little, and when I went to college I did a whole lot of research into them. Without really meaning to I became something of an international expert.'

'Is your mother still alive?'

I shook my head. I didn't want to talk about my mother just now. I didn't want Jill to know how intent I was on hunting down Duca, and destroying it, and why. In any case, anger was unprofessional. Anger could lead to fatal mistakes.

Bullet led us across the field and back into crowded residential streets. Soon I found that we were walking down a street that I recognized. It was the same street where the birthday-party massacre had taken place. We passed the same house and the same Victorian church, and soon we were back on the busy main road, just opposite the Red Deer pub. I would have given £5 for a beer right then, even a warm one, but of course the pub's doors were closed.

We passed a small parade of shops, a barber's and a chemist's and a sweet-shop. Outside the sweet-shop there was a colour poster for *The Curse of Frankenstein*, starring Christopher Lee and Peter Cushing, showing next week at the Regal Cinema.

'I can't stand horror films,' said Jill, and then she looked at me with a self-deprecating smile. 'I'm really not very good for this job, am I?'

'Jill – nobody's good for this job, believe me, but some poor sucker has to do it. You're doing fine.'

Jill bent down to take hold of Bullet's collar and we crossed the main road. On the other side, the streets were even narrower and the houses were smaller and closer together – orange-brick Victorian terraces with black slate roofs. We walked up a short steep hill into Bynes Road, which backed on to the main London to Brighton railroad line. We were only halfway up the road when – just above the rooftops – a Pullman express train flew past, with its distinctive brown-and-cream carriages, and pink table lamps shining in every window. *Whoosh*, bang, a decompression of air, and it was gone.

'That was the Brighton Belle,' said Jill. 'London to Brighton in sixty minutes flat, and a good lunch, too.'

'Well – we'll have to do that one day, you and me, when this is all over. And paddle in the sea.'

'*Yes*,' she said, 'that would be lovely.'

Bullet continued to sniff his way along the sidewalk, but then I said, 'Grab his collar, Jill! Look.'

About a hundred yards further up the street, a glossy black Armstrong-Siddeley saloon was parked. Apart from a ten-year-old Morris and a motorcycle, it was the only vehicle in the street, and it was far more expensive than anything that the people round here could have afforded – well over $4,000 new, I would have guessed.

Bullet whined and strained, but Jill pulled him back across the street, and we took shelter in the doorway of a small laundry on the corner. The woman behind the counter looked at us oddly, but didn't come to ask us why two grown people and a dog were playing hide-and-go-seek in the front of her shop.

We waited over ten minutes, and then the front door of the house opened. After a further pause, a tall grey-haired man in a grey suit appeared. He was too far away for me to be able to see his face clearly, but he had a very upright bearing, and he was carrying a cane. He opened the garden gate, and as he did so he turned back to the house, as if he were saying something to the occupant. Then he climbed into the Armstrong-Siddeley and drove off.

Bullet made another strangled noise, as if he were disappointed that the man had gone. 'I'll bet money that was Duca,' I said.

'Well, we have his registration number,' said Jill. 'All we

have to do now is get the Ministry of Transport to look it up for us. NLT 683.'

'I'll call Terence. Then I want to take a look in that house.'

I went into the laundry and asked the woman if she had a phone I could use. 'Of course,' she said. 'Is everything all right?'

'Oh, sure. My girlfriend and I are just playing a trick on somebody. It's his birthday.'

'Oh,' said the woman, blinking at me. Then, 'You're *American*, aren't you?' as if that explained why I was behaving so strangely.

When the MI6 operator put me through to Terence, he sounded distracted. I gave him the licence number of Duca's car, and told him that I'd call him back later.

'But, Terence – on no account take any action, even when you've found out who the car belongs to.'

'Don't worry, old man. I wouldn't have the first idea.'

We walked up Bynes Road toward the house. It had a peeling, brown-painted front door, and a knocker in the shape of Mr Punch. The tiny front garden was covered over with concrete but dandelions were growing up between the cracks. I tried to see into the front window but a pair of sagging net curtains were drawn across it, and all I could make out was the sunlight shining in the back yard. In Louisville they would have called this a 'shotgun' house, in the sense that you could fire a shotgun in through the front door and the pellets would go clear through the house without touching anything.

The front door of the adjoining house opened, and an elderly woman appeared, wearing a flowery summer dress that appeared to have been modelled on a bell-tent, and wrinkled red socks. From the open door I could hear 'Diana' playing on the radio. '*I'm so young and you're so old.*'

The elderly woman made a phlegmy noise in her throat and said, 'If you're looking for the Browns, mate, they've been poorly.'

'Really? When was the last time you saw them?'

'Three days ago. The doctor's been round twice a day. He even came round in the middle of the night. I asked him what was wrong with them and he said meningitis.'

'Was that their doctor? The guy in the black sedan?'

'That's right. He's not their usual doctor, though. Their usual doctor's Dr Bedford. I suppose he's on his holidays, Dr Bedford.'

'Yes, I imagine he is. Well – thank you for telling us.'

The elderly woman didn't appear to be in any hurry to go back into her house. She said, 'I go to Dr Cotterill myself. She's a woman doctor. You don't want to go to a man doctor at my age. I get this rash on my legs, see.'

'I see.'

I thought we were going to be delayed there for hours, talking about the woman's skin problems, but after two or three minutes a younger woman appeared at her front door and told her that her tea was getting cold, so she went inside.

I said, 'Thank God the British can't survive for more than ten minutes without a cup of tea.'

'I think there's somebody in the living room,' said Jill. 'I saw a shadow moving across toward the door.'

I shielded my eyes with my hand, and she was right. There was definitely somebody in the house, moving around, although it was impossible to tell what they were doing. I decided to go in cold. Normally, I would have made sure that we had covered the back of the house, but the railroad embankment was very steep and trains were rattling past every three or four minutes, some of them at fifty or sixty miles an hour, and even a Screecher would have thought twice about trying to escape that way.

I opened the garden gate and went up to the front door. It may have been bolted on the other side, but the main lock was only a cheap Yale. I turned my back on it, and at the same time I reached behind me and took out my gun. Jill said nothing, but held on to Bullet's collar and waited. 'Don't let Bullet go,' I warned her. 'These bastards are capable of breaking his neck without blinking. And once I'm inside, bring my Kit in, will you, as quick as you can?'

'All right,' said Jill, apprehensively.

I had started to count to three, '*One – two—*' when I heard the young man's voice inside the house.

'Who's there? Is there somebody outside? Beryl – there's somebody outside, I can smell them!'

Without any more hesitation I kicked backward and the

door burst open. I barged into the hall and hurled myself sideways so that I virtually bounced off the wall. There were three or four coats hanging up and for one desperate moment I was entangled in empty sleeves, as if the coats were trying to catch hold of me, but then I fought my way out of them and pushed my way into the living room.

The young man we had seen in the park was standing in the far corner, behind a frayed brown couch. Lying on the couch was the gingery-headed girl, with its knee heavily bandaged. The living room was stuffy and hot, and there was a sickening smell of putrescent flesh and dried herbs, the unmistakable stench of Screechers.

'Jill!' I yelled, pointing my gun at them with both hands. 'Get in here, now!'

'What do you think you're going to do with that?' the young man sneered at me. '*Kill* us?'

'We'll suck you empty,' said the gingery-haired girl. 'You and your girlfriend. *And* your bleeding dog.' There was no doubt where the piece of skin in the park had come from: the girl's face had a pale greenish tinge to it and its eyes were already starting to milk over. It was very close to becoming a *strigoi mort*.

Jill came in with my Kit. Bullet was close behind her, eager to get at the two Screechers, but Jill said, '*Stay*, Bullet!' and he reluctantly waited in the hallway, panting, his tail thumping against the umbrella stand.

Keeping my gun pointed at the young man, I went down on one knee and opened up my Kit. The young man started to come around the side of the couch, and as it did so it took his kitchen knife out of its belt.

'I'm going to split you wide open, mate, and there's nothing you can do to stop me!'

I was reluctant to shoot it. For one thing, I didn't want the neighbours to call the police. For another thing, I had only six Last Supper bullets left, and I wanted to conserve them. The young man came up to me, crouching slightly, holding out its knife, and grinning. Like most Screechers, it thought that it was immortal, and that even if I shot it, it would survive.

'I think that's near enough, son,' I warned it. Out of my case, I lifted the Bible with the ash-wood cover and the silver crucifix, and held it up in front of it. Immediately, it turned its face away, as if I had shone a blinding light in its eyes. The gingery-haired girl clamped both her hands over its face and cried out, 'What's that? Micky, *what's that*?'

'I'll tell you what this is. This is the first Bible that was translated into Romanian for Serban Cantacuzino, of Wallachia, when he swore to rid his country of unholy vermin like you.'

'Take it away!' the girl screamed at me. 'Take it away, it's hurting my eyes!'

The young man raised one hand to protect its face, and started to edge its way toward me again. But then I handed the Bible to Jill, and said, 'Open it where it's bookmarked, and hold it up high.'

She took the Bible and found the faded red ribbon. Then she opened it wide and held it up. It was marked at Revelation, Chapter 20: '*A prins balaurul – arpele cel veche, care este Diavolul i Satan, l–a legat pentru o mie de ani.*'

Both Screechers found it almost impossible to see. When I had first used this Bible on a Screecher, during World War Two, I hadn't been able to believe that the word of God could have such a blinding effect on them. But they were totally unholy, and it did. It was like throwing salt on slugs.

I shoved my gun back into its holster and took out my silver-wire whip. I made Jill take a step backward, toward the door, and then I lashed it sideways so that it wound itself around the young man's chest, pinning its arms. I gave the whip a sharp yank, and the young man fell on to the worn-out carpet, struggling and swearing.

'What you done to me, you bastard? What you done?'

You never forget how to restrain a Screecher. After you've done it often enough, you could almost do it in your sleep. Kneel on its chest, fasten its thumbs together with the silver thumbscrews, then drag off its rancid shoes and fasten its big toes together, until you hear the screws crunch into the bones. The gingery-headed girl kicked and wrestled me, too, but for a Screecher it was very weak. I must have hurt it badly when I shot it, and Jill helped me by holding the Bible right in front of its turquoise-mottled face so that it was completely dazzled.

When I had tightened up their thumbscrews and toescrews, I pulled the young man so that it was sitting upright, and unwound the whip. Then I dragged the girl off the couch so that *it* was sitting upright, too, back-to-back, and I wound the whip around both of them, so hard that it was cutting into their arms.

Jill looked at me, and I could see that she was disturbed.

'You're going to regret this, you bastard,' the young man told me.

'Not half as much as you are, sunshine.' You see how British I was becoming, and I'd only been there a couple of days. 'Especially if you don't tell me what I need to know.'

'I'm not telling you nothing. You can effing eff off.'

'I want to know where Duca is, that's all.'

'Micky'll split you wide open and I'll drink you dry,' the girl spat at me.

'Um, I don't think so. You seem to be labouring under the misapprehension that I can't kill you. The truth is, I *can*, and I'm going to.'

Jill was still holding up the Bible. I said, 'It's OK, Jill, you can put that down now. The only way these characters are getting out of here is in a sack.'

She slowly closed the Bible and put it back into my Kit. 'You're not really going to . . .?'

'Kill them? Of course. They're half-dead already. But I need some information first.'

'Why should we tell you anything?' said the young man. 'If you're going to kill us anyway, what's the effing difference?'

'The difference is that if you don't tell me what I want to know, I'm going to hurt you both very badly.'

Jill said, 'Jim – can I talk to you? Outside, if that's all right.'

'Sure. These two aren't going anyplace.'

She went out into the front garden. I could see that she was very agitated. Bullet stayed close to her and kept looking up at her anxiously.

'Jim, they told me that you were going to kill the Screechers, when you found them, but I never realized that it was going to be like this.'

I didn't know what to say. She was a lovely and sensitive

111

young woman and I really didn't want to distress her, but she had to realize that we were hunting some of the most disgusting parasites on the face of the earth and there was no easy or humane way of exterminating them.

'Listen,' I said, 'why don't you go back to that laundry and call Terence for me again? Tell him where we are and tell him that we're going to need an unmarked van. He'll know what you mean.'

'I don't know how you can do this,' she said.

'If it's any consolation, neither do I.'

'How long do you need?'

'Give me ten minutes, OK? If they're going to talk, that should be long enough.'

'And if they don't?'

The Curse of Duca

The two Screechers looked up at me as I came back into the house and I don't think that I have ever seen such hatred on any creature's face, human or not.

'You still don't want to answer my questions?' I asked them. 'All I need to know is where Duca is hiding himself, and how many people he's infected.'

'You can kill us but we won't die,' said the young man, contemptuously. 'You can even cut our heads off and we won't die.'

'Oh, yes, I know that. But that can only happen if your body is able to escape from the place where I put it, and your head is still reasonably intact. Since I'm going to bury your bodies in consecrated ground, and I'm going to boil your heads until there's nothing left of your brains but soup, which I'm going to pour down the drain, there isn't much chance of that happening.'

'Duca will find you, and Duca will make sure that you suffer.'

'Duca doesn't have to worry about finding me. I'm going to find it first. I have a score to settle with Duca.'

'Well, *we're* not going to help you find him,' said the gingery-haired girl.

'You want to bet?' I asked it. I went to the windows which overlooked the back yard, and pulled down the grubby net curtains. Then I came back and wrapped the curtains around the Screecher's heads.

'What are you doing, you tosser?' the young man said, spitting to get the net curtain out of its mouth.

'Guy Fawkes' Night just came early,' I told it.

'What?'

I took the holy oil out of my Kit, unstoppered it and poured it over their wrapped-up heads.

'Bloody hell, that burns!' the young man shouted, tossing its head violently from side to side. The girl didn't say anything, but sucked in its breath because the oil hurt so much.

I took a box of Swan Vestas and struck one, holding it up in front of them so that they could see the flame.

'Now do you want to tell me where Duca is hiding?'

'You're mad, you are!' the young man screamed. 'I'm not going to tell you nothing!'

'The choice is yours, buddy. How about *you*, sweetheart, are *you* going to tell me where Duca is?'

'Go to hell,' the girl retorted, its voice muffled under the nets.

'In that case, you don't leave me any alternative.' The match had burned right down to my fingers and I had to blow it out and take out another one.

At that moment, though, Jill came back into the living room. She looked wide-eyed at the two Screechers with the net curtains wrapped around their heads, but she didn't ask me what I was doing. Instead, she said, 'I've just spoken to Terence. He's identified the car.'

'Well, that's good news for these two. Comparatively speaking.'

Jill had written the car-owner's address on the back of a laundry bill. 'It belongs to Dr Norman Watkins, the Laurels, Pampisford Road, South Croydon. He's in general practice, but most of his patients are private.'

'So . . . I wonder what a *strigoi mort* is doing, driving his car around?'

'Terence is leaving now. He's going to collect his car from Beddington Park, and then he's coming over here with a van. He says that he shouldn't be more than an hour.'

'That's plenty of time. Do you want to take Bullet for a walk while I do the necessary?'

Jill said, 'All right. Come on, Bullet.' But when she reached the door she hesitated. 'Do you have to do this? I mean, is there really no other way?'

'Come on, Jill – you saw for yourself what these two jokers are capable of. And once they become *strigoi mortii* they'll spread their infection like wildfire.'

'Can't they be given a proper trial?'

'Jill – justice is a human right. These goddamn things are halfway to losing their humanity already.'

'Duca will drain your blood, even if we can't,' said the gingery-haired girl. 'I promise you that, you piece of shit. I promise both of you.'

'Watch your language,' I told it.

Smoke and Mirrors

Terence arrived just after 5:00 pm, followed closely by a dark blue Austin van. Jill and I were sitting on the low brick wall in front of the house, with the mid-August sun in our eyes.

The van was driven by a whippet-thin man in a brown boiler suit, with a sharp purple nose and hair that stuck up at the back of his head. His companion was big and silent, with a blue-shaved head and a scar under his nose where his harelip had been sewn up.

Without a word, the two of them opened the back doors of the van and carried two folded-up coal sacks into the house. Terence went in after them and came out almost immediately, looking queasy. 'My God, "Jim".'

114

'Nobody said that it was pleasant.'

'I know, but all the same.' He pressed his hand over his mouth and held it there for a while, his eyes watering. 'My God. I wish I hadn't had those sausages for lunch.'

Micky and Beryl hadn't been easy to kill, especially since I was on my own, and I wasn't nearly as young and as fit as I used to be during the war. The only way to kill them together was to force Beryl face down on to the floor, with Micky on top of her, facing upward. Even though they were both restrained, they still twisted and fought and cursed, and I had to wedge their shoulders underneath the legs of a dining chair to keep them still. I hammered each nail directly into Micky's eye sockets, and at nine inches they were just long enough to penetrate the back of Beryl's skull, too, which was sufficient to numb her. Then I got out my saw and cut through their necks, leaving both of their heads in the kitchen sink.

The driver and his companion came shuffling out of the house, with one of the sacks swaying heavily between them. Terence winced and looked in the opposite direction. 'What do you plan to do about Duca?' he asked.

'Go after it,' I told him. 'But this isn't something we can rush. Duca's going to be a hell of a lot wilier than these two, and much more difficult to nail down. We need to do some reconnaissance first.'

'What's your suggestion?'

'Well, it's posing as a doctor, isn't it? So let's make a doctor's appointment.'

Pampisford Road was a three-mile-long avenue that ran along the east side of Croydon Aerodrome. Most of its houses had been built in the mid-1930s – large detached residences hidden behind laurel hedges – but they weren't as opulent as Jill's parents' house, and most of them weren't nearly so well maintained. Their front gates were sagging on their hinges and their gardens were overgrown with weeds.

We parked on the grass verge about fifty yards away from the Laurels and walked the rest of the way, leaving Bullet in the car. On the gatepost there was a tarnished brass name-plate with the name Dr Norman Watkins, FRCS, General Practitioner, engraved on it. Beyond the gate there was a shingled driveway, where Dr Watkins' Armstrong-Siddeley was

115

parked. The house was pebble-dashed and painted white, although the pebble-dash was grey from years of weathering and there was a bright green streak of damp down one wall, where the guttering was broken.

I said, 'You can see why Duca chose a practice like this. Dr Watkins was running it single-handed, and from the looks of things, he was probably pretty old. He wouldn't have been able to put up much of a fight.'

'What's the plan, then?' asked Terence. The windows of the house were black and curtainless, and the interior looked deeply forbidding, with dark antique furniture and mirrors on the walls. In the dining-room mirror, we could see ourselves standing in the driveway, our faces pale and distorted, like reflections in a lake.

'Why don't you keep watch from the road?' I told Terence. 'Jill and I will go in and try to see Duca.'

'You're actually going to go in and talk to him?'

'*It*,' I corrected him. 'Never forget that it's an it. But, yes. We can make out that we're just about to get married, and we need some information on birth control.'

Jill looked at me and gave me a nervous smile.

'Well,' I said, 'we don't want a whole lot of baby Falcons around, do we? Not just yet.'

'Do you need your Kit?' asked Terence.

I shook my head. 'This is a recce, that's all. But if you hear any gunfire, bring it in – and bring it in quick.'

Terence retreated to the sidewalk just outside the Laurels, standing behind the hedge and lighting a cigarette. Jill and I crunched over the shingle to the maroon-painted front door. There was another brass sign on it – polished, this time – which said Kindly Enter. I turned the doorknob and we went inside.

The house was stuffy, as if nobody had opened a window in a very long time, and there was an underlying smell of boiled fish. The hallway was tiled in a diamond pattern of black and white, with a hideous oak coat stand, and four or five dead flies lying on their backs on the windowsills.

A doorway to the left-hand side was open, and I could hear typing. I went in, and Jill followed me. A middle-aged woman in a pale green tailored suit was sitting very upright at a desk, her head slightly raised so that she could see through the lower half of her bifocal spectacles, pecking away at a huge black typewriter.

Opposite her stood a row of bentwood chairs, and a low table with a collection of dog-eared magazines on it – *John Bull* and the *Illustrated London News* and *Horse & Hound*.

The woman looked up and said, sharply, 'Can I help you?' as if helping us was the last thing she wanted to do.

'I – ah – we don't have an appointment, but we were wondering if we could see Dr Watkins.'

'I'm afraid surgery finished half an hour ago, and in any case Dr Watkins is away.'

'It's just that this is the last chance we'll get before Saturday.' I gave Jill an indulgent smile and took hold of her hand. 'We're getting married, and there were one or two things we wanted to talk about. You know, personal things.'

'Are you regular patients of Dr Watkins? I'm afraid I'm only temporary here myself.'

'Oh, sure. I mean, my fiancée is. Dr Watkins helped to deliver her, so I'm sure that he'd want to help her as much as he could.'

'Well, all right. I'll ask Dr Duca if he can see you. He's the locum.'

'That would be great. It's just that we want to make absolutely sure that – you know – we don't have any little surprises.' God, I must have sounded dumb.

'Who shall I say?' asked the receptionist, clicking down the switch of her intercom.

'Mr Billings and Miss Erskine.'

The receptionist leaned forward and shouted, '*There's a Mr Billings and a Miss Erskine here, Doctor! They're going to be married on Saturday and they were wondering if they could have a word!*' She didn't really need an intercom: I was sure that Duca must have been able to hear her across the corridor.

There was a moment's silence, and then I heard Duca's voice for the very first time, and I felt as if centipedes were crawling over my shoulders. '*Of course. Why don't you ask them to come through?*'

Suave, measured, with that distinctive Romanian accent that reminded me of all the other *strigoi mortii* I had encountered. I almost felt that the past twelve years had shrunk away completely.

The receptionist led us across the hallway to a door marked Private. She knocked, and showed us in. My heart was beating in slow, painful thumps, as if I had been running for my life.

Duca was standing by the window, looking out over the back garden. It was very tall, over six foot three, and it was wearing an immaculate light-grey suit, with a dark-grey shirt underneath it, and a white starched collar. Its grey silk necktie was tied just a little more flamboyantly than the average Englishman would have tied it in those days, and its grey, combed-back hair was just a little longer than the average Englishman would have allowed it to grow, so that it curled over its collar at the back. It had a single diamond sparkling in the lobe of his left ear, which the average Englishman would have thought was incontestable proof of homosexuality. Not only that, it was wearing some kind of lilac cologne, at a time when even Old Spice was considered a little suspicious.

But like most *strigoi mortii*, it was devastatingly handsome, even in my eyes – and I detested Duca more than anything alive or dead. Its face was angular, with hooded, sea-green eyes, and a sharp, straight nose. Its jaw was clearly defined and it had lips of extraordinary sensuality, as if it had just finished giving a woman the most intimate kiss imaginable, and had not yet wiped its mouth. The girl at the house in Schildersstraat had been right: it strongly resembled a male incarnation of Marlene Dietrich.

It turned away from the window and smiled at us. Behind it, in the garden, I could see a dilapidated pergola, so wildly overgrown with creepers that it looked as if it were infested with green snakes. Beside it stood a marble statue of a pensive woman, holding a water jug.

'So, you are to be married,' said Duca. It turned its head toward me, but it never once took its eyes off Jill. 'You are a very lucky man, Mr . . .'

'Billings. John Billings.'

'And your very desirable bride-to-be?'

'Catherine Erskine.'

'Catherine . . . ah, yes. In my country you would be called Katryn, which means "pure". You are an extremely beautiful woman, Catherine. You deserve many years of joy.'

'Thank you,' said Jill. Although Duca was being so absurdly flirtatious, I had the feeling that, in a way, she was enjoying it. Its voice was so mellow and yet it had an air of intense danger about it that was both alarming and attractive at the same time. It gave me the same sensation as standing too close to the edge of a cliff. For some reason, I always feel insanely tempted to throw myself over.

'Why don't you both sit down?' it asked us. 'Then you can tell me what it is that you wish to know.'

We sat down in two leatherette armchairs facing Duca's desk. Or rather Dr Norman Watkins' desk, because it had Dr Watkins' nameplate on it, and a sepia photograph of a rather overweight family standing by a sea wall somewhere. Duca eased itself into a high-backed chair and tilted itself back, still keeping its eyes fixed on Jill.

'We were wondering about birth control,' said Jill, and blushed. Either she was a very good actress, or else she was genuinely embarrassed. 'We're not at all sure what the best method is.'

'Well, you are both mature adults, capable of deciding what your priorities are,' Duca replied. 'Are you looking for complete safety, or are you looking for unmitigated pleasure?'

'Both, I hope,' I told him, but Duca still didn't look at me.

Duca raised his eyebrows. 'No method of course is foolproof. But there are four different ways in which you can lessen the risk of conception. The occlusive cap, sometimes known as the Dutch cap, which would cover the neck of your desirable young lady's womb and prevent the entry of spermatozoa. The sheath, or condom, which would prevent spermatozoa from entering your desirable young lady at all. Then there are chemical pessaries or solutions which kill the spermatozoa on contact.

'You can practise *coitus interruptus*, withdrawing yourself from your desirable young lady immediately prior to ejaculation; or you can try the rhythm method, whereby you should only have intercourse with your desirable young lady during that time of the month when she is not ovulating.'

The way in which its tongue lingered around the words 'your desirable young lady' would have really raised my hackles, if I had genuinely been intending to marry Jill. But all I did was nod, and say, 'Unh-hunh, I see,' as if I were taking this all very seriously, and didn't realize how lubriciously it was talking to her.

'It's difficult to decide, isn't it?' said Jill. 'Which method do you personally recommend?'

'Well . . . ' said Duca, 'the rhythm method of course is the best for natural pleasure, but it is very unreliable for contraceptive purposes. *Coitus interruptus* is also unreliable in that some spermatozoa can escape prior to ejaculation, or the husband may not be prompt enough in his withdrawal. Also, somewhat *messy*.'

'The sheath sounds the most effective to me,' I put in.

For the first time, Duca really looked at me. 'You may think so, my dear sir. But it is only effective if you can be relied upon to wear one.'

'Is there any reason why I shouldn't? I've always used one before.'

'Perhaps one night you may have drunk too much wine, and forget. Perhaps one night you may decide that you are tired of sheaths, that they diminish your pleasure. After all, what does it matter to you? You are not the one who will have to carry the child, and go through the agony of labour.'

'Well, no, I guess not.'

'In my opinion, the Dutch cap is the best protective, because your desirable young lady herself will ensure that she always fits it.' Duca lifted its thumb and two fingers, as if it were folding a Dutch cap prior to insertion. It was one of the most sexually suggestive gestures I had ever seen anyone make.

'Where can I get one?' asked Jill. 'Do they sell them at the chemist's?'

'No, no. Your doctor has first to measure your cervix so that you have the correct size. Then he has to demonstrate to you how to insert the Dutch cap so that it snugly seals the neck of your womb. Usually I insist that my young ladies insert it for themselves at home and then visit the surgery so that I can ensure they have learned how to fit it correctly.'

Jill looked at me, her eyes wide, and the look on her face said *absolutely not*.

I cleared my throat and said, 'That was – uh – very enlightening, Doctor, thank you. I think you've told us just about everything we need to know. Maybe my fiancée and I should go away now and talk this over between ourselves.'

'Of course,' said Duca. 'But you are to be married in only a few days' time, so if your desirable young lady has need of my services it would be better if you made your decision sooner rather than later.'

'Sure,' I said, and stood up. As I did so, however, Duca looked at me again and this time its sea-green eyes narrowed a little and a crease appeared in the middle of its forehead, as if it had suddenly remembered something.

'You know, my dear sir, it's very strange. You remind me very much of somebody I once knew well.'

'I do?'

Duca nodded 'I can't quite put my finger on it. It's in your expression. You don't have any Romanian blood in you, do you?'

'Me? My parents were Irish.'

'Irish? It's still very strange. I have a long memory for faces, and your face . . . it's so much like this person I knew.'

'Can't help you, I'm afraid,' I told him. But he kept on staring at me and I was convinced that he could see my mother looking out of my eyes.

Night Fever

At around six that evening, the sky clouded over from the west and it grew so dark that Terence had to drive with his headlights on. Rain began to fall on the windshield, big fat drops as warm as blood.

We drove to Jill's house in Purley and Terence parked in the driveway. We had decided that there was no point in my going all the way back to central London, so Jill had invited me to stay over. Terence would find me a local bed-and-breakfast in the morning, and have my cases brought down.

Charles Frith had arranged with Inspector Ruddock for a watch to be kept on the Laurels throughout the night. The police would alert us immediately if Duca left the house, and follow it, although they were under strict instructions not to attempt to stop it. If they did, they wouldn't stand a chance.

'What's next, then?' asked Terence, tugging on the parking brake.

'We need to get into the Laurels sometime during the day when Duca's out. What I'm looking for is his wheel, the talisman that he wears around his neck.'

'Why do you want that?'

'Two reasons. When a live Screecher becomes a dead Screecher, its physiology changes. It can slide through the narrowest of gaps, and it can run so fast that you can barely see it, but it has very poor night vision. The wheel has properties which realign the rods and the cones in its eyes, so that it can see in the dark.'

'But if Duca wears it around its neck—' said Jill.

'It doesn't – not during the day. If it did, its eyes would be much too sensitized, and it would practically be blinded, especially if the sun came out. If we can find Duca's wheel, and take it, Duca is absolutely certain to come looking for it.'

'And I suppose we'll be waiting for it, when it does?'

'You've got it. We'll catch it in a sealed and darkened room, so that it won't be able to see us and it won't be able to escape.'

'Then what?'

'We'll tie it up, nail it down, decapitate it, and dispose of the body, just like the other Screechers. The only difference between exterminating a live Screecher and a dead Screecher is that the dead ones' bodies have to be cut into four pieces and each piece has to be buried well away from the others.'

Terence looked queasy. Jill said, 'I don't have to be there when you kill it, do I?'

'Not unless you want to. It's dangerous, and its pretty damned disgusting, and the dead ones usually scream blue murder.'

'In that case, I think I'll pass.'

*   *   *

As we went into the house, lightning flickered over the trees at the end of the garden, followed by an indigestive rumble of thunder. Jill's mother was in the dining room, wearing an emerald-green sari, and setting the table for dinner. Her father was in the living room, standing in front of the fireplace.

'Captain Falcon! Good evening! Perhaps I can offer you a snifter?'

'I'll have a Scotch, if that's OK.'

He went over to a large drinks cabinet and opened it. 'I've just been given some very palatable single malt, as a matter of fact.'

'That sounds . . . very palatable.'

He handed me a heavy cut-crystal glass brimming with whisky. I didn't usually drink this much alcohol in a week.

'Jill's mother has been having a bit of a word with her,' said Jill's father, leaning forward confidentially and lowering his voice to make sure that Jill and her mother couldn't hear him.

'Oh, yes?'

'It turns out that Jill's rather taken with you.'

'Oh. I didn't realize. But what she has to understand is—'

'I suppose it's partly the danger that she finds attractive. Women do, don't they? They get starry-eyed about racing drivers and test pilots and mountaineers and suchlike.'

'I'm afraid I'm not doing anything nearly as glamorous as that.'

'Well, whatever it is, it's certainly had an effect on our Jill, or so her mother tells me. She was very upset about what you were doing, no question about it. But she was even more upset that she might not have the gumption to go on working with you.'

'Oh. I see. I'm sorry. But I think she needs to know that—'

Jill's father lifted his hand. 'All I'm saying to you, old boy, is that I'd appreciate it if you didn't take advantage of her. No offence meant. But I'm her father, and obviously I have to have her best interests at heart.'

'Of course. I totally understand.'

'Good man. Just thought that it would be better to get things straight.'

I sipped my whisky. Jill's father was right. It was very palatable, and I began to feel much more relaxed. But I couldn't help asking myself why I hadn't quite managed to admit that I was married.

Dinner was strange but very good. I had never eaten any kind of curry before, and this was a Burmese curry, with fishy-tasting rice and chicken simmered in coconut and a bewildering selection of pickled vegetables and fried chillies and chopped cilantro leaves.

We ate out of small decorative bowls, and drank very cold light ale, making a toast every time we took a drink. 'Here's to international friendship!' 'Here's to Bullet!' 'Here's to Harold Macmillan!'

Jill's parents asked me about my family and my life in Connecticut, but they assiduously avoided the subject of what I was doing here in England, and why I needed Jill and Bullet to help me.

'Jill's always had such a passion for dogs,' said her mother. 'I'll show you some of her Kennel Club trophies, after supper.'

'I'd like that,' I said. 'You can take it from me that what she and Bullet are doing for me – it's invaluable. I only wish I could tell you what it is.'

'Well, it was the same during the war,' said Jill's father. '"Careless talk costs lives" and all that kind of thing. Have some more of those noodles, they're absolutely top-hole.'

Jill's mother showed me to a large bedroom on the third floor, with sloping ceilings and a window that overlooked the tennis court. It was decorated with red-and-gold Regency-striped wallpaper and all the furniture was antique. I took a bath and then I lay on the bed in a blue towelling robe that they had lent me, reading one of the books that were stacked on top of the bureau – a crime novel called *The Tiger In The Smoke*, by Margery Allingham. 'The Smoke' in the title referred to London.

I suddenly felt very tired and very alone. I had tried to book a telephone call to Louise after dinner, but after forty-five minutes the international operator had come back to say that there was no chance of my being able to talk to the United States until the early hours of the morning. I had thought about trying to call my father, too. It was his sixty-first birthday in a week's time. But I wasn't sure how I was going to talk to him, now that I knew that he hadn't told me the truth about my mother's death. I very much doubted that the counterintelligence people in Washington had given him the full details of how she had died, but he must have known that she was on some kind of secret mission.

My eyes started to close. When I opened them again, my watch said ten after midnight and I was still lying on the bed with the bedside light on, with the book open in front of me. I rolled over and put the book aside, and I was just about to turn off the light when I heard floorboards creaking outside my door. Immediately, I pulled my gun out from under my pillow, pointed it directly at the centre of the door and cocked it.

Screechers aren't easily deceived, especially the dead ones, some of whom are twenty or even thirty generations old. If Duca had managed to remember who I looked like, then the chances were that it had worked out why I was here, and why I had paid it a visit.

There was a cautious knock. 'Jim? It's Jill. Are you still awake?'

I swung myself off the bed, went to the door and opened it. Jill was standing out in the corridor wearing a short white baby-doll nightdress.

'Are you OK?' I asked her.

'Not really. I was wondering if we could talk for a bit.'

I peered out on to the landing. 'What about your parents? I don't want to ruffle any feathers here.'

'Oh, they're dead to the world. They always go to bed early, and you saw how much whisky Daddy puts away.'

'Maybe it could wait till the morning?'

'I won't be able to sleep.'

'OK, then.' I opened the door wider and it was then that she saw my gun.

Her eyes widened. 'What's that for? You don't think that Duca might follow us?'

'Never underestimate a Screecher, sweetheart.'

She came into my room and sat down on the edge of the bed. 'I suppose you think I'm being hysterical.'

'Why should I think that?'

'They gave me this assignment because I had so much experience with murders, and I accepted it because I thought I was pretty hard-boiled. But hunting these Screechers – I didn't expect anything like this. Not only do we see them murdering people, right in front of our eyes. *We* have to murder *them*.'

'That's right,' I said, sitting down close to her. 'That just about sums up the noble sport of Screecher-hunting. Are you trying to tell me that you want out?'

'No. *No*. I don't know. It's partly *you* that's making me feel so confused. I find it so hard to reconcile who you are with what you're capable of doing. I don't understand you at all.'

'Do you think that's necessary? To understand me, I mean? So long as you know that I'm on your side. So long as you're confident that I'm never going to let you down.'

She looked directly into my eyes. She was incredibly beautiful, even down to the small pattern of moles on her left cheek. She smelled so good, too, fragrant and soapy like Cusson's Imperial Leather. The bedside light shone through the layers of nylon net that made up her nightdress, and I could just make out the darker tinge of her nipples.

'I've never felt like this before,' she said. 'Not about anyone.'

'I'm just a garden-variety academic, Jill. There's nothing special about me. I got involved in Screecher-hunting by accident, more than design. You know that.'

'Yes, but you couldn't do it, could you, if you didn't have that special quality in you?'

'What special quality? Stupidity?'

'No,' she said. 'Cruelty.'

She reached up her hand and touched my face. I thought about Louise but this was something very different. This was something dreamlike, something that was taking place on the other side of the mirror. Jill opened her lips and kissed me, and I kissed her back, our tongues touching and licking each other as if we were trying to discover what kind of people we were through our sense of taste, the way that Bullet did.

She loosened the tie of my bathrobe, and reached inside, running her fingers down my sides, so that I shivered. Her fingernails were very long, and when she ran them down my back the soft scratching was incredibly arousing. I could feel myself rising, and then there was no turning back.

Jill raised both of her arms like a ballerina and I drew the baby-doll nightdress up over her head. Her breasts were rounded and heavy, and they performed a complicated double-bounce when her nightdress came off. Her nipples were dark crimson, with very wide areolas, and as I rolled them between my fingers they knurled and crinkled and stood up erect.

'I don't have any rubbers,' I told her.

'What?'

'I don't have any protection.'

She pressed her forehead against mine and laughed. '"Rubbers" are Wellington boots. Well, they are in England.'

'That doesn't help. I don't have any Wellington boots, either.'

She kissed me and kissed me and kissed me again. Then she opened up my bathrobe and took hold of me and squeezed me hard, digging her nails into me as if she wanted to prove that she could be cruel, too.

She lay back on the bed. The hair between her legs was fine and dark, like Burmese silk. I climbed on top of her and all the time she kept her eyes open, staring up at me, trying to read the expressions on my face. I made love to her very slowly, because I had the feeling that this would be the first and only time, and I wanted it to last as long as possible.

As I rose up and down, she drew her fingernails across my shoulders. 'You're so lean,' she said. 'All muscle and bone and sinew. Like a greyhound.'

She smiled all the time we were making love, as if she were harbouring some secret. Her breasts swayed in a gentle, undulating rhythm, and her hips rose to meet me with every thrust so that I penetrated deeper and deeper. At last I began to feel that tightening sensation between my thighs and I knew that I couldn't hold off much longer. 'I'm afraid it's going to have to be *coitus interruptus*,' I told her.

'Oh, no! Dr Duca doesn't approve of it! He says it's *messy*.'

'It'll be a darn sight messier if I knock you up.'

127

I took myself out of her and climaxed. The warm drops fell in a pattern across her stomach. Outside, rain began to patter on the roof.

She said, 'Do you think, when this is all over, and you've gone back to America, that you'll remember me?'

'Are you kidding me? I'll remember you for the rest of my life.'

She sat up and kissed me. 'I know you will. Because I'm never going to let you forget me. Ever.'

Wheel of Ill Fortune

Terence came to pick me up at 9:30 the next morning. He smelled of cigarettes and fried bacon.

'Any movement from Duca?' I asked him as I climbed into the passenger seat.

'Not a dicky bird. If he did leave the house, he didn't use his car.'

'Have you found us someplace we can use to trap it?'

'I believe so. It's in an old newspaper office in South Croydon. The paper closed down about a year ago, and the building's been empty ever since then. But there's one room they used to use as a darkroom. No windows, double-sealed doors, and we can easily cover up the ventilator.'

'That sounds ideal. Did you find me a bed-and-breakfast?'

'Better than that, old man. You can come and stay with me. I live in Thornton Heath, and that's only ten minutes away from here. It was my mother's idea. She said you must be feeling homesick.'

'Well, that's very thoughtful of your mother, but—'

'Excellent, that's settled, then! One of the chaps will bring your cases down, and you can borrow a clean shirt from me, until they arrive.'

Terence and his mother lived in a semi-detached Victorian house in a long street of semi-detached Victorian houses.

Inside it was gloomy and narrow with very high ceilings. The furniture was reproduction rustic with tapestry uphol-stery, and there was a gilt-framed reproduction on the wall of *The Haywain* by John Constable, as well as decorative dinner plates and a selection of Spanish fans with sequins on them.

Terence's mother was a small, flustered woman with very red cheeks and wild grey hair. She wore a cotton print frock with huge yellow flowers on it. 'As soon as Terence told me you were looking for a B-and-B, I thought, the poor fellow can't stay in a place like that. What he needs is his home comforts.'

'That's very generous of you, Mrs Mitchell.'

'Oh, please. Call me Dotty. I hope you like shepherd's pie.'

Terence showed me up to my room. 'It used to be my sister's, before she moved out.' There was a dressing table with a pink frilly valance around it, and a dark mahogany closet, and a poster of Pat Boone on the wall, stuck with Scotch tape.

'Tell me when you want a bath, won't you,' said Terence, 'and I'll put the immersion heater on. It only takes about an hour to heat up.'

I changed into a clean blue shirt and then Terence drove me to South Croydon, to the abandoned offices of the *South Croydon Observer* – a squarish three-storey building of brown brick, right on the noisy main road. The same blue Austin van was parked outside, and when Terence parked behind it, the whippet-thin driver and his shaven-headed friend climbed out, and came toward us.

'Everything OK?' asked Terence.

'Yes, Mr Mitchell. Want to come and have a look?'

The driver unlocked the double doors that led into the reception area. The parquet flooring was gritty with dust, and there were yellowing bundles of old newspapers stacked up against the walls. He led the way up the staircase to the second floor, and then along a corridor. The darkroom was right at the very end.

'What do you think?' Terence asked me, ushering me inside. The darkroom measured about ten feet by twelve. The walls and ceiling were painted entirely matt black, and not a chink of light showed anywhere. There was a ventilator grille over the sink, but the driver and his friend had screwed a rectangle of plywood over it.

I tugged the cord which turned the light on and off. 'Looks ideal,' I nodded.

'It won't be too small, will it? If Duca puts up a fight, there isn't going to be very much elbow-room.'

'No, this is fine. The less space you give a Screecher to manoeuvre, the better.'

Terence chafed his hands together, nervously. 'I can't wait to get this over with, to tell you the truth.'

I slapped him on the shoulder. 'You'll be all right. Once you get in close, you won't have time to be frightened, I promise you.'

We collected Jill and Bullet from Purley and drove up to Pampisford Road. Jill was unusually subdued. When I turned around in my seat to smile at her, she smiled back briefly but then she looked away. I wondered if she regretted what had happened between us last night. It was so hot that Bullet kept panting and licking his lips so that his warm slobber flew all around the inside of the car.

When we arrived, we parked close behind a grey Hillman saloon. Two plain-clothes detectives were sitting in it, smoking and reading the *Daily Mirror.* One of them was fat and sweaty and the other was thin and drew in his cheeks when he smoked as if he were sucking on a lemon.

'All quiet on the Western Front,' said the fat one. 'Some woman arrived about fifteen minutes ago, answering the description of the suspect's receptionist, but so far that's all.'

'You haven't seen Duca at all?' I asked him.

'Not a sausage, sir.'

'OK, Terence,' I said. 'Now it's your turn to play patients.'

'Supposing Duca rumbles me?' asked Terence.

'It won't. It's so preoccupied with pretending to be a doctor that it won't think that you're pretending to be a patient.'

'All right, then. But if things start going pear-shaped—'

'I'll be right behind you, Terence, I swear to God.'

Terence walked across the shingle driveway and went in through the front door. We could see him talking to the receptionist, and nodding. Then he sidled up to the waiting-room window so that we could see him, and tapped his wristwatch, to indicate that Duca was making him wait. We saw him pick up a copy of *Picture Post* and sit down.

A pigeon started up a monotonous mating call from the chimney tops. 'Are you OK?' I asked Jill. 'You've been acting kind of pensive this morning, if you don't mind my saying so.'

'I didn't sleep much,' she said. 'Oh – nothing to do with you. Nothing to do with *us*. I kept having horrible dreams, that's all.'

'Goes with the job, I'm sorry to say. I used to have a nightmare almost every single night, during the war.'

'I dreamed about this man who was walking around with no head. I was sitting in the living room, at home, and he tapped on the windows, as if he wanted me to let him in. I was so frightened I thought my heart was going to stop. I woke up, but every time I went back to sleep I had the same dream.'

The thin detective said, 'There you are, sir. He's going in.'

Terence was standing up. The receptionist showed him out of the room and then she came back in again, alone.

'Right,' I said. 'Let's see how long Terence can keep Duca talking about his imaginary hay-fever.'

I entered the front garden with Jill following close behind me. We ducked our heads low, so that we were out of the receptionist's line of sight. Skirting around the laurel bushes, we went up to the front door and I gently pushed it open. Inside, I could hear the receptionist typing, but she was interrupted by the telephone ringing.

'Dr Watkins' surgery!' she shrilled, at the top of her voice. 'No, madam, Dr Watkins is on his holidays at the moment! No, I don't know how long for, I'm only temporary! But if you need to see a doctor right away, Dr Duca is standing in for him! *Duca*, that's correct!'

While she was screaming into the receiver, Jill and I crept into the hall. 'Let's start by making a search upstairs,' I whispered. 'Let's hope that Duca leaves the wheel in its bedroom during the day.'

'If your foot's really painful, you should come in!' said the receptionist. 'The doctor is only here until half-past twelve, but I could fit you in at a quarter to!'

Luckily for us, the door to the waiting room was open only three or four inches, and while the receptionist was talking on the phone her back was half-turned, so we were able to make our way along the hall without her seeing us. As we reached the bottom of the stairs she banged down the receiver and started typing again.

'I'll take the bedrooms on the right,' I told Jill. 'You take the bedrooms on the left. If the wheel isn't in plain sight, go through every single drawer, but make sure you close them afterward. Ideally, I don't want Duca to find out that we've taken it until it starts to get dark.'

I was just about to climb the stairs when the door to Duca's surgery suddenly opened, and Duca came out. He looked at us in surprise, and then smiled.

'Well, well! So you two lovebirds have decided!'

'Ah, *yes*,' I said. 'We talked it over, and – ah – decided.'

Duca laid its hand on Jill's shoulder. 'In my opinion, my beautiful young lady, I think you have made the most sensible choice. I have always believed that a woman should be in charge of her own destiny, at least as far as her *womb* is concerned.'

Terence came out of the surgery, too. He gave me an apologetic grimace. Duca turned to him and said, 'Your allergy doesn't seem to me to be so bad, Mr Mitchell. The prescription I have given you for antihistamine tablets should alleviate your symptoms. They will make you a little drowsy, so if you are thinking of driving a steamroller, I suggest that you don't.' It gave a sharp, humourless laugh.

'All right, Doctor,' said Terence. 'Thanks very much.'

Duca turned back to Jill. 'Now let me see what I can do to give your desirable young bride the protection she requires.'

This was a seriously horrible moment. It had been one thing to pretend that we were engaged, and listen to Duca's lip-licking descriptions of various methods of contraception. But to allow it to give Jill an intimate examination, when both of us were fully aware that it wasn't even human, was enough to bring me to the edge of panic.

'On second thought – maybe we're being too hasty,' I suggested. 'Maybe we should leave it for today and come back tomorrow.'

'I have no surgery tomorrow, I regret,' said Duca. 'Tomorrow I have . . . other obligations.'

'In that case, maybe we should leave it till after we're married.'

'Is something *wrong*, my dear sir?' asked Duca, and there was something very knowing in his tone of voice, something very arch. I wondered if he might have remembered who I looked like, and guessed why I was here.

'Wrong? No, of course there's nothing wrong. It's just that this is a very important decision and I don't want us to rush into doing something that we both regret.'

'I don't see why you are so concerned. If you find that you dislike this particular method of birth control, all you have to do is to stop using it. But look at you. You seem very agitated. You are perspiring. Perhaps something else is worrying you.'

'Of course not. It's a very warm day, that's all.'

But it was then that Jill said, 'It's all right. Why doesn't Dr Duca examine me, and you can wait outside?' At the same time, she lifted her eyes toward the upstairs landing, and I realized what she was trying to tell me. While Duca is busy measuring my cervix, you can go looking for the wheel.

I didn't know what to say. I felt that I had lost control of the situation, and to my own surprise I also felt both protective and jealous. Jill was trying to prove herself to me, trying to show me that she was brave enough to be a Screecher-hunter. But the proof that she was offering me was the same proof that she had offered me last night, as proof that she was attracted to me.

Duca laid his arm around her shoulders. His fingernails were very long, and pale, and immaculately manicured. Jill said, 'Don't worry, darling, honestly. I'll be quite all right.' The way she called me 'darling' made me feel even worse.

'You're absolutely sure about this?' I asked her.

She nodded. What could I say, without arousing Duca's suspicions? 'All right,' I said. 'I'll wait for you in the car.'

Duca ushered her into its surgery and closed the door. I said to Terence, 'Go get my Kit. Stay right outside. If I shout out, come on in as fast as you can.'

'God,' said Terence, 'you're not going to let it—?'

133

'I don't have any choice. *Hurry!*'

Terence went out of the front door, and I ran up the stairs as quietly and as quickly as I could. If the worn-out stair carpet and the dusty window ledges were anything to go by, Dr Watkins lived alone. No woman would have kept a vase of dried honesty on the landing, so old that the leaves had turned skeletal.

First of all I opened the bedroom door on the left. A guest bedroom, quite small and smelling of damp. Next to it was a bathroom, with a large pale-green bath that was streaked with rust. I went to the bedrooms on the right. A medium-sized room, which must have been a schoolboy's room once upon a time, with athletics trophies on the windowsill and a single model Spitfire still hanging from the ceiling, thick with woolly dust.

In the master bedroom stood a large mahogany bed with a pink satin quilt. The quilt and the pillows had been so fastidiously arranged that I knew that Duca must be sleeping here. Or resting, anyhow. Screechers don't sleep in the same way that humans do, and so of course they never dream. The nearest they ever get to dreaming is a reverie about their lost humanity, and the people who used to love them.

I found Duca's wheel at once. It was hanging on a fine gold chain from the side of the mirror on the dressing table. On top of the dressing table stood several bottles of hair lotion and cologne, as well as a miniature portrait of a young woman in an oval frame. I picked it up and looked at it more closely. I could see why Duca was so attracted to Jill. This young woman looked more Slavic than Jill, but she had similar features, with high cheekbones and feline eyes. The name *Anca* was written on the bottom of the portrait, in faded mauve ink.

I lifted the wheel off the mirror and dropped it into my coat pocket. Then I left the master bedroom on tiptoes and started to make my way downstairs. The door to the surgery was still closed and the receptionist was still pecking away at her typewriter.

I was only a little more than halfway down, however, when the surgery door opened and Duca appeared, sleeking back its hair with both hands. It looked up and saw me and said,

'*Aha!*' It didn't look angry, or outraged. Instead, it looked triumphant, as if it had known all along what Jill and I were doing here.

'Sorry,' I said. 'I was looking for the bathroom.'

Duca pointed to a door right behind me. It had a hand-lettered card pinned to it: *Patients' Toilet.*

'Oh, sorry! I didn't see that! I must think about getting myself some eyeglasses.'

Duca glanced upstairs and then it looked back at me. 'I think perhaps you were looking for something else, not a bathroom.'

'I don't know what you mean.'

It held out its hand. 'I think perhaps you have taken something that does not belong to you.'

'Still don't know what you mean.'

'I am not a fool, Mr Billings, or whatever your real name is. I recognized your Romanian ancestry the moment you walked into my surgery. You think that I cannot *smell* where you come from, by your blood?'

It took a step toward me, still holding out its hand. 'I can also sense what you have stolen from me, Mr Billings. I think it would be wise of you to return it to me, now.'

'Terence!' I shouted. '*Terence!*'

The front door was flung wide and Terence appeared, carrying my Kit. Duca swung around and spat, 'You too? You with your ridiculous allergy to timothy grass? I should have guessed!'

'Oh, bugger,' said Terence.

'*Jill!*' I called her. 'Jill – are you OK?'

Duca turned around again and faced me. I could see how furious it was, by the way it kept wincing, but its voice was cold and utterly controlled. 'So it was *you*, then, who caught my two protégés? I am going to kill you for that, my friend. I am going to kill *both* of you, with much pain.'

'*Jill!*' I yelled. I was getting worried about her now. 'Terence – bring me the Kit!'

Terence came toward us, holding up the Kit in both hands as if he were quite prepared to smash Duca on the head with it. I hoped that he didn't, because I didn't want anything broken.

I reached behind me and tugged my gun out of my belt. I

pointed it directly at Duca's chest and said, 'I've had to wait a long time for this, Duca.'

'You *know* me? You know who I am?'

'Oh, yes. I know who you are. I also know *what* you are.'

'That is very flattering. But if you know me so well, you will know that you have absolutely no chance of catching me.'

'Terence,' I said, 'do you want to open the Kit for me?'

'What?' said Duca. 'You really believe that I am going to stand here and allow you to work your ridiculous hocus-pocus on me?'

'Terence, open the Kit and take out the Bible. Open it up where the ribbon is.'

Terence flicked open the catches, but before he could lift out the Bible, Duca lunged at me, and snatched my wrist. I fired at point-blank range, right through his perfectly tailored vest and into his lungs. The bang was so loud that the receptionist shrieked and dropped her telephone.

Duca stared at me, still holding my wrist. The expression on its face was unreadable. That's one of the things about Screechers: they've lived so long and they've seen so much that you can never really understand what they're thinking.

There was a three-second pause, and then Duca coughed, so that blood sprayed out from between its lips, all over my right cheek and all over the front of my coat. Then it smiled and said, 'I want you to give me back my wheel, Mr Billings.'

I tried to raise my gun so that I could give it a head shot, but it was far too strong for me. I strained and strained, with my teeth gritted and my elbow juddering, but I couldn't manage to lift my arm more than a couple of inches. Duca had almost managed to pry the gun out of my hand when Jill appeared in the surgery doorway, unbalanced and bewildered. 'What's happening?' she said. She looked as if she was walking away from a car accident. 'What's happened to me?'

Duca turned, and as it turned, Terence held up the Bible – open, like before, at Apocalipsa, the Book of Revelation.

'*Dah!*' Duca protested, raising its hand to shield its face. It wasn't totally blinded by the scripture, the way that Micky and Beryl had been, but all the same it twisted its head from side to side to keep the dazzle out of its eyes, and it had to let go of my wrist.

'*Jim!*' said Jill, reaching out for me.

Duca made a grab for her arm, presumably to use her as a human shield, but I fired at it again. I missed it, and blew a large chunk of plaster out of the wall, but Duca must have decided that it had had enough. It disappeared out of the front door, so fast that it was nothing but a grey flicker, like a moth's wings.

'Terence!' I shouted. 'Don't let it get away!'

We hurried out of the house. We looked left and right, and at first we couldn't see Duca anywhere. But the thin detective pointed upward and called out, 'There, sir! Right behind you! Gone up the wall like a bleeding ferret!'

Terence and I turned around. Duca was climbing the ivy-covered wall, so fast that it had already reached the bedroom windows. The ivy rustled and tore as it surged its way upward, and it looked as if it were *swimming* through it, like a man swimming up a waterfall, rather than climbing. I raised my gun to take a shot at it, but by the time I had steadied my hand it had already reached the guttering and disappeared over the roof.

I ran around to the side of the house, just in time to see Duca leaping on top of the garage, and then to the roof of the garage next door, and then it was gone. There was no point in going after it now.

'That was bloody rotten luck,' said Terence, as I came back round to the front of the house.

I reached into my pocket and took out the wheel. 'Not entirely,' I said, swinging it from side to side. 'Duca's still going to come looking for this.'

'You *found* it? That's terrific. But now Duca knows who we are, doesn't it, and what sort of a game we're playing? You don't think it's just going to walk into a trap?'

'Of course not. We'll have to be a little more ingenious, that's all.'

The thin detective came up to me, shaking his head. 'Never seen anything like that, sir. Never.'

'Never seen anything like *what*, detective?'

'Oh. Yes, sir. Sorry, sir. Take your point. Never happened, sir, did it?'

'No, detective. It never happened.'

Field of Blood

I went back into the house to look for Jill. I found her sitting in the waiting room, with the receptionist leaning over her, offering her a glass of water.

'Your poor fiancée's had a *very* nasty turn,' said the receptionist. 'Mind you, I'm all in a tither myself.'

Jill was pale and trembling and there was perspiration on her upper lip, as if she were running a temperature. Her pupils were dilated, too, and she didn't seem to be able to focus properly.

'Jill? Are you OK?'

'I don't know . . . I don't know what happened to me. Duca told me to lie on the couch. He said, "Lie on the couch, my dear," and that's all I can remember.'

'It didn't inject you with anything, did it?'

She frowned down at her arms. 'I don't think so. I can't feel anything. I just feel so strange, as if I've been asleep.'

Terence came in. 'I think we'd better get Jill home,' I said. 'I don't know what Duca did to her, but she's not feeling too good.'

'I don't understand what's going on,' said the receptionist. 'Why were you shooting at Dr Duca? What am I supposed to do now?'

'I guess you'll have to start looking for another job.'

We drove Jill back to her parents' house in Purley and helped her out of the car.

'Jill! What's happened to her? What's wrong?' demanded her mother, as we brought her in through the front door.

'I'm sorry, Mrs Foxley, we simply don't know. It could

be delayed shock from yesterday. It could be the heat.'

'I should call the doctor.'

'Not just yet, if you don't mind. Give her some time to rest first.'

Bullet clearly sensed that something was different about Jill because he stayed very close, nuzzling at her and whining in the back of his throat. Jill lay on the couch in the living room and covered her eyes with her hand.

'Do you have a headache?' I asked her.

'No, not really. I feel feverish, that's all. Hot and cold, like when you have flu.'

'Maybe it *is* flu,' said Terence. 'There's a lot of it going about. I mean, that's why we—' He remembered at the last moment that Mrs Foxley knew nothing about Operation Korean Flu, and finished his sentence with a meaningless flap of his hand.

Mrs Foxley said, 'I'll bring you some Aspro, Jill. Would you like a cold drink?'

I used Mrs Foxley's phone to call Charles Frith at MI6. I explained that Duca had found out who we were, but we had taken its wheel and it was sure to come looking for it. I also asked that he send a forensic team down to search the Laurels from attic to basement, and the garden, too.

Charles Frith said, 'Very well. But we really need to wrap this business up, old man, and as soon as possible. The press have been chasing the minister all day, and I don't think we're going to be able to keep it under wraps for very much longer.'

'I can't make any promises, sir, but Duca's going to want its wheel back, and if I know anything about Screechers, it's going to be looking for revenge.'

I didn't tell him about Jill, because I wanted to see how quickly she would recover, but I was seriously beginning to think that I would have to ask him for a substitute dog handler.

Ten minutes later, when I returned to the living room, Jill was asleep, with her mother sitting close beside her. I leaned over to make sure that she was still breathing, and then I lifted her eyelid with my thumb. She was staring at nothing at all, and her pupil was fixed, which told me that she wasn't dreaming.

'Is she going to be all right?' asked her mother.

'I'm pretty sure of it. But call me if you notice any change in her condition.'

Terence and I drove back to the *South Croydon Observer* building. The morning had started sunny but a heavy bank of bronze-coloured clouds had slowly rolled over from the south-west, and now it was gloomy and humid. I felt that I could hardly breathe.

'Any ideas what Duca might have done to her?' asked Terence.

'I'm not sure. Dead Screechers have a way of draining their victims' resistance, so that they don't struggle, even when the Screecher is actually cutting them open. Their victims know that they're being killed, but they feel so lethargic that they can't do anything to stop it. In Romania they call it the Weakness.'

'It doesn't look as if Duca's hurt her, though, does it?'

'I hope not. I think Duca sensed that I was upstairs, and that interrupted it. God, I blame myself. I should never have let her go in there.'

'What else could you do?'

'I could have gone straight in there and cut its goddamned head off.'

'Without your Kit? It would have cut yours off, first.'

Terence was parking outside the former newspaper office when his radio-telephone crackled, and a brusque woman's voice said, 'Control to Three-Four-Zero. Control to Three-Four-Zero. Position, please, Three-Four-Zero.'

'Three-Four-Zero,' said Terence. '*South Croydon Observer*. We'll be here for the rest of the day.'

'Can you go immediately to Chalmer's Boys' School in Haling Park? Three-Three-Nine will meet you there. There's been another incident.'

'What kind of an incident?'

'Operation Korean Flu.'

'Ask her when it happened,' I told him.

'Control? Do we know when this incident occurred?'

There was a lengthy pause, and then the woman's voice said, 'It was logged about two hours ago, apparently. A few minutes past eleven.'

'Thank you, Control,' said Terence. 'Roger and out.' Then he looked at me and said, 'Bloody hell. It's happened again.'

'You know what this means, don't you? Duca couldn't have done this. Two hours ago Duca was still at the Laurels.'

'You mean we've got ourselves *another* dead Screecher, apart from Duca?'

'There has to be. One of the live Screechers must have transformed already. If they're transforming as quickly as this, there could be dozens of them by now. Damn it, we really need a dog right now.'

'I'll get on to Control, see if they can fix us up with one.'

'OK . . . but don't tell them what's happened to Jill yet. Tell them – tell them that Bullet's eaten something that's upset his stomach.'

Terence raised an eyebrow, but didn't make any comment. He may have appeared to be puppyish, with all his talk of cricket and Nevile Shute stories and collecting cigarette cards, but he was perceptive and very discreet. Whatever a chap did, a chap's own business was a chap's own business, especially when it came to women.

We turned into Haling Park Road and drove up a steep curving hill toward the entrance of Chalmer's Boys' School. Chalmer's looked more like a cathedral than a school, a large red-brick building built in 1930s Gothic, complete with stained-glass windows and flying buttresses. A green copper weathervane surmounted the roof, in the shape of Time, carrying his scythe over his shoulder.

The courtyard in front of the school was crowded with shiny black Wolseley police cars and ambulances. I could see some reporters and photographers, too, but they were being kept well back by police officers.

As we parked, one of the young MI6 agents who had met us outside the birthday-party massacre came hurrying over to meet us. His linen sport coat was crumpled and his red necktie was askew.

'I don't know how the *hell* we're going to keep the lid on this one,' he said.

We climbed out of the car. 'What's happened?'

'Follow me.' He led us between the ambulances and around the side of the school. 'The school is closed for the holidays at the moment, but they were holding a friendly seven-a-side cricket practice . . . First Eleven versus Old Chalmerians.'

At the rear of the school buildings there was at least an acre of wooded copse, with beech trees and oak trees and horse chestnuts. The young agent took us through the shadows and the bracken to the other side, where there were five bright green sports fields. On three of the fields, red-and-white-painted rugby posts had already been erected in preparation for the fall term, but the furthest field was still being used as a cricket pitch.

Three ambulances were parked on the grass, and two more police cars, and there were police photographers taking pictures, and forensic scientists in brown lab coats, and coroner's assistants, and over a dozen police officers. Even from a quarter-mile away, I could see bodies lying on the grass. The bodies were red and white, too.

We crossed the fields. My old friend Inspector Ruddock was there, pacing backward and forward and bristling his moustache.

'Captain Falcon!' he barked, as we approached. 'I was rather hoping that you and I wouldn't be seeing each other again.' He was trying to be fierce but I could tell that he was badly upset. Anybody with any human feelings would have been distressed. The cricket pitch was strewn with nearly twenty bodies, all of them wearing white cricket flannels. Half of them were men in their twenties and thirties. The other half were boys of sixteen and seventeen.

Two bloodstained cricket bats lay on the grass, and the wickets were splayed at an angle, as if both players had been bowled out.

'God Almighty,' said Terence, and he actually took a staggering step backward, as if somebody had pushed him.

We slowly walked around the cricket pitch. All of the victims had been stabbed in the stomach, and their white shirts were crimson with blood. A few of them had their hearts bulging out of their chests, like gory fists. They looked so youthful and innocent, especially the schoolboys, and for the first time since World War Two I felt myself close to tears. Not only tears of pity, but tears of fury. I hated those goddamned Screechers. I hated their moral filthiness, and

142

their cruelty. I knew that Terence was right, and that if I had attacked Duca at the Laurels without my Kit, it probably would have beheaded me on the spot. But right then, walking around the glistening bloodstained grass of that cricket pitch, between those bodies, I bitterly wished that I had tried.

'How could anybody do this?' said Terence, shaking his head. 'I mean, honestly, how *could* they?'

As I looked at the bodies, though, something began to dawn on me. Even though all of the players had been killed, only a few of them looked as if their chest cavities had been opened up. To make absolutely sure, I walked around the cricket pitch a second time, and peered closely at every body. All twenty of them had been sliced open, yes, and some of them lay with their intestines coiled on the grass beside them. But only five of them had had their chests pulled wide open, and their hearts dragged out.

I turned round to say something to Terence, but Terence was standing a long way off, by one of the sight screens, smoking a cigarette. I can't say that I blamed him.

I walked over to one of the forensic pathologists, a plain fortyish woman with very red lipstick. Her coppery hair was fastened in a tight French pleat, like the coil of an electric motor. She was standing beside one of the older victims, making notes on a clipboard.

I introduced myself, and held up my security pass, although she didn't bother to look at it.

'This poor guy here, he had his aorta cut, right?'

'That's right. He probably lost twenty-five per cent of his blood.'

'That's around two and a half pints, correct?'

She nodded, and carried on making notes.

'These others who had their hearts cut out . . . would you say that they lost roughly the same amount of blood?'

'I can't make an accurate assessment until we get them back to the mortuary, but I would say so, yes – give or take a few pints.'

So only five victims had been drained of any blood, and only two to two and a half pints each. Simple math indicated that they had been attacked by no more than four or five Screechers – or even as few as three, if they were particularly thirsty. Terrifying as the Screecher infection still was, maybe I had been wildly overestimating how rapidly it was spreading.

But why had the Screechers felt it necessary to attack so many people? If there had been only three of them, and they had wanted no more than four pints each, they would have needed to kill only *two* people, not twenty.

Not only that, out of the five victims who had been drained of blood, four of them were Old Chalmerians. I would have thought that the Screechers would have had a taste for the youngest blood they could find, yet they had pulled out the heart of only one of the school's First Eleven.

'Can I talk to you again later?' I asked the coppery-haired pathologist.

'Of course. Here's my telephone number. You can always leave a message for me, and I'll get back to you.'

She handed me a card with *Rosemary Shulman, MD, FRCPath* printed on it.

Inspector Ruddock came up to us, blowing his nose on a large white handkerchief. 'Any ideas, then?'

'I don't know yet,' I told him. 'But I'm beginning to think that only three Screechers did this. They usually go out in threes – two living Screechers and one dead one. The question is, why did they need to kill two entire cricket teams just for a few pints of blood?'

'Off their bloody rockers, if you ask me. Mental cases.'

'Screechers are lots of things, but they're not mad. They killed all of these people for a reason.'

'They were *witnesses*, weren't they?' said Inspector Ruddock, as if he were talking to a very slow child. 'That's why they killed all of those people on the 403. They were *witnesses*.'

'But why attack so many people when you don't need their blood and so many of them are going to be able to identify you, unless you slaughter everybody in sight? It doesn't make any sense. Why not attack a young couple walking home at night, or a couple of cyclists in a country lane? Nobody would see you do it, and so you wouldn't need a wholesale massacre to cover it up.'

'I told you,' said Inspector Ruddock. 'Mental cases. Lunatics. They do it for the thrill of it, that's all.'

Black Trap

We spent the rest of the afternoon at Chalmer's School. Charles Frith pulled some strings with Scotland Yard and at 3:30 pm a dog and a trainer arrived. The dog was a German shepherd called Skipper and his trainer was an ex-military policeman called Stanley Kellogg.

Skipper was far from being an ideal dog for Screecher-trailing. The scent of Screechers made his fur bristle and he was very reluctant to follow it, keening and barking and trotting around in circles. Sergeant Kellogg wasn't much more help. He was boneheaded and pedantic and he repeatedly made it clear that he strongly objected to taking orders from an American attached to MI6.

'This isn't an easy one for me, sir, as you can probably appreciate. I have been instructed to look for persons or objects about which I have been told absolutely nothing except that I am going to be told absolutely nothing.'

'This isn't personal, Sergeant,' I said. 'It's just that we didn't have time to get you the necessary security clearance. I'm sure that you and Skipper have all the necessary skills to do us proud.'

'With respect, sir, whatever persons or objects that Skipper is supposed to be trailing, the scent of them is causing him considerable apprehension, and since Skipper and me is so closely bonded, I would very much appreciate some idea of what they is or are.'

'Sergeant, what they are is irrelevant. All you need to know is that they have murdered twenty people on a cricket field and we have to track them down before they murder anybody else.'

The bodies had been removed now, but Skipper was quick to pick up the scent, as much as it unsettled him. Although it was only mid-afternoon, the sky was dark maroon, as if the clouds had been soaked in blood. I could see lightning over Croydon Aerodrome. We followed Skipper across the playing fields to the far side of Chalmer's School, which bordered on to a suburban street. The Screechers had obviously entered the school from this direction, climbing over the green iron railings.

Skipper led us along the street to a quiet dead end street, or 'cul-de-sac'. There, the trail ended. The Screechers must have arrived here by car – parked, and then walked to the school playing fields.

'Sorry, sir,' said Sergeant Kellogg, with undisguised smugness. 'Think your persons or objects have been spirited away.'

'Thank you, Sergeant. I'll call for you again if I need you.'

'Let's hope not, sir.'

I raised an eyebrow, but he quickly added, 'Wouldn't want to see any more fatalities, sir, would we?'

I walked back to the school. I found Dr Rosemary Shulman in the parking lot, beside a dark blue Home Office van, packing up her medical bag and her notes and taking off her lab coat.

'Who's going to be carrying out the autopsies?' I asked her.

'Well, I am, in conjunction with the Croydon coroner.'

'Did you deal with any of the previous killings?'

'All except the first ones, at the Selsdon Park Hotel. I was on holiday then.'

'Have they all been the same – with only a small proportion of the victims with their hearts pulled out?'

'No, they haven't, as a matter of fact. Each incident has been very different. In one case we had a family of five killed in a caravan in Warlingham, and four out of five of them were exsanguinated. But in another case, in Streatham, seven were killed at a Boy Scout get-together but only two were exsanguinated.'

'Those victims who *weren't* exsanguinated,' I asked her. 'Did they have anything in common? I was looking at the victims here, and it occurred to me that whoever did this, they mostly cut the hearts out of the older people.'

Dr Shulman folded her lab coat neatly and tucked into the back of her van. 'I can't be sure without checking my records, but it's worth looking into, isn't it? The only victim in the caravan killing who wasn't exsanguinated was a girl of eleven. Everybody else in the family was older – older brother, parents, uncle and aunt, cousin.'

'OK . . . that's interesting. Can you go through the figures for me, with a particular focus on age? Also, can you look for any other distinctions between the victims who were drained of blood and the victims who weren't. Such as – I don't know – blood type, or medical history, or ethnic background?'

'Of course. I'll get in touch with you as soon as I can.'

'Even if you don't find anything, can you still let me know?'

'Naturally,' said Dr Shulman, and climbed into her van, and drove off.

It was past 6:00 pm by the time Terence and I had finished at Chalmer's School, so we drove back to his mother's house for supper. We sat at the kitchen table and she served us shepherd's pie with carrots and cauliflower. I had never eaten shepherd's pie before – ground lamb topped with mashed potato – but I was hungry and I think I enjoyed it. At least Mrs Mitchell seasoned her meat with plenty of salt and pepper and Lea & Perrins sauce. Apart from Mya Foxley's Burmese curry, most of the food that I had been served since I had arrived in England had been very inferior quality and almost tasteless. You wouldn't have believed that the war had been over for twelve years.

While Terence went upstairs to visit the bathroom, I helped his mother by drying the plates.

'He's a good boy, my Terence,' she said. 'Very thoughtful. Always brings me a bunch of flowers on pay day.'

'I'm glad to hear it. A young man should always respect his mother.'

'How about your mother, Jim? Do you get to see much of her?'

'My mother passed away before the end of the war.'

'Oh, I'm sorry. She must have been quite young.'

'Forty-eight, but she didn't look it. She was Romanian. Dark-haired, very beautiful. I can still remember the songs she used to sing me. In Romania they call them *doina*. They have sad *doina* and happy *doina* and love *doina* and *doina* for singing your kids to sleep.'

'You miss her,' said Terence's mother.

'Yes. I never had the chance to say goodbye to her. Not the way I wanted to.'

I thought of my father and I standing on the dock at Bodega Bay, letting those light-grey ashes run between our fingers into the sea, and they weren't even hers. For all I know, my father had dug them out of the living-room hearth, and they were nobody's.

Terence and I drove back to the *South Croydon Observer* building. We unlocked the front doors and let ourselves in. We had checked every single office before we left it, making sure that the doors and windows were all closed tight. I hadn't wanted to come back here to find that Duca had slid in through some inch-wide aperture, and was waiting for us.

Our footsteps echoed along the corridor as we made our way to the darkroom. I was carrying a flashlight but I didn't switch it on. There was a faint orange glow from the main road outside and that was enough for us to find our way upstairs. The darker the building was, the more difficult it was going to be for Duca to be able to see where we were.

There was a loud bang. Terence had collided with a metal filing cabinet that had been left abandoned in the corridor. 'Are you OK?' I asked him.

'Fine. Stubbed my toe, that's all.'

'You're sure you're up to this?'

'Bit apprehensive, if you must know.' He paused, and then he said, 'I was in the Eve Club last year, in Mayfair. A lot of security people go there – MI5, MI6, Soviet agents, all sorts. I was spotted by this East German agent and I had to hide in the ladies' for two hours. He would have shot me, no questions asked, if he could have found me.'

He gave a self-deprecating snort. 'I thought I was scared *then.*'

I opened the darkroom door, and switched on my flashlight. 'Try to keep your nerve, Terence, OK? When you're dealing with Screechers, the last thing you need to do is to show them that you're frightened. They latch on to fear, the same way a shark will go after your leg if you're bleeding.'

'Well, that's reassuring.'

We entered the darkroom and took a quick look around. It still smelled faintly of photographic developer.

'So what exactly are we going to do when Duca gets here?' Terence asked me. '*If* Duca gets here.'

'Oh – it'll get here, don't you worry about that.' I hunkered down and opened up my Kit. 'When it does, I want you to open up the Bible, just like you did before, but I want you to do something else, too. I want you to hold up this silver mirror, right in front of Duca's face, so that it has no choice but to look at it.'

'All right, then. What will that do?'

'It will show Duca what it really looks like. It's pure silver and it was blessed by Pope Urban VIII, so it can only reflect purity and truth. Did you ever read *The Picture of Dorian Gray*?'

'No . . . but I saw the film. George Sanders, wasn't it?'

'Oscar Wilde based that novel on stories that he was told about the *strigoi*. Dorian Gray's portrait grew older while Dorian Gray himself stayed young and handsome, just like a *strigoi mort*. You wait until Duca sees its true face in the mirror. I promise you, its own image will stop it dead in its tracks. Or *un*dead in its tracks.'

I took out my whip, my hammer and my nails, and my surgical saw, and I laid them out on the darkroom drain-board. 'That's when we slam the door shut and do the rest of the business.'

'But it'll be totally dark, won't it?'

'Not entirely.' To give Terence a demonstration, I took out the screwtop lid from a pickle jar. I had cut a thin three-inch slit in the centre of it and then painted it matt black. It screwed tight over the top of my flashlight, so that only a faint glimmer managed to escape. Terence and I could only just make out each other's outlines, and the dark glitter of each other's eyes. Duca didn't have its Screecher wheel so it was going to be 99.9 per cent blind.

'So . . . how long do you think we'll have to wait?' asked Terence, checking his watch.

'Who knows? But I don't think it's going to be very long. From my experience, Screechers have better noses than bloodhounds. They can smell what you had for yesterday's breakfast. In Holland, I've known them go through hospitals, drinking the blood of everybody in sight, except for the patients on morphine, because morphine affects their sense of balance.'

Terence said, 'How do you *do* this? This Screecher-hunting. Bloody hell, I couldn't do it.'

I shrugged. It was too complicated to explain.

We waited for over an hour. Terence took out his cigarettes but I shook my head. 'Let's keep the air clear, shall we?'

'Well,' he said, 'I'm trying to give them up, anyway. Too expensive. Two and fourpence for twenty, these days.'

'Maybe you should try gum,' I suggested.

'Does that really work? But you'll never guess what I saw the other day. A chewing-gum machine. You put in a penny and turn the handle and you get a packet of Beech-Nut chewing gum.'

'Miraculous.'

Terence glanced at me. 'You're twitting me, aren't you? You've got all those automats in America.'

Right then, we heard a door banging, somewhere downstairs. Then a metallic squeak, and another bang. I lifted out my gun and cocked it.

Terence said, 'Do you think that's Duca?'

'I don't know. It could be. Ssh.'

We strained our ears, but all we could hear for the next few minutes was the swooshing noise of traffic from the main road. Then I thought I heard a faint scrabbling noise, like a caged animal scratching at chicken wire.

'Want me to take a look?' asked Terence.

I heard the noise again. It certainly wasn't footsteps. Terence eased open the darkroom door and peered out into the corridor – right, and then left.

'I can't see anybody. Perhaps it was squirrels, or rats.'

Outside, a police car sped past, with its bell urgently ringing. Then silence again.

'No, nobody there,' said Terence.

He was just about to close the door when there was a sharp pattering sound, quite loud, and approaching us very quickly. I looked out into the corridor and for a split second I still couldn't see anybody there. But then I looked up and saw that Duca was hurrying rapidly toward us on its hands and knees.

It was crawling along the ceiling, upside down, so that each of the conical glass lampshades started to sway as it came rushing past them.

I stepped back into the darkroom and pulled Terence after me, by his shoulder.

'*It's on the ceiling!*' said Terence.

'Hold up the mirror!' I told him. 'As soon as it comes through the door!'

At the same time I holstered my gun and picked up my silver bullwhip. I gripped the handle in my right hand and the claw-like tip in my left.

There was a last flurry of scrabbling and we saw Duca climb headfirst down the wall on the opposite side of the corridor. It unfolded itself like a great grey praying mantis, until it was standing up straight. It fastidiously brushed the ceiling dust from its sleeves – its green eyes staring at us with unblinking fury. Its spine was straight, its handsome head was tilted slightly backward, its lips were scarlet, like a bloody razor cut. It was slightly out of breath, which lent it a false humanity that for some reason made it all the more frightening.

'So here you are,' it announced. 'I have come to recover what is rightfully mine.'

'Well, my friend,' I told it. 'You can certainly try.'

'You have stolen it from me and I want it back.'

'Oh, really? Haven't you forgotten what *you've* been stealing? You've been stealing the lives of innocent men and women, and children, too, for centuries, fellow, and I've come here to stop you stealing any more.'

'You are a pathetic fool. You cannot stand in the way of fate.'

'You don't think so? I've exterminated more *strigoi mortii* than you can count on the fingers of three hands, my friend, and now it's your turn.'

He stepped forward, with his left hand held out. 'I will give you the chance to return my possession. If you refuse, then I will take it anyway, and I will unravel your viscera all the way along this corridor.'

'How do you know I have it? This possession of yours?'

Duca looked at me with derision. 'Because it is mine, and it sings out to me, like all of my possessions, animate or inanimate.'

It held its hand to its chest, and of course it was right. I was wearing the wheel around my neck.

'If you want it, Duca, you'll have to come get it.'

'You think I won't?' Without hesitation, Duca stepped through the doorway into the darkroom. I shouted, '*Now, Terence!*' and Terence held up the silver mirror and pointed it directly at Duca's face. Duca turned toward Terence with obvious irritation. Terence was shaking with fright but he managed to hold the mirror still enough for Duca to see its own reflection.

From where I was standing, I couldn't see what Duca could see in the mirror – its own face, as it should have appeared, if it hadn't been transformed into a *strigoi mort*. Corrupt, centuries-dead, and heaving with grave-worms. Duca seemed to be confused at first – not understanding what it was looking at. But it slowly raised its hand toward the mirror like somebody recognizing a long-forgotten acquaintance and as it did so it realized what Terence was showing it, and it was shaken to the very core of its self-belief. It bunched up its shoulders and let out a harsh roaring scream, and shook its head wildly from side to side.

It was almost a mythological moment: when the beast catches sight of its own reflection and realizes what it really looks like. That was my moment, too. I looped my silver whip right over its head, and pulled it down to its waist. Then I lifted its coat and crunched the claw right through its vest and its shirt, into the muscle of its back, just below its ribcage. Duca screamed even more furiously as I wound the whip around its waist, trying to pinion its arms.

'*Lights, Terence!*' and Terence switched off the lights, so that the darkroom was swallowed in black. Duca ducked and thrashed and struggled, and even though I had managed to lash both of its elbows against its sides, it was incredibly strong, and it was pulling at the whip so furiously that I wasn't sure that I would be able to restrain it.

'*Hammer and nails! Quick as you can!*'

Without warning, Duca dropped to the floor, so that I had to drop down beside it to keep my grip on my whip. My eyes were becoming accustomed to the darkness now. The faint glow from the flashlight on the workbench was just enough for me to be able to make out Duca's glittering eyes.

Duca itself would have been totally blind. But its blindness didn't prevent it from twisting and wrestling and trying to bite me.

The only sound in the darkroom was scuffling and grunting and cursing, and the clatter of our shoes as we kicked against the cupboards.

Terence held out my hammer and two nails. I dropped my whip and tried to reach out for them, but Duca abruptly rolled over on to its side, trying to unwind itself.

'*Hit it!*' I shouted.

Terence pushed his way past me and flailed at Duca with my hammer. The first blow hit the floor, but the second struck Duca on the shoulder, and the third caught it just above its left ear, with a hollow knocking sound. Its head abruptly fell backward, and it stopped struggling, although it kept twitching and jerking as if it were suffering an epileptic fit.

Terence gave me one of the crucifixion nails. I positioned it over Duca's right eye and held out my hand for my hammer. Duca's eye was closed but I had no qualms about driving the nail through its eyelid. I had seen what Duca had done – how many innocent people he had killed. This was for Ann De Wouters, and everybody else that Duca had murdered during World War Two. This was for my mother.

'Oh, God almighty,' said Terence.

I lifted the hammer high, trying to keep the nail steady. As I did so, however, Duca suddenly rolled over again, and then again, until he reached the opposite wall. I made a desperate grab for my whip, but it snaked out of my hands, and Duca began to stalk up the wall, completely horizontal, until it reached the ceiling. Then it turned itself around and faced us, although it was still virtually blind. The light was too dim even for us to see it clearly, but there was no mistaking the contempt in its voice.

'I have escaped such people as you so many times before, and I will escape you, too.'

'Don't bet on it,' I told him, and took hold of my whip, which was still embedded in Duca's back. I yanked it with both hands, as hard as I could, hoping that I could drag Duca down from the ceiling. But I heard a sharp tearing noise, and the claw came free. As I later found out, all I had pulled out was a bloody lump of muscle and a triangular piece of silk from the back of its vest.

'*Terence!*' I said. '*Mirror! We have to start this over!*'

But at that moment, Duca reached into his coat pocket and took out something cylindrical. As Terence reached for the mirror, Duca tugged the end of the cylinder and the darkroom was suddenly filled with intense white light – so bright that Terence and I could see nothing at all. I took three steps backward, shielding my eyes. Although I was blinded, I could tell by the magnesium smell and the sharp fizzing noise that Duca had set off a hand-held marine flare – ten thousand candle-power, at least. It dazzled us totally, but it gave Duca the extra light he needed to see.

I hauled out my gun but the light was so intense that all I could see in front of my eyes were dancing scarlet amoebas, and Duca was so quick that I didn't stand a hope in hell of hitting it. I heard it leap from the ceiling, and the next thing I knew it pushed me squarely in the chest, so that I stumbled backward over my Kit. It twisted the gun out of my hand and threw it aside. Then it tore open the front of my shirt, and pulled the wheel from around my neck, breaking the chain.

'Thank you for my property,' it breathed, and its breath was actually chilly, like an open icebox. 'Now you will get what you deserve for stealing from me.'

Through the glare, I saw Duca take out a broad-bladed knife. I had never let a Screecher get the jump on me before, ever, but I suddenly realized that I could die here, with my heart cut out, and my guts lying all over the floor. I felt like a skydiver on his thousandth jump, who discovers that his chute won't open.

'You think you're going to live for ever?' I asked it. 'Whatever you do to me, you're not going to see another winter.'

Duca pointed his knife at my throat. 'There is a war here. There is always a war. On one side, the living. On the other side, the eternals. You can never win, for all of your religion, for all of your so-called morality. For all of your piety.'

It pulled my shirt open even wider. 'Maybe now we can see what you are made of.'

It prodded my navel with the point of its knife, and the

pain made me jump with shock. But as its drew back its elbow to stab me, it tilted backward. I heard struggling and swearing. Although I was still half-blinded, I managed to roll over and pick myself up. The flare had almost burned out now, but in its last flickering moments I could see that Terence had thrown himself on Duca and dragged it to the floor. They were hitting each other and grunting with effort.

I stood up, and hauled out my gun. 'Right there!' I shouted. 'Hold it right there!'

But Duca was too quick and too strong. It dragged Terence up off the floor, and swung him around in a circle, so that he was standing between us. By the sputtering light of the flare, I could see that it was holding its knife across Terence's throat. Terence was staring at me in panic.

'Now I am going to leave you,' said Duca, its voice hoarse with effort. 'But in case you are thinking of showing me any more of your mirrors, or opening any more of your Bibles, I am going to take this fellow with me, for my security.'

'*No!* I'll let you go, I promise you. You can walk out of here and take your wheel and I won't do anything to stop you. Just don't hurt him, OK?'

'Do you think I believe you? I know who you are. I know *what* you are.'

'I'm coming after you, Duca,' I warned it. 'If you so much as scratch him, I'm going to make sure that you have the most agonizing death that any Screecher ever suffered, and that's a promise.'

'*Jim—*' choked Terence, but Duca pressed the blade of his knife right up against his Adam's apple, so that he couldn't say any more.

'Just stay calm, Terence,' I told him. 'Do what Duca tells you, and you won't get hurt.'

Duca smiled. 'Who are you to make promises on my behalf? We shall see what happens to your friend when it happens.'

With that, it pulled Terence back toward the darkroom door and opened it. Then, with unbelievable speed, it dragged him off along the corridor toward the stairs. It was like watching a flickery old black-and-white horror movie.

I ran after them, but before I could even reach the head of the stairs I heard the front door slam, and I knew that they were gone.

155

Body Count

I clattered down the stairs and into the street, but there was no sign of them. I saw a black saloon pulling away from the kerb on the opposite side of the road, with a puff of exhaust, but I couldn't make out who was driving it.

I needed a man-trailing dog, and I needed it fast. But Terence had the keys to the car and without the keys I couldn't get access to the radio-telephone to call for assistance. The counterintelligence corps had trained me how to fire a whole variety of weapons from crossbows to bazookas, and how to break down a reinforced door using explosives, but they had never taught me how to hot-wire a car.

I looked around. Only about thirty yards along the road, on the corner of Allenby Avenue, stood a lighted red phone booth. I panted my way up to it. Inside, chattering and laughing and smoking a cigarette, there was a plump-faced girl with a pony-tail. She was wearing a pink skirt with so many net petticoats underneath it that it practically filled up the whole booth, and a white back-to-front cardigan, and pink popper beads. I rapped on the window and mouthed, 'Are you going to be long, honey? I have an emergency!'

She opened the door and a cloud of smoke came out. 'What's the matter with you, mate? I'm talking to my boyfriend!'

'I have an emergency. I really need to use the phone.'

'I just put three bob in. Go and have your emergency somewhere else.'

I took out my wallet and pulled out a ten-shilling note. 'There. You've made seven bob profit. Now can I use the phone?'

I called MI6 control. As it happened, Charles Frith was still in his office, and the operator put me directly through to him.

'Captain Falcon? You were lucky to catch me, old man. What's the latest? Mission accomplished, I hope?'

I told him what had happened. He listened in silence. The only time he interrupted was when he said, 'A *flare*?'

'Just because the *strigoi* come from a bloodline that's over three thousand years old, that doesn't mean they're not technically sophisticated. Duca turned the tables on us completely. It blinded us, and at the same time it gave itself all the light it needed to see in the dark.'

'Well, look here, I'll get in touch with Inspector Ruddock and get him to start looking for Mitchell right away. As for a dog, perhaps Miss Foxley has recovered sufficiently to help you out. She's nearest, after all. If she's still hors de combat, let me know right away, and I'll arrange to have another dog handler sent down.'

'OK . . . I'll call you when I get to Miss Foxley's.'

'Good man. By the way, a Mrs Rosemary Shulman has been trying to get in touch with you, from the Home Office. She rang two or three times, so far as I know. Daphne's got her number.'

'Thank you, sir. I'll talk to you later.'

'Captain Falcon—'

'Yes, sir?'

'You *will* keep a very low profile, won't you? I've had the press hounding me all day. Sooner or later, one of the buggers is going to find out what we're up to.'

'Yes, sir.'

I hung up. The girl with the petticoats said, 'About bloody time, too. My boyfriend's probably left me for somebody else by now.'

'A terrific-looking girl like you? He'd have to be nuts.'

'Oh,' she said, flattered, and giggled.

I went back into the *South Croydon Observer* building and collected up my Kit. The building was dark, and it echoed, and it smelled strongly of burned-out flare. I was reminded of World War Two, searching through bombed-out apartments for signs of Screechers.

When I had reassembled my Kit and shut the case, I went back outside to flag down a black taxi. I asked the cabbie to take me to Jill's house in Purley, which was only about five minutes away.

'I'll be glad when this bleedin' 'eat lets up,' complained

the cabbie, with a skinny cigarette dangling between his lips. 'Makes me feet swell up like bleedin' balloons.'

'Sorry to hear it.'

'Then there's all this Korean Flu going around. People dropping like bleedin' flies. That's all because of the 'eat, if you ask me, and they say that next year's going to be even 'otter. Do you know what I was readin'? By the year nineteen-seventy-nine, the 'ole of England's goin' to be like the Sahara desert, and we'll all be ridin' around on bleedin' camels.'

We reached the Foxleys' house and I asked the cabbie to wait. The Foxleys were obviously at home, because the drapes were drawn and the living-room lights were on, but the house seemed unusually quiet. I couldn't even hear a TV.

After a few moments, however, Mr Foxley opened the door, holding Bullet by his collar.

'Captain Falcon!' he blinked. 'We weren't expecting you, were we?'

'No, you weren't. But we have a crisis on our hands, and I was wondering if Jill could maybe help us out.'

Without hesitation, Mr Foxley shook his head. 'I'm sorry, Captain, but Jill isn't very well at all. She's been in bed since yesterday, and we've had the doctor around twice.'

'Do you know what's wrong with her?'

'She's very feverish. The doctor thinks it might be Korean Flu. He's given her something to keep her temperature down, but I don't think she's out of the woods yet.'

'I'm very sorry to hear it. The problem is, I desperately need a tracker dog.' I looked down at Bullet, who was straining so hard against his collar that he was wheezing. I thought: *I've seen how Corporal Little handled Frank. I've seen how Jill handles Bullet. It can't be too difficult to manage a man-trailer. They go running off on their own most of the time.*

'Maybe I could take Bullet myself,' I suggested.

'Oh. I'm not so sure about that. I mean, Jill and Bullet, they're tremendously close. I don't know whether he'd take instructions from anybody else.'

At that moment, Mrs Foxley appeared, in an orange silk robe. 'Who is it, dear? What's going on?'

'Hi there, Mrs Foxley,' I said. 'I'm sorry that Jill is feeling so low. I was wondering if I could borrow Bullet for a few hours.'

Mrs Foxley looked dubious. 'You could *try*, I suppose.'

I hunkered down on the front doormat and held out my hand. 'Here, Bullet. Good boy, Bullet. How about coming out to play with your Uncle Jim?'

I stroked his ears and he seemed to like that. 'Do you have a leash?' I asked Mrs Foxley.

She went to the hall closet and came back with Bullet's leash. 'Here, boy,' I said, soothingly. 'Let's go walkies, shall we?'

I started to clip the leash on to his collar, but Bullet immediately snarled and twisted his head round and his teeth crunched into the fleshy part of my thumb. I toppled back, knocking over all of the Foxleys' empty milk bottles.

'Oh, I am *so* sorry!' said Mrs Foxley, coming outside to help me up.

'You're a wicked dog!' snapped Mr Foxley, slapping Bullet's nose. 'What are you? You're a very wicked dog!'

I stood up, holding my bleeding hand. The bite wasn't too deep, but it damn well hurt. 'Hey, it's not Bullet's fault. Poor mutt hardly knows me. I'll just have to call for another dog handler, that's all. Can I use your phone?'

Just as I was about to go inside, the cabbie came up, carrying my Kit. 'Sorry, mate. I can't wait any longer. It's me mother-in-law's wedding anniversary tonight. If I turn up late for that, I'll get all kinds of grief from 'er indoors.'

'It's all right,' said Mr Foxley. 'You can borrow Jill's car. It's the least we can do. I'll get the keys for you.'

I called MI6 again. Charles Frith had left the office, but his deputy George Goodhew said that he would arrange for a dog handler to meet me in South Croydon as soon as he possibly could. I prayed that it wasn't Skipper and that pompous Stanley Kellogg.

I was anxious to see Jill. I wanted to find out what Duca had done to her, if anything. Her doctor might have believed that she was suffering from 'Korean Flu' but I knew damned well that there was no such illness. It could have been nothing more serious than stress. After all, I had left her in Duca's surgery for only a matter of minutes. But she had been very disoriented when she came out, and I would have liked to check her out.

159

There was no time. I had to get after Duca without delay, and in any case Mr and Mrs Foxley seemed to be keen for me to leave. I didn't blame them. Since I had first arrived on their doorstep, I had brought them nothing but trouble.

It was past 9:30 pm now. I tried to think where Duca might have gone. It must have infected at least a dozen *strigoi vii*, so maybe it had taken refuge in one of their homes. Once I had a man-trailing dog, I would have a much better chance of hunting these Screechers down. But it also occurred to me that many of Duca's recent victims were likely to have been patients of Dr Norman Watkins. Once Duca had installed itself as Dr Watkins' 'locum', it wouldn't have had to go out searching for new people to infect. Every day, unsuspecting victims would have come to the Laurels expecting medical treatment, and it would have been simplicity itself for Duca to taint their blood with an injection of its own blood, or simply give them an oral dose of cough linctus blended with its own saliva.

I drove to the Laurels. There were still two bobbies standing outside, with cigarettes cupped behind their backs, and a line of marker tape was fluttering across the gates. I parked outside and showed the officers my MI6 pass.

'I need to take a quick look inside.'

'Rather you than me, squire. I reckon it's haunted, that house.'

'Haunted?'

'We thought we saw somebody looking out of that upstairs window.'

'When was that?'

'About nine o'clock, just before it got dark. We went inside and made a search. Cupboards, under the beds, everywhere.'

'Not a sausage,' said the other officer, emphatically.

'Well, maybe you're right, and it *is* haunted,' I told them. 'On the other hand, reflections can play some pretty funny tricks.'

I went into the house, switched on the lights and headed straight for the receptionist's office. The police and MI6 had obviously searched it, because all of the drawers of the filing cabinet had been left open, and the pictures taken down from the walls. Two of the chairs were tilted over and magazines were scattered all over the floor.

I found what I wanted almost at once, but then of course the police and MI6 hadn't been specifically looking for it. The receptionist's diary was still lying open on her desk, and the name and address of every patient who had visited 'Dr Duca' was meticulously listed, along with the time of their consultation. Once my new dog handler had arrived, we could visit every one of these patients, starting with the earliest, and it wouldn't take us too long to sniff out any Screechers.

I closed the diary, tucked it under my arm, and I was about to leave the office when I thought I heard a creaking noise upstairs. It wasn't like somebody walking across floorboards – it was more like hinges, followed by a complicated click. There was something else, too: a noticeable change in atmospheric pressure, as if a window had been opened, and a draft was blowing in.

I went out into the hallway and stood at the foot of the stairs, listening. I was sure that I heard more creaking, and then a shuffling sound. The police officers hadn't been mistaken. There *was* somebody in the house. I listened and listened, but I didn't hear anything else. I had the impression that whoever it was, they were listening to me, too.

I waited a few moments longer, and then I went outside to Jill's car. I opened my Kit and put the receptionist's diary inside it, along with all the other artefacts I needed for hunting Screechers.

'Everything all right, sir?' one of the bobbies asked me.

I gave him a thumbs-up but I didn't say anything. The less that anybody else knew what was really going on, the better.

Back in the house, I laid my Kit on the receptionist's desk and unfastened the clips. I took out my Screecher compass and opened the cover. Immediately, the needle swung around and pointed, shivering, toward the stairs. Its response was so quick and so positive that I knew there must be more than one Screecher in the house.

I could guess what had happened. Once they were infected with the Screecher virus, several *strigoi vii* had been forced to leave their homes, or had left voluntarily because they didn't want to be tempted to kill their loved ones or their neighbours. I had seen this happen many times before, during

161

World War Two. They had gathered together in a nest, close to the *strigoi mort* who had infected them.

Judging by the way my compass needle was trembling, Duca's nest of living Screechers was here, someplace upstairs, in this house.

I took out my Bible and my whip, coiling my whip loosely around my waist. Before I attempted to destroy the Screechers, I had to find out how many there were, and *where* they were. And this wasn't wartime. I couldn't throw in a hand grenade and attack them while they were still stunned and maimed and disabled.

I went to the foot of the stairs again and looked up. The house was silent again, and the second-floor landing was in darkness. I tried the light switch but the bulb had burned out, or the Screechers had removed it.

Holding my gun in my right hand and my Bible in my left, I carefully mounted the stairs. They creaked, so I stopped every two or three stairs and stood totally still, in case the Screechers had heard me. Somewhere in the distance a plane was droning.

I reached the top of the stairs and looked right and left. No Screechers on the landing. I went into the bedrooms, one by one, switching on the lights. I opened the wardrobes and looked under the beds. No Screechers here either.

I nudged open the bathroom door. There was a huge black spider halfway up the side of the bath, but no Screechers.

Maybe the police officers had been hallucinating. Maybe I had been hearing things.

I was just about to go back downstairs when I heard a sharp shifting sound right above my head. I looked up and saw a trapdoor, and finger marks on the white ceiling all around it. That's where they were: in the attic. The noise of springs and clicking must have been a loft ladder coming down.

This was going to be difficult. I would have to pull down the loft ladder to get into the attic, so there was no chance of my taking them by surprise, and as soon as I stuck my head through the trapdoor they would tear my face off. There was only one way to deal with them, so far as I could see, and that was to seal them in the attic so that they couldn't get out – at least until I had thought of a way of rousting them out of there and killing them.

I went into the main bedroom and carried out an antique wooden chair, which I positioned directly underneath the trap-door. Out of my Kit I took a large ball of yellow wax, and two full heads of garlic. The wax had once formed part of a death mask of St Francis of Assisi, and I had used it several times before to prevent *strigoi mortii* from sliding out through narrow gaps around windows and doors.

I rolled a large lump of wax between the palms of my hands until it was warm and soft. Then I climbed up on to the chair and started to press it into the crack around the edge of the attic door.

I had only filled in a few inches when I heard a loud scrape, and a clatter. Before I could jump down from the chair, the trapdoor was pulled upward, and a staring-eyed man in a grey suit appeared, his grey hair sticking up as if he had been walking through a hurricane. He lunged down and seized my wrists, trying to drag me upward. I kicked and struggled, and the chair tipped sideways, so that I was left in the air with my feet furiously pedalling.

Another man reached down and grabbed my left sleeve. My shirt tore, but he got a grip on my elbow. Between the two of them, the Screechers started to haul me upward through the trapdoor, scraping my shoulders on the wooden frame. It was dark inside the attic, but I could see five or six more of them, including two women, and they all came clustering around me, snatching at my shirt and pulling at my hair. I saw knives shining, and I suddenly felt a sharp wet cut across my knuckles, and another one across my fore-head.

Christ, they were going to cut me open and drink my blood, and there were enough of them in this attic to drink me dry.

I realized then that they were too strong for me, and that they were going to pull me up into the attic no matter how hard I struggled. So I stopped kicking and swinging my legs, and instead of trying to wrench myself free, I took hold of the grey man's coat and hauled myself upward.

The Screechers were all pulling me so hard that I almost jumped up into the attic, and the grey man lost his balance and fell backward. I rolled over and rolled over again, colliding with a stack of suitcases and knocking over an old standard lamp, but as I rolled over the second time I was able to reach behind me and pull out my gun.

The grey man was practically on top of me, so close that my nostrils were filled with the sweet smell of his rotting insides. I pointed the gun at his face and fired, and even in the semi-darkness I could see a large lump of his head fly off, including his ear. He fell sideways on top of the suit-cases, his heels drumming on the floorboards like a stricken horse.

I fired again. The noise of the shot made my ears ring, and the attic was filled with gunsmoke. I fired a third time, and one of the women Screechers fell backward and toppled through the open trapdoor. A fourth shot brought down another man – and even though their knives were raised, the rest of the Screechers hesitated. They knew that I couldn't kill them, even if I blew bits off their heads, but they weren't impervious to pain, and even Screechers don't relish disfigurement.

I stood up and approached them, pointing my weapon at each of them in turn. The dim light that came up through the trapdoor showed me what a sorry, hideous collection of lost souls they were – their faces haggard, their clothes caked in dried blood, their eyes milky. They were in the last stages of degradation as *strigoi vii*, and it wouldn't be long before they would be craving one final poisonous drink of Duca's blood – the blood that would transform them forever into *strigoi mortii*.

From down below I heard shouting. 'You all right, sir? What's the 'ell's going on?'

'I've found your ghosts!' I shouted back. 'There's a woman down there . . . hold on to her and don't let her get away!'

I edged toward the open trapdoor, keeping my gun pointed at the Screechers. They were growing bolder now, and one of the women lunged toward me, hissing in contempt, and criss-crossing her knife in the air. I pointed my gun at her head and pulled the trigger but all that I heard was a metallic click. All of my Last Supper bullets had been fired, and the clip was empty.

I didn't hesitate. I swung myself through the trapdoor and jumped down to the landing below, stumbling over the fallen chair. The woman who had fallen through was already halfway down the stairs, her hair wild and her blue cotton dress spattered with dried blood. The two police officers had just reached the foot of the stairs below her, and they were staring up at her in horror.

'Bloody 'ell, you've shot 'er!'

'Stop her! Don't let her get away!'

The woman threw herself down the stairs toward them, screeching. The officers made a fumbled attempt to hold her, but she flailed her arms and wrenched herself free and ran along the hallway to the open front door.

'There's another one!' exclaimed one of the officers, pointing to the trapdoor above my head.

Another woman Screecher was climbing out of the attic. She was wearing a green skirt and a stained yellow cardigan. Unlike the first woman, she didn't drop to the floor. Instead, she crawled upside down along the ceiling, so that her skirt hung down and I could see her laddered stockings and her garter belt. She crawled all the way down the sloping ceiling above the staircase, above our heads – all the way along the hallway ceiling, and out of the front door. We couldn't have reached her to pull her down to the floor, even if we had had the nerve to do it.

As soon as she had gone, the man in the grey suit appeared in the trapdoor. His hair was sticking up wildly and the left side of his skull looked like broken, bloodstained china. I could see the other Screechers crowding close behind him, and I knew that it was time to get the hell out of here.

I jumped down the stairs, three and four at a time. 'Come on, there's too many of them!'

The man in the grey suit was already crawling across the ceiling, and a balding middle-aged man with liver-spotted hands was following him. There must have been more Screechers in the attic than I had realized, because they came pouring out like spiders, swarming down the walls. I didn't stop to count them, and neither did the two police officers. I grabbed my Kit from the receptionist's office and we ran out into the night.

Halfway toward the front gates, one of the officers turned around and drew out his baton. 'Right, then!' he said, defiantly. 'Let's see how they like having their 'eads cracked!'

I seized hold of his arm and pulled him away so violently

165

that he almost fell over. 'You're out of your frigging mind! They'll kill us! Let's go!'

'Come on – they're only a bunch of women and old geezers!'

'Listen to me – do you want to have your goddamned heart cut out? Because that's what they'll do to you!

The officers hesitated. 'Let's *go*, guys!' I shouted at them – and, confused, they followed me. We all scrambled into their unmarked Wolseley and slammed the doors. The officer in the driving seat immediately reached for the radio, but I said, 'Let's get out of here first, OK?'

The Screechers were already running out of the front door and across the shingled driveway. The officer suddenly realized that they were intent on coming after us and doing us serious harm, even if they were women and middle-aged men. Three or four of them reached the car and started to beat their fists on the windows and pull at the door handles, and it was then that the officer started up the engine and jammed his foot on the gas pedal. We roared off the grass verge and bounced on to the roadway, with the Screechers still banging on the roof and trying to mount up on to the running board.

A mile up the road, the officer slowed down, although he kept looking nervously in his rear-view mirror.

'What the hell were *they*?' said his fellow officer, turning around in the passenger seat.

'What the hell were what?'

'Those people. Normal people can't crawl across the ceiling. Jesus Christ.'

I was dabbing at my forehead with my handkerchief. The cut extended all the way from my hairline to the side of my left eye, but fortunately it wasn't very deep.

'We never saw any people, crawling on the ceiling or otherwise.'

'But—'

'Official Secrets Act, OK? Now, can you patch me through to George Goodhew at MI6? He needs to know what hasn't happened.'

Blasphemy

The two police officers drove me to Croydon Police Station, a monumental red-brick Victorian building in the centre of town. Just as we climbed out of the car the Town Hall clock struck twelve midnight, but the air was still humid and warm, and moths still swarmed around the blue police-station lamps. We walked along corridors with shiny brown tiles and highly polished linoleum floors and the whole building echoed like a public swimming bath.

I found Inspector Ruddock in the main operations centre. The room had high vaulted ceilings but it was badly lit and hazy with cigarette smoke. Fifteen or sixteen young officers were sitting at rows of desks, wearing headsets with trumpet-shaped Bakelite speakers.

Inspector Ruddock was standing in front of a large map of South London, drinking very strong tea from a Coronation mug. This time he didn't even say how irritated he was to see me. He simply grunted and lifted his mug toward the map.

'We've had one sighting outside the Swan and Sugar Loaf public house and another at West Croydon station. Not confirmed, mind you, but it looks as if your Duca might be trying to make his way to Central London.

'He was seen in the back seat of a brown Ford Consul, with another man driving. The other man could be Mr Terence Mitchell, although we can't confirm that either.'

'How soon can I get a dog?' I asked him.

'A dog's not much good for following a car.'

'I need a dog, Inspector. If I have a dog, I can track down all of the people that Duca has infected, and if I can find them, I can find Duca. They know where it is.'

George Goodhew arrived, looking tired and hot and harassed. He was a short, podgy young man, with a wave of thinning blond hair, and he always wore his suspenders too tight, so that his pants flapped around his ankles. He was only thirty-three, but he had been appointed Deputy Director of MI6 because he had graduated from Birmingham University. The government were trying to look egalitarian, while at the same time quietly trying to dismantle the Oxbridge elite who had dominated the British security services for so many years.

'Bloody hell,' said George, when I told him what had happened at the Laurels. 'So now we've got *how* many Screechers on the loose?'

'Ten, maybe a dozen. It wasn't easy to count. But this could be the chance we've been waiting for. Now that we've smoked them out of their nest, they'll have to go to ground some-place, and my guess is that most of them will make their way back home, to their original addresses. Which I believe I may have, in Dr Watkins' appointments book.'

George checked his wristwatch. 'Your dog handler shouldn't be long. He comes highly recommended, from RAF Brize Norton. I must say, though, you'll have your work cut out for you.'

The search for Duca and Terence went on throughout the night, until it began to grow light. The *Daily Express* had got wind of the fact that dozens of police were combing the streets of South London, but they were told that a Soviet spy had escaped from custody at Paddington Green, and police suspected that he might be seeking refuge with his former contacts in Norbury.

At a quarter of eight, my dog handler still hadn't arrived, and I was hungry, sweaty and exhausted. I decided to go back to Thornton Heath for a bath and a change of clothes and a couple of hours' sleep. I hadn't yet decided what I was going to tell Terence's mother, but she was used to him not coming home for days on end, and I doubted if she would even ask me where he was.

I was just about to leave when George held up his tele-phone receiver and said, 'Call for you, Captain Falcon. Dr Shulman. The switchboard passed her through from MI6.'

'Thanks,' I said, and took the phone from him.

'Captain Falcon?' said Dr Shulman, making no attempt to

conceal her impatience. 'I've been trying to get in touch with you since yesterday evening.'

'Yes, Doctor, I know. I've been kind of . . . tied up.'

'I carried out the tests that you suggested. I think you may be on to something quite significant.'

'Go on.'

'Out of the total number of known victims since these attacks began, which is now one hundred and twenty-seven, only forty-eight had their hearts removed and any blood drained from their circulatory system. That's less than thirty-eight per cent. A very high proportion of these forty-eight were notice-ably older than the remaining seventy-nine – twenty-five years old and upward.'

'Which led you to conclude what, exactly?'

'It was the blood that told us the story. We took samples from every single victim and analysed them exhaustively. We found considerable variations in the proportions of red and white corpuscles, as well as other indicators such as urea and salts and proteins. However none of these variations seemed to bear any relation to whether a victim had been drained of blood or not.

'There was only one consistently common factor which was shared by the victims who had been killed but not drained of blood. They had all recently been vaccinated against polio.'

'Polio?'

'Well, I expect you know that there's been an epidemic of polio, especially in London and the Midlands. Scores of people have been killed or paralysed. The Health Ministry have been vaccinating schoolchildren in their hundreds.'

'I've been reading about that, yes.'

'They sent six hundred doses to Coventry, and they're desperately trying to get more.'

'That's the Salk vaccine, isn't it?'

'That's right. They inject children with the dead polio virus, but it immunizes them against the live polio virus.'

I felt an extraordinary surge of emotion – almost triumph. It all made sense to me now. The Screechers hadn't been killing such large numbers of people because they were wantonly sadistic – or because they were trying to silence any witnesses, as Inspector Ruddock had believed. They had been desperately trying to find victims whose blood didn't yet contain the new vaccine against poliomyelitis.

They didn't dare to drink the blood of anybody who had been vaccinated, and it was easy to understand why. The Salk vaccine was made of dead polio viruses. Dead polio viruses didn't affect humans. But when a *strigoi vii* was transformed into a *strigoi mort*, all of the dead and dying cells in its body were revived. Not only revived, but enhanced so much that the *strigoi mort* became immortal. So if it had polio viruses in its bloodstream, the viruses would be revived, too. The *strigoi mort* might be immortal, but it would be totally paralysed.

'Dr Shulman,' I said, 'you're an angel. You've made my day.'

'Well, I think you must be some kind of an angel, too, Captain Falcon. We certainly wouldn't have thought of making comparative blood tests if it hadn't been for you.'

I put down the phone. George said, 'Has something happened?'

'Yes, George, I believe it has. I believe we've found the way to wipe out these goddamned Screechers for good and all.'

'You mean it? You really mean it? That's a bloody relief.'

I was just about to leave the operations centre when a young man in a blue RAF uniform appeared, with his cap tucked under his arm.

'I'm looking for Captain Falcon.'

'That's me. You must be the dog handler I asked for.'

'That's right, sir. Warrant Officer Tim Headley, sir. Keston's outside in my van.'

W/O Headley was a serious-looking young man with very thick eyebrows and very blue eyes and very red cheeks. His hair stuck up in a sprig at the back as if he were about six years old, and he had been sleeping on it.

'I'll tell you what we'll do, Warrant Officer Headley. I'll call you Tim and you can call me Jim.'

'Yes, sir. Very good, sir.'

'Listen, Tim, I have to go back to my diggings right now to change my clothes and take a bath, but then we'll be ready for action. I have a list of addresses for Keston to go sniffing around, and I'm pretty confident that we've found a way of dealing with the characters we're likely to find there. How much have you been briefed?'

Tim's cheeks flushed even redder. 'I've got a rough idea of what's going on, sir. I've been told to keep it very hush-hush.'

'Do you know what it is we're going after?'

'I was told some pretty odd types.'

'"Some pretty odd types"?' I hesitated, wondering if I ought to tell him more. But then I said, 'Yes, OK. "Pretty odd types". I guess that just about sums them up.'

Tim drove me to Thornton Heath in his RAF Police van. I felt as if I had gone through fifteen rounds with Rocky Marciano – bruised, exhausted, with a thumping headache. But Dr Shulman's discovery had got my adrenaline going and I couldn't wait to start hunting down Screechers.

Keston turned out to be a large German shepherd with a shaggy coat and a black face. It was hot in the back of the police van, and he panted on the back of my neck all the way to Terence's mother's house.

'Keston's a whiz at finding deserters,' said Tim. 'One chap was hiding in an empty water tower, fifty feet above the ground. Keston sniffed him out, didn't you, boy?'

Keston barked about two inches behind my head.

'You found him, didn't you, boy? None of the other dogs could, but you did!'

Another bark. I turned to Tim and said, 'No more compliments, OK? My head won't take it.'

We parked outside Terence's mother's house. 'Do you mind if I bring Keston in for a bowl of water?' asked Tim.

'You can bring him in for a cup of tea and a sausage sandwich for all I care.'

Tim was opening up the back of the van when I noticed that the front door of Terence's mother's house was open. I looked up and down the street. Although it wasn't yet 9:00 am, the morning was glaringly bright and very hot. There were only two other cars parked anywhere nearby, and a motorcycle with sidecar.

I approached the front door cautiously. Maybe I was overreacting. After all, the temperature was almost in the 70s already, and Mrs Mitchell might have left her door open for a cooling draft. But the house was unusually silent. Mrs Mitchell always kept her wireless on, humming along to *Sound Track Serenade* and *Johnny Duncan's Song Bag*.

'Mrs Mitchell!' I called out. 'Mrs Mitchell!'

There was no answer. Tim was coming through the front gate now, with Keston.

'Everything OK?' he asked me.

'I'm not sure. Probably.'

But as I opened the front door a little wider, Keston started to whine and lower his head, like a dog who has been smacked on the nose for misbehaviour.

'Mrs Mitchell!'

I stepped into the narrow hallway. Tim tried to bring Keston in after me, but he scrabbled his claws on the path and refused to come into the house.

'Keston! Scent, boy! Come on, boy!'

Still Keston refused to come any further. Tim dragged at his leash, but he wouldn't budge.

'He's never acted up like this before, never.'

'Maybe there's something here that he seriously doesn't like the smell of.'

'Keston! Come along, lad! Keston!'

I took out my gun and cocked it. I had no more Last Supper bullets left, but I had reloaded with a clip of regular bullets, rubbed with garlic. Not nearly so effective at stopping a *strigoi vii*, but hopefully still enough to give me a few seconds' advantage.

I went down the hallway and eased open the kitchen door. The green floral curtains were drawn, and the main overhead light was still burning. There was a single saucepan on top of the New World gas cooker, and the table was laid for one, with a place mat and a soup spoon.

Tim came up behind me. 'Keston won't budge. I've had to put him back in the van. I'm really sorry about this.'

'He's been spooked, Tim. And I can't say that I blame him. I'm spooked too.'

We both listened. All I could hear was the droning of those hairy blue blowflies the British call bluebottles. Scores of bluebottles.

I stepped into the kitchen. I could smell vegetable soup,

but I could also smell that distinctive rotten-chicken odour of dried human blood. At the far side of the kitchen there was a door with frosted-glass panels which led through to the scullery and then to the back yard. The frosted-glass panels were spattered with dark brown spots.

Tim said, 'Oh, God.'

'How about going back to your van and calling George Goodhew for me?' I asked him.

'Somebody's been killed here, haven't they?'

'It sure smells like it. But if you don't want to see it – look, I lost my last dog handler because she couldn't take the sight of people with their insides hanging out.'

'Is that what you're expecting to find?' Tim's face was very pale, although his cheeks were still fiery.

'I don't know. Let's take a look, shall we?'

I opened up the scullery door. I had been prepared to see all kinds of horrors, but at first I couldn't really understand what I was looking at. Tim made a retching noise and clamped his hand over his mouth. Then he hurried back through the kitchen and out into the hallway and I could hear him noisily vomiting in the front garden.

On the side wall of the scullery, in a grisly display of blasphemy and butchery, both Mrs Mitchell and Terence had been nailed, completely naked and upside down, their feet together but their hands outspread.

Their heads had been sawn off, and underneath each of their gaping necks an enamel basin had been placed to catch their blood. A zinc bucket stood in the corner, and I could see a bloody tangle of grey hair in it, so I knew what had happened to their heads.

The scullery was thick with bluebottles, most of them crawling in and out of the blood-filled basins. In one of the basins there was a soup ladle. I could only guess that Duca had fed before he left.

I went through to the living room, just as Tim was coming back into the house.

'Sorry about that,' he apologized. 'Thought I had a strong stomach.'

'Don't worry about it. I think Keston had the right idea, staying outside.'

I looked around the living room. It would take a police

forensics team to work out exactly what had happened here, but I could guess. Duca had forced Terence to drive him here to his mother's house – the last place that we would have thought of looking for him. Then it had probably questioned him about our investigation – who I was, how much we knew, what we were going to do to hunt it down. After that, it had murdered both Terence and his mother and had fastened their bodies to the scullery wall in a deliberate mockery of Christ and Christianity.

While I waited for George Goodhew to arrive from MI6, I made a systematic search of the living room. I even got down on my knees and looked underneath the sofa, where I found dozens of dog-eared knitting patterns and three crumpled Mars Bars wrappers.

I opened drawers crammed with cut-out recipes from *Woman's Weekly* and stray buttons and cotton reels. In the right-hand corner of the room stood a semicircular telephone table, with a crochet tablecloth on it, and a framed photograph of Terence's mother on her wedding day. The telephone receiver was off the hook. I picked it up and listened but it was dead. I jiggled the cradle a few times but it stayed dead. In those days, if you left your phone off the hook for long enough, they cut you off.

On the carpet underneath the table I found a crumpled piece of notepaper. Somebody had written on it SOTON QE = 1200, in blunt pencil, in shaky, childlike letters. On one side of the piece of paper there was a dark brown oval which looked very much like blood.

'Tim,' I said. 'What do you make of this?'

Tim peered at it, and then handed it back. 'Soton . . . that's short for Southampton.'

'What about the rest of it?'

'Well . . . QE could mean the *Queen Elizabeth*, I suppose. She docks at Southampton. Twelve . . . I don't know, that could mean a twelve o'clock sailing.'

'You mean Terence could have made a reservation to cross the Atlantic?'

'Yes, I suppose it could.'

I jiggled the cradle a few times and eventually an impatient voice said, 'Operator?'

'Oh, yes. Hi. I was wondering if you could tell me the last number dialled on this phone.'

'Wait a minute, sir. I'll have to check.'

A minute became two minutes and then five. At last the operator came back on the line and said, 'Southampton seven-two-two-seven.'

'Can you tell me whose number that is?'

'It's the new twenty-four-hour reservations office for the Cunard Shipping Line, sir.'

'And what time was that call made?'

'Seven minutes past two this morning, sir.'

Tim looked at his watch. 'I really think Keston is going to need a bit of a walk now, sir. He's had his breakfast, he always has to stretch his legs afterwards, if you know what I mean.'

'Do you think he's going to be OK? I really need a dog right now.'

'To be honest with you, sir, he's looking a bit dicky.'

'This thing I'm after – I think it's trying to leave the country.'

'Sorry, sir. *Thing*?'

'The thing that killed those two people in there.'

Tim looked perplexed. 'Whatever it is, sir, I don't think that Keston will go after it. I've never seen him like this before. Well, only once. Out in Suez, somebody put him off the scent with lion manure.'

I rang the Cunard Line reservations number. After another lengthy wait, I was answered by a chippy young girl. 'Somebody made a reservation on a Cunard ship at about ten after two this morning,' I told her. 'This is an urgent security matter. I need to know who it was, and what ship they're booked on.'

She wouldn't tell me, of course, so in the end I had to talk to her supervisor, and her supervisor had to call MI6 to verify my credentials. This wasted another fifteen minutes, and meanwhile Duca was putting ever-increasing miles between it and me.

At last, the supervisor came back to tell me that Mr Terence Mitchell had telephoned to book a cabin on the *Queen Elizabeth* bound for New York via Cherbourg, sailing at noon today.

In Pursuit

George Goodhew arrived just as I was leaving the house. His grey Rover was closely followed by three other cars and a plain navy-blue van. A dozen young men in suits climbed out of the cars, and two Home Office pathologists climbed out of the van.

'I think that Duca's trying to get out of the country,' I said. 'It forced Terence to make a booking for it on the *Queen Elizabeth*.'

'Yes, but hold on. Duca hasn't got a passport, has he – or *it*, I mean. They won't let it on board without a passport.'

'It won't need a passport, George. It can move so fast they won't even see it. It can slide through a gap that's half an inch wide.'

'All the same, I can alert the police and customs at Southampton. And we can hold the sailing if necessary.'

'Well, OK. But tell the police, don't try to detain it. It can rip them apart as soon as look at them, and we don't want any more casualties. I have to get down there, with my Kit.'

'I'll drive you.'

'That's great, thanks.'

Tim came up, with Keston trotting behind him on his leash. 'How is he?' I asked him. 'That *Queen Elizabeth*'s a hell of a big boat. I could really use a good dog.'

'I'm sorry, sir. I don't think he's going to be up to it.'

I looked down at Keston and I had to admit to myself that I had never seen a dog look so cowed. His head was lowered and he couldn't stop trembling, as if he was suffering from hypothermia. 'All right, Tim,' I told him. 'I'll just have to find another man-trailer, that's all.'

I picked up my Kit and put it on the back seat of George's Rover. We left Terence's mother's house just as the Home Office pathologists were walking in with their brown overalls and their cameras and their forensic equipment, and headed south through Croydon town centre. George managed to change gear and smoke and talk on his radio-telephone all at the same time, blasting his horn impatiently at anybody who slowed him down.

'Cunard won't postpone the sailing,' he said, as we came closer to Purley. 'Charles Frith doesn't want to postpone it, either. It'll attract too much publicity. The Foreign Secretary's on board, as well as Loretta Young, and some Russian bigwigs, too.'

'In that case, we'll have to make sure we get to Southampton before she sails.'

I directed him to the Foxleys' house. He parked in the driveway with the engine running while I went to the front door and rang the doorbell.

Mya Foxley answered, almost at once. Her hair was fraying and she looked as if she hadn't slept.

'Mrs Foxley, I know Jill isn't feeling too good, but I really have to talk to her.'

'I'm sorry, she isn't here.'

'She's not here? She hasn't had to go to hospital?'

'No, no. A man came round to call for her, about two hours ago. She said that he was something to do with the police, and she would have to go with him. She even packed an overnight bag.'

At that moment, Bullet appeared, his crimson tongue hanging out in the heat. He looked up at me and wuffed.

'Jill was on police business and she didn't take Bullet? That doesn't make any sense.'

'I don't know. She asked me to take care of him, that's all.'

'This man who called for her . . . what did he look like?'

Mya Foxley frowned. 'He was very tall, with his hair brushed back.'

'Did you notice the colour of his eyes?'

She shook her head.

'Would you say that he was good-looking? Handsome?'

'Oh, yes. He would stand out in a crowd. And very well dressed, too. A dark suit, and a dark silk tie.'

'Mrs Foxley – Mya – this man had nothing to do with the police. If he's the man I think he is, he's taken Jill against her will. He's abducted her.'

'But I don't understand. She seemed quite happy to go with him. He didn't say anything to threaten her.'

'That's what makes him so dangerous. Listen – do you think that Bullet might come with me, and help me find her?'

Mrs Foxley looked down at Bullet dubiously. 'I don't know – you've seen for yourself that he is a dog who obeys only his owner. That was the way he had to be trained.'

I bent over and held my hand out. Bullet sniffed at my fingertips, and growled in the back of his throat.

'Bullet,' I said, 'we have to go find Jill. Do you understand that, boy? We have to go find Jill.'

Bullet barked, and his tail slapped wildly from side to side.

'Mrs Foxley, would you bring me Bullet's leash, please? I think he realizes what I want him to do.'

Mya Foxley went inside, and while she did so I tugged Bullet's ears and rubbed his throat and he didn't seem to mind at all. At least he didn't try to take another chunk of flesh out of my thumb.

'Let's go find Jill, boy, yes? Let's go find that mistress of yours!'

Bullet grew more and more excited, and when I clipped his leash on his collar, he immediately ran out across the driveway, dragging me after him. He was a hell of a lot stronger than I had anticipated, and he seemed to be even more determined to find Jill than I was.

'I'll call you!' I shouted back to Mya Foxley.

As we turned on to the main London to Brighton road, I had a sudden thought.

'George – can you take me to Dr Watkins' house?'

'We're going to be pretty pushed for time, old man.'

'How long will it take us to reach Southampton?'

'It's about sixty-five miles. If I really step on it, we should make it in an hour.'

'OK . . . but I really need to go the Laurels first.'

I directed him to Pampisford Road, and he slewed to a halt on the grass verge outside the Laurels. The two bobbies on duty recognized me, and they saluted and said 'Morning, sir!' and let me through without any trouble. Inside the house, I went directly to Dr Watkins' surgery and opened up his fridge.

Inside, there were dozens of bottles of various vaccines – smallpox, diphtheria, yellow fever. On the middle shelf, on the right-hand side, there were a dozen bottles of Salk anti-poliomyelitis vaccine, with their distinctive red caps. I grabbed a handful and put them in my coat pocket. Then I went to the stainless-steel trolley beside the examination couch and took two 5cc syringes.

Bullet barked excitedly as I returned to the car, and we pulled away from the Laurels with the Rover's rear end sliding side-ways in the grass.

I checked my watch. It was ten minutes of eleven already.

'Don't worry,' said George. 'If I keep my foot flat on the floor, we should get there in time.'

'OK, then,' I told him. 'Try not to kill us, that's all I ask.'

The sky began to grow increasingly thundery as we sped south-westward through Surrey and Hampshire. The clouds rolled in so quickly they looked like a speeded-up film, and by the time we reached the town of Havant, huge warm drops of rain had begun to patter on to the windshield of George's Rover.

I had never been frightened by anybody's driving before, not even during World War Two, when I was driven in a Jeep between Brussels and Nijmegen by a stogie-chewing marine sergeant who had drunk a bottle and a half of Napoleon brandy. But George drove so furiously that I found myself gripping the door handle to keep myself from sliding from one side of my seat to the other, and constantly jamming my foot on an imaginary brake pedal.

He hardly ever dropped below 50 mph. He drove the wrong way along dual carriageways. He even drove right over the middle of a traffic circle, leaving parallel tyre-tracks in the grass. He ran countless red lights and blasted his horn at anybody who looked as if they might slow him down. All this time he smoked one cigarette after another, lighting a fresh one from the burned-down butt of the last.

'Do you know who I admire the most?' he asked me, as we slewed around the corner into Havant High Street. 'Fangio. What a driver. The last lap of the German Grand Prix, he averaged ninety-one-point-seven miles an hour. *Averaged.*'

We reached the outskirts of Southampton at three minutes of twelve. It was raining hard and the Rover's windshield wipers were having difficulty in coping, so that George had to drive more slowly. But as we approached the docks, I could see the *Queen Elizabeth*'s two red funnels over the rooftops, and as we turned the corner to the Cunard Terminal, and the sheer black wall of the liner's sides came into view, it was clear that she wasn't yet ready to sail.

George parked by the railings at the terminal entrance. A policeman in a raincape came up and knocked on the window.

'Can't leave it here, mate.'

George produced his identity card. 'I think you'll find that I can,' he said, with public-school self-assurance. 'Look after it for me, will you, constable?'

'Yes, sir,' said the policeman, grudgingly. 'You'll be wanting Chief Inspector Holloway, sir. He's inside the terminal, at the information desk.'

We climbed out of the car. I turned my coat-collar up against the rain, which was hammering down all across the docks. 'Come on, Bullet,' I urged him. 'Let's find Jill, shall we? Come on, boy.'

We crossed the wet, reflective asphalt. Close up, the *Queen Elizabeth* was enormous, over a thousand feet long and nearly two hundred feet high, its sides streaked with runnels of rain. Passengers were looking down on us from the upper decks and waving, even though the ship's gangways were still down, and the dock was still cluttered with vans and trucks and luggage. The air smelled strongly of brine and diesel.

We went through the swing doors into the reception area, which was still noisy and crowded with passengers and relatives. We found Chief Inspector Holloway next to one of the stainless-steel counters, surrounded by detective constables and at least fifteen uniformed officers. Chief Inspector Holloway was very tall and lugubrious-looking, with a thin sallow face and a nose like a fire axe. His brown trilby hat was soaked with rain and the lapels of his flappy brown double-breasted suit were curled up.

'I don't know why Hampshire Constabulary can't be trusted to deal with this,' he said to George, even before George had introduced himself.

'It's what you might call a specialist operation,' I put in.

'You're *American*,' said Chief Inspector Holloway.

'That's correct, sir. Captain James Falcon, seconded to MI6.'

'This is all *very* irregular.'

'Yes, sir. You're right. It is irregular. Have you checked the passenger manifest?'

One of the detectives held out a clipboard. 'Mr Terence Mitchell made a telephone reservation early this morning and booked a middle-class cabin, M64. He hasn't checked in yet. Cunard have promised to let us know as soon as he does.'

I said, 'OK, officer, thanks.' Then I turned to George. 'I need to get on board now. Duca's here already, I can feel it.'

'But he hasn't checked in yet.'

'It won't. It doesn't have to. It can get on board without anybody seeing it. Christ – it could climb straight up the side of the ship if it needed to. All it needs is a cabin for itself and Jill while it crosses the Atlantic.'

I looked down at Bullet. I think Bullet had picked up the scent, too. He was quivering, and staring toward the doorway which led out to the pier.

'Come on, boy,' I told him. 'There's one little thing we have to do before we go on board.'

I asked one of the uniformed girls behind the Cunard counter if there was a spare office I could use. Then I led Bullet into the back, and opened up my Kit. I took out two pots of white and black paint, and a paintbrush.

'What on earth are you doing?' asked George.

'Hold Bullet's head still, would you? I'm giving him an extra pair of eyes.'

Duca At Bay

Bullet and I walked up the gangway with the rain drumming on the canvas awning above our heads. Two detectives came with us, so that we wouldn't have any trouble getting on board. A smooth-faced Cunard purser greeted us at the top of the gangway and he looked down at Bullet with amusement.

'I've seen plenty of four-eyed people, but this is the first time I've ever seen a four-eyed dog.'

'Please,' I said. 'He gets embarrassed very easily.'

'Yes, sir. Sorry, sir.' I guess the purser was experienced in dealing with eccentric passengers.

Once we were on board, I told the detectives to wait where they were.

'Can't really do that, sir. We're supposed to stick close, just in case you need us.'

'You're that eager to die?'

One detective looked at the other detective. 'If you put it that way, sir, we can wait here, yes. But call if you need us.'

The *Queen Elizabeth* was supposed to have sailed over twenty minutes ago, and her turbine engines were making the whole ship vibrate, but the decks and promenades were still crowded and chaotic. Passengers were saying tearful good-byes, pageboys in pillbox hats were hurrying about with messages and bunches of flowers, porters were carrying suit-cases on board. As Bullet and I made our way down to M Deck, we shared the elevator with a strongly perfumed woman in a green Dior dress and a veiled hat, who was openly sobbing as if her world were coming to an end.

We hurried along the corridor to M64. Bullet's claws pattered on the highly polished Korkoid flooring. 'Come on, boy,' I encouraged him. 'Find Jill for me, OK?'

A Cunard official had given me a pass key, but as it turned out I didn't need it. The door to cabin M64 was unlocked. I put down my Kit, turned the handle, and cautiously eased it open.

There was nobody around. The bed was neatly made, the blinds were drawn down over the portholes. The only indi-cation that anybody had been here was the pale blue overnight case in the corner, and the rucked-up throw on the floor.

I led Bullet into the cabin and let him sniff around. He trotted over to the overnight case, licked it and then turned to me and gave a high-pitched whine.

'Good boy, Bullet! Go find Jill!'

Bullet nudged the cabin door open with his nose and began to patter his way along the passageway. The scent that he had picked up must have been very strong because I could hardly keep up with him. Several passengers looked at his extra pair of painted-on eyes and laughed. They wouldn't have found it so amusing if they had known why I had done it.

Bullet made his way to one of the elevators aft and sat down outside the closed doors, keening. Duca and Jill could have gone upward or downward to any number of decks. But I took a guess that they had gone up to the promenade deck or the sun deck, like most of the other passengers, and I took out my *strigoi* compass to confirm it.

The elevator took over five minutes to come down, and when it did it was jam-packed with passengers and their luggage and they took another two or three minutes to jostle their way out of it, with lots of 'sorries' and 'do excuse mes'.

We rose slowly upward. The pageboy who shared the elevator with us kept making kissing noises at Bullet, which Bullet disdainfully ignored. I kept my compass open, and as we came to the promenade deck the needle sharply swivelled and pointed forward.

The elevator doors opened and Bullet immediately trotted out and started sniffing around the deck. It was still raining, but not as heavily now, and over the Solent the sky was gradually beginning to clear. The ship's horn blew, deep and deafening, and Bullet looked up at me in alarm.

'It's OK, boy. Just find Jill for me.'

Bullet picked up the scent almost at once. I followed him along the wet planking of the promenade deck and twenty yards in front of me, leaning against the railings with their backs to me, I saw Duca, wearing a grey fedora and a dark grey suit, and Jill, in a light fawn summer coat. They were standing so close to each other that anybody would have thought they were husband and wife, or lovers.

Bullet started to run even faster, but I yanked on his leash and forced him to slow down. 'Careful, Bullet. Careful, boy.' He gave a strangled whine but I think he must have understood that something wasn't right, because he didn't bark or strain at his leash, and he obediently came to heel.

183

'Here, boy. Hold up a minute.' I went into the doorway of the cocktail lounge and put down my Kit. 'Sit, boy. Stay.' I took out one of the hypodermics that I had found in Dr Watkins' consulting room. My hands were shaking, but I filled it with anti-poliomyelitis vaccine and squirted a few drops out to make sure that the needle was clear.

'Come on, boy. This is it. Showdown time.'

I approached Duca and Jill until Bullet and I were standing less than ten feet away from them. Neither of them turned around but Duca must have sensed that I was there, because it took a step sideways, away from Jill, and let go of her hand.

Over Southampton Water, the sun suddenly broke through, and shafts of light shone down from the clouds as if they were the windows of a great grey cathedral.

'So, Captain,' said Duca, still with his back to me. 'You have found me.'

Bullet barked, and Jill turned round at once. Her face was so bloodless that I hardly recognized her. She stared at me in shock, and then she said, 'Bullet! Bullet – what are you doing here? What's that on your face?'

Instead of running toward her and jumping up, Bullet sat down, and gave another whine. 'Bullet,' she said. 'Bullet, what's wrong with you, boy?'

She stepped toward us but Duca reached out and held her wrist. Then it turned around and faced us.

'Let me tell you something, Captain—' Duca began, but then it saw Bullet and Bullet's extra pair of eyes. Its reaction was astonishing. It raised one hand to shield its face, and it jolted convulsively backward until it was up against the ship's railings. Then it seemed to slide away sideways, still holding up its hand.

'You *dare*?' it rasped at me. 'You dare to bring a devil-dog with you?'

Jill looked bewildered. 'Bullet!' she said. 'Bullet! Here, boy!'

But Bullet stood up now, with his fur bristling, and he started to stalk toward Duca with his teeth bared, growling. I came right behind him, holding my hypodermic in the palm of my right hand. Several people stopped and stared at us, but nobody could have understood what Duca was, and what was really happening here.

'Stay back!' Duca warned me. 'Take that dog away from me, Captain Falcon, or I will make sure that you die the most agonizing of all possible deaths!'

'Sorry, Duca. This is where you find out what it's like to be mortal.'

'Jill!' snapped Duca. 'Take this devil-dog away!'

'Jill!' I said, without looking at her. 'Just stay back!'

'Bullet!' Jill called him. 'Here, boy! Bullet!'

Bullet was confused now. He knew that I wanted him to keep Duca at bay, but at the same time he had grown up with Jill, and she had trained him since puppyhood to obey her implicitly.

'Bullet!' I ordered him. 'Stay!'

But Jill crouched down and held out her hands toward him and Bullet didn't really have any choice. He trotted toward her, and even though he still seemed to be unsure about her, he allowed her to take hold of his collar.

'Take it away!' Duca ordered her. 'Take that cursed animal out of my sight!'

'Jill!' I appealed, but Jill led Bullet away, and the two of them disappeared around the curved windows of the cocktail lounge.

'Well, Captain,' said Duca, lowering its hand. It looked more relaxed now, but I thought that its face was greyer and more strained than the last time I had seen it. Its sea-green eyes seemed to have faded, and its lips were redder, almost as if they were bleeding. It was beginning to look more and more like a creature whose time was coming to an end, a creature that had survived for too many centuries, and committed too many acts of murder and cruelty.

'This is the finish, Duca,' I told it. 'You're not going to get away this time.'

'Oh, that's where you're very wrong, Captain. Nobody will ever find me on this vessel, even if they search it from stem to stern. And I have a new love in my life, to give me succour and support.'

'Jill won't stay with you.'

It smiled and raised its eyebrows. 'You really don't think so? She reminds me so much of my Anca. She could almost be Anca reincarnated. I will certainly love her just as much, and give her just as much devotion, for ever.'

185

'What have you done to her?'

'What do you think? I have won her heart.'

'Won her heart? You're kidding me. Jill knows exactly what kind of creature you are.'

'Oh, yes. But I have won her heart all the same, and now I am going to win your heart, too, but in a very different way. I am going to cut it out of your body and drink your life's blood fresh and warm, and watch the light in your eyes go out while I do so.'

'Oh, I see. You're going to kill me right here, in front of all of these people?'

'Of course not. You and I, we're going to go below, to the privacy of my cabin, and you can feed me there.'

'And what makes you think that I'm going to come with you?'

'I am ten times stronger than you, Captain, and a hundred times quicker. And what will you do when I take hold of your arm and force you to walk through these crowds with me? Will you shout out for help? I don't think so. You know what I will do to any of these innocent people if they try to intervene.'

Duca lifted its hat and smoothed back his hair with its hand. Then it took a step toward me, holding out its right hand.

'What do you think, Captain? Shall we walk together? There's no way that you can stop me, not even with your box of tricks. You think a Bible can stop me? You think a silver mirror can stop me? You think whips and nails and poppy seeds can stop me?'

I stayed where I was, even though several passengers had to push their way past me.

Duca came right up to me. There was no denying how handsome it was, what good bone-structure it had. But, close up, there was an unhealthy transparency to its skin, which reminded me that for all of its good looks, it was dead.

'Why don't you put down your box?' it smiled.

There was a moment when I considered running, and opening up my Kit, and taking out my silver mirror and my silver whip and trying to destroy Duca with all the religious and superstitious paraphernalia that I had used for so long. But Duca was infinitely faster than me, and somehow I knew

186

that the time for all of those ancient and medieval artefacts was past. This was the modern age, and both Duca and I had to get used to the idea.

I set down my Kit, and pushed it with my foot underneath one of the varnished benches that ran around beneath the fascia of the cocktail lounge.

'There you are,' I told it. 'Satisfied?'

Duca took hold of my left elbow. Its grip was painfully strong, and its thumb dug deep into my nerve, so that my forearm felt numb.

'I assume you know which cabin I reserved?' said Duca.

'Yes,' I told it.

'In which case—' it said, and started to steer me along the deck. The *Queen Elizabeth*'s siren blew again, and then again, which was the signal for those who weren't sailing to go ashore. Duca was saying something else – something which caused it to smile, but I couldn't hear what it was.

Blood Feud

We reached the elevator and waited. Duca's grip on my elbow was unrelenting.

'You really think you're going to get away?' I asked it.

'You know I am.'

'So where are you going?'

'I have an appointment to keep in America.'

'An *appointment*? Who the hell with?'

This seemed to amuse Duca even more. 'Before you and I finish our business together, Captain, I will tell you. I want to see the expression on your face.'

'Oh, yes?'

The elevator doors opened. Duca had to step back to allow half a dozen people to get out, and as it did so I half-twisted myself around and stabbed it in the forearm with my hypodermic. Duca flinched, but dead Screechers are not as sensitive as we are. Before it could turn its head and realize what I was doing, I had jammed down the plunger with my thumb and injected it with the full 5cc of polio vaccine.

Duca slammed me against the side of the elevator door. Two women were trying to get into the elevator and one of them shrilled in alarm.

'What have you done to me?' Duca shouted at me. It seized my wrist and forced the hypodermic out of my grasp. 'What is this? What have you done to me?'

'You're just about to find out, friend,' I told it.

Duca dropped the hypodermic on the deck and stamped on it. Then it struggled out of its coat, yanked out its cuff links and pulled up its shirtsleeve. The needle-prick was clearly visible, and the skin around it was already looking inflamed.

'What have you done to me?' Duca raged. It lowered its head and tried to suck the needle-prick, but it was out of its reach, and it let out an incoherent roar of utter frustration. I backed away, intending to retrieve my Kit, but Duca came after me, as fast as a camera shutter. It seized my arm and threw me across the deck, so that I collided with the rail. Then it came after me again, as if it was going to rip me apart.

It twisted my coat in both hands and shouted directly into my face, so that I could feel its freezing breath. 'Tell me what you have done to me!' it screamed. 'Tell me what poison you have given me!'

'Like I said, Duca,' I panted. I felt as if my shoulder was dislocated. 'You'll soon find out for yourself.' At least I hoped it would. Supposing I were wrong, and anti-polio vaccine had no effect on dead Screechers at all? Or supposing – even if it *did* work – that it took hours before the dead viruses came back to life, or even days?

There was a crowd around us now, but Duca was too enraged to take any notice of them. A white-jacketed steward came up to us and said, 'Now, then! Pack it in, you two, or I'll call the police and have you thrown off the ship!'

Duca jerked its head up and snarled at him like a wild beast. Its face was so distorted with fury that the steward raised both hands and said, 'OK, mate. OK. Just take it easy, all right?'

188

The rest of the crowd shuffled back, too, some of them stepping on each other's feet.

Duca gripped my coat even tighter and its fists trembled with effort. 'I am going to drag out your intestines for this, Captain. I am going to hoist you on a pole and watch the crows eat your eyes out!'

It was half-choking me, and I could barely speak. But I managed to say, 'Wrong country, Duca. You're not in Romania any more. Worse than that – wrong century.'

Duca began to shudder, and its breathing started to become more laboured. It looked into my eyes and I could tell now that I had compromised its immortality.

'I have an appointment in America,' it said. 'I swore that I would get my revenge, and I shall.'

'Come on, gents,' said the steward, warily. 'Get up off the floor and let's be having you. This is the *Queen Elizabeth*, not the bloody Isle of Wight ferry.'

Duca grasped my throat and pressed its thumbs into my Adam's apple. I took hold of its wrists and tried to pull its hands away, but it was still far too strong for me.

'I have an appointment,' it repeated, and now its voice was softer and hoarser. 'I have an appointment . . . in America.'

I tried to cough, but I couldn't. I could see tiny prickles of light swimming in front of my eyes. I thought with a strange feeling of serenity that I was going to die here, with all of these well-dressed people watching me, and none of them lifting a finger to help me.

But Duca's hands began to tremble more and more violently, and little by little its grip began to weaken. I managed to take a breath, and then another.

'Come on, mate,' said the steward, and laid his hand on Duca's shoulder.

Only a few minutes before, Duca would probably have twisted the steward's arm off, but now it reached out and held on to him for support. Slowly, painfully, it managed to climb on to its feet, and to lurch across to the handrail. It stood there for a while, its chest rising and falling as if it had been running a marathon, its face ashy, its blood-red mouth gaping open.

Two men helped me to stand up, too. 'What's the matter with your sparring partner?' said one of them. 'Is he ill or something?'

'I'll call the ship's doctor,' said the steward.

'There are two police detectives down by the main gangway,' I told him. 'I'd like you to call them, too. And please—' I coughed ' – can we clear all of these people away?

I took out my identity card and held it up. 'Please – MI6. This man is a dangerous suspect.'

The steward said, 'Blimey.' Then, 'Come on, ladies and gentlemen, if you'd be so kind. Can we give this gentleman a bit of breathing space?'

As the crowds of passengers reluctantly began to disperse, I approached Duca and stood facing it – although I made sure that I didn't get too close. Duca stared back at me with utter hatred, one hand pressed against its chest, but it didn't have enough breath to be able to speak.

'What did I tell you?' I said. 'This is where you find out what it's like to be mortal.'

Duca took one step forward, and then another, and slowly shuffled its way toward the cocktail lounge. I followed it, but I still kept my distance. It may have been affected by creeping paralysis, but I didn't trust it one inch. It turned to me and said, 'You are going to die for this, Captain.' Then it opened the door to the cocktail lounge and disappeared inside.

I hurried along the promenade deck and dragged my Kit out from under the bench. Then I shouldered my way into the cocktail lounge, urgently looking left and right to see where Duca had gone.

The lounge wasn't open yet, and it was deserted, although a syrupy orchestral version of 'Diana' was playing over the loudspeaker system. It was decorated in the highly contemporary 1950s style of all of the *Queen Elizabeth*'s public spaces, with sycamore-panelled walls dyed to the colour of lobster shells, inlaid with marquetry pictures of scenes from the circus. Behind the bar stood scores of shining bottles – crème de menthe and Pernod and grenadine, and rows of chromium cocktail-shakers.

I couldn't see Duca at first, but then I saw a spasmodic movement halfway up the panel that depicted a trapeze artist. Duca was slowly and painfully climbing up the wall, clinging to the panelling like a dying man crawling across a desert. When I came in, it managed to turn its head around, but it didn't speak. Instead it continued its climb, gasping for breath with every few inches that it managed to ascend.

I set down my Kit on one of the polished wood tables and opened it. I took out my Bible, my holy oil, my hammer and my nails. I felt like a priest, taking out everything he needed for an exorcism. This was the day when the devil got what the devil deserved.

'Duca! Dorin Duca! Are you going to come down from there, or do I have to pull you down?'

Duca had nearly reached the top of the wall now. The polio virus was already stiffening its arms and its legs, because it clawed feebly at the ceiling two or three times before it managed to get a grip, and I thought for a moment that it was going to fall. Eventually, however, it started to creep upside down toward the central light fitting.

I couldn't understand where Duca thought it was going, or how it was going to escape me. Maybe it was giving me a final demonstration of its supernatural abilities, its superiority, its differentness. I opened my Bible at Revelation and stood directly underneath Duca.

'You feel this, Duca? You feel the power of the Word?'

There was a long silence, punctuated only by Duca's agonized breathing.

'I will kill you, Captain. You and all your kin.'

'I don't think so, Duca. There are too many people who want their revenge on *you*.'

I laid down the Bible and unstoppered the bottle of holy oil. Taking a couple of steps backward, I flicked my wrist in a crisscross pattern so that the oil sprayed all over Duca's back, and over its hair. Duca's evil was so intense that the oil actually *smoked* on contact with it, and it let out a howl of pain.

I sprayed it again and again, and the smoke poured out thicker and faster. It reached around with one hand, trying to tear the oil-soaked shirt from its back, and as it did so it spontaneously burst into flames.

These weren't the flames that I would have expected from olive oil, no matter who had blessed it. These flames were fierce and bluish-white, like burning naphtha. Duca clung on to the ceiling, screaming hoarsely with its half-paralysed lungs,

191

while all around it the light grey paint was blackened with twists and whorls of sooty smoke.

Suddenly, Duca dropped to the floor. It rolled over and over, still blazing, and I had to step smartly sideways to avoid it. It rolled up against the cocktail bar and lay there, not moving, while the flames subsided and flickered out. I picked up my hammer and my nails and approached it.

Its face was charred and raw and most of its hair was burned off. Its shirt had been reduced to a few blackened shreds. But when it opened its eyes and looked up at me I wasn't surprised: a *strigoi mort* couldn't be killed by fire, or by bullets, no matter what the bullets had been cast out of; and it couldn't be killed by polio, either, even if it remained paralysed for all eternity.

Duca whispered, 'I will kill you for this, I promise. You and all of your kin.' Smoke actually leaked out of its mouth.

I knelt down beside it. I detested it, and all of the death and bereavement it had caused, and I only wished that its suffering could have lasted longer. I thought of Ann De Wouters' children, and all of the other children who had been orphaned by Duca and its disciples. Most of all I thought of my mother.

I lifted one of the nails and held it over Duca's right eye. It didn't even blink. Then I raised my hammer.

At that moment, the doors to the cocktail lounge swung open and the two detectives came running in, closely followed by George.

'Bloody hell!' said one of the detectives. 'What's all this bloody smoke? What the bloody hell's happened to him?'

'Keep away!' I warned him. But in that split second of distraction, Duca snatched my wrist, and wouldn't let go. The skin on its fingers was crusted and split, like pork crackling, but its grip was bony and incredibly strong.

With a deep grunt, it seized the shaft of my hammer, and twisted it around so viciously that I dropped it. It bounced across the Korkoid floor, well out of my reach.

'Jim – *Jim*!' asked George, in a panic. 'What do you want us to do?' One of the detectives pulled out a large Webley revolver and waved it at us, but Duca and I were so close together that he was obviously too scared to shoot. Not that a bullet would have done any good, even if it had hit Duca right between the eyes.

'Oil!' I told George. 'There, on the table!'

'What?'

'There's a bottle of oil on the table! Pour it over it!'

Now that it had relieved me of my hammer, Duca was concentrating on the crucifixion nail that I was holding in my left hand, trying to screw it around so that it was pointing at my heart. Duca's breathing was harsh, and it kept coughing up a thick, bloody mucus. Its eyes were bloodshot and unfocused, but it was absolutely determined to kill me. I could hear the cartilage in my wrist crackle as it gradually bent my hand around the wrong way, and I couldn't stop myself from saying, '*Gah!* Shit! *Agh!*'

'You want to talk – about mortality?' it wheezed. It had managed to lodge the point of the nail underneath my ribcage, and was pressing hard. 'You want to talk about – death?'

I felt the point of the nail break my skin. The pain was so intense that I went cold all over. Even my blood felt cold, as it soaked down the front of my shirt.

'You want to talk about revenge?' said Duca. 'This is my revenge!'

It hooked its left arm around my back, trying to pull me downward, so that the nail would penetrate my ribcage, and force its way upward at an angle of forty-five degrees, into my heart. It was making thick, animal-like grunts, almost as if it were trying to violate me.

I didn't see George. But I suddenly felt something slippery slide down the side of my face and pour directly onto Duca's forehead, and into its eyes. The holy oil couldn't harm me at all, but it had a devastating effect on Duca. Its face began to crackle, and what was left of its skin began to crumple up like cellophane thrown into an open fire.

'*No!*' screamed Duca. Smoke poured out of its face, and its eyes literally fried in front of me, so that they turned opaque.

The young detective with the Webley revolver came up close now, and pointed the muzzle at Duca's right temple.

'Don't!' I warned him. 'You won't be able to kill it! Bring me that hammer!'

But Duca let out a terrible screech, and the detective jerked backward and pulled the trigger. There was a deafening bang and a bony chunk of Duca's right eye socket was blown away, but at the same time the shot ignited the holy oil.

Duca exploded into flames, still relentlessly gripping my wrist. I felt a scorching blast of heat on my face, and I heard my hair crackle. My silk necktie caught fire and flared up around my neck.

'Get it off me!' I screamed out, but Duca was blazing so fiercely that George and the two detectives couldn't get close.

There was only one thing I could do. I heaved myself upward, so that I was kneeling, and then I gave another heave, so that I was on my feet. The pain was horrifying. I felt as if my face was being blasted with a blowtorch. All of my clothes were alight now and I was sure that I was going to die.

Duca was a dead weight, and a burning dead weight, but somehow I managed to drag it across the cocktail lounge to the doors.

'Open the doors!' I shouted at George. 'Open the goddamned doors!'

George and one of the detectives ran ahead of me and opened them. I pulled Duca out of the cocktail lounge and on to the deck.

Even today, I find it hard to believe that I managed to manhandle Duca across the deck, and over to the rail. I can't actually remember doing it. I do remember falling, though, and hitting the water over a hundred feet below. It was like hitting a cold concrete sidewalk.

Both of us went under, but at least Duca released its grip. I went down and down, and I thought that I would never come up again. But I managed to kick my legs and paddle with my hands, and at last I began to rise to the surface. When I finally broke out into the daylight, I found that there were crowds of people staring down at me, and it was raining red-and-white lifebelts.

Two young sailors stripped off their sweaters and dived into the water to help me. I circled around and around, looking desperately for any sign of Duca.

'There was another man!' I panted, as the sailors swam up to me.

One of them dived under the water and disappeared for what seemed like five minutes. When he reappeared, he shook his head and shouted out, 'Can't see anyone, mate! Think we've lost him!'

The sailors swam with me to the dockside. Between them they half-carried me up a ladder, and when I reached the top there were willing hands everywhere, all of them outstretched to help me. I was wrapped warmly in a blanket and a wheel-chair was brought from the office so that I could sit down. I was shaking uncontrollably with shock.

'How are you feeling, mate?' said an elderly man in a cloth cap, leaning over me with a worried frown. He reached into his pocket and took out a pack of Woodbine cigarettes. 'Bet you could do with a fag.'

For some reason, I couldn't stop myself from bursting into tears.

Days of Silence

I was taken by ambulance to East Grinstead, in Sussex, to the Archibald McIndoe Burns Unit, which had cared for so many young Spitfire pilots during World War Two. I spent six weeks there, recovering from my injuries, while August turned to September, and the sweltering heat of the summer became a memory.

My burns were mostly first-degree, although I needed a skin graft on the left side of my neck and two fingers on my left hand were permanently crooked. I broke my collar-bone, too, when I hit the water, and fractured three ribs.

It was a peaceful, almost dreamlike time. Out of my window I could see a red-tiled rooftop and the top of a large horse chestnut tree, with bright green conkers beginning to ripen on it. The sky seemed to be the same pale blue every day, as if it were a child's painting, rather than a real sky.

I had plenty of visitors, of course. Charles Frith came to see me two days after I was admitted, along with George Goodhew and a bespectacled woman from the Home Office, who said nothing at all but took pages of notes in Pitman's shorthand.

Charles Frith brought me a large box of Cadbury's Milk Tray chocolates, which he immediately opened and proceeded to eat.

'Hope you don't like coffee creams,' he said. 'They're my favourite.'

'No sign of Duca, I suppose?' I asked him.

Charles Frith picked out another chocolate and shook his head.

'We've had Royal Navy divers searching the whole area,' said George. 'They've even been diving as far away as Pilsey Island, where they found Commander Crabb.'

'Thanks to your efforts, Captain,' Charles Frith added, 'I think we can safely say that Mr Dorin Duca has had his chips. Not only that, we've tracked down three of your dead Screechers and given them polio jabs, too. Two in London and one in Birmingham.'

'Heads removed, bodies buried in consecrated ground?'

Charles Frith put his fingertip to his lips. 'The Health Minister is going to announce to the press tomorrow that the Korean Flu epidemic has been successfully contained.'

'Isn't that kind of premature? We still don't know how many *strigoi mortii* there might be.'

'True. But when we *do* find them, we know how to deal with them, don't we, thanks to you.' He stood up. 'By the way, the police dug up the back garden at the Laurels. They found poor old Dr Watkins, and his receptionist, and they found Professor Braithwaite, too, and his two assistants from the Royal Aircraft Establishment. All of them gutted like herring.'

He put another chocolate into his mouth, but promptly spat it into my waste basket. 'Ye gods! *Pah!* Turkish delight!'

On the afternoon of my third day in hospital, I phoned Jill. Her father answered, and he didn't sound at all pleased to hear from me.

'Jill's not here, Captain.'

'Is she OK?'

'I said, she's not here.'

'Well, can you ask her to call me, please? I'd really like to talk to her.'

'I'm sorry, old man, but I think you've already caused us enough trouble, don't you?'

He hung up. For a moment, I thought of calling back, but then I hung up, too.

I telephoned Louise every day, however, and on the third week she flew over from New York to see me. I was out in the hospital garden by then, in a wheelchair, with a thick plaid blanket wrapped around me. She came across the lawn carrying a large bunch of flowers and a shopping bag full of books.

Her hair was cut short and pixie-feathery, so that she looked even more like Audrey Hepburn than ever. She was wearing a smart lemon-yellow suit with white piping around it. She smelled of Chanel No. 5.

'I'm sorry,' I told her. 'You can't kiss me yet. Risk of infection.'

She sat down on the green-painted bench next to me. 'My God, Jim. Your poor face.'

'Don't worry, it's not so bad as it looks. My left hand got the worst of it.'

'Jean and Harold send you their best. So does Mo. When do you think you'll be able to come home?'

'Soon as the doctors give me the all-clear. Three or four weeks, not much longer.'

'I wish you could tell me what happened.'

I laid my bandaged right hand on her knee. 'I think it's better if you don't know. Sometimes ignorance is bliss.'

'You won't have to do this again, though?'

'No. But it's possible that I'm still at risk.'

She raised one of her perfectly plucked eyebrows. 'I don't understand. What kind of a risk?'

'Well . . . the people I was brought over here to deal with . . . they're not very good at forgiving and forgetting. I think we've managed to catch up with most of them, but there's always a chance that one or two of them might have slipped through the net.'

'Meaning what? That they're going to come after you?'

'Something like that.'

'Even in the States?'

'They don't give up easy, I'm afraid.'

'So what are you going to do?'

'Move, I'm afraid. Go live someplace else, under a different name.'

'*Move?* Are you serious? Where? I can't move . . . I have all my friends in New Milford. My work. Besides, I don't want to move. And I happen to *like* the name Falcon.'

'Sweetheart . . . these people are very, very dangerous.'

'So why did you agree to get mixed up in this at all? Didn't you spare one single thought for me?'

'I didn't have any choice. I'm sorry.'

'Oh – you're sorry? That makes it all right, then.'

Louise stayed all afternoon but I guess I already knew that our marriage had been torpedoed below the waterline. Louise lived for her social life – her dinner parties and her charity drives and her craft classes. She would never be able to tolerate a solitary existence in a strange city, under an assumed name, jumping every time the phone rang and checking every stranger who came knocking at our door.

But until I was sure that Duca's remains had been quartered and beheaded and buried in holy ground, and until I was sure that every other *strigoi mortii* had been hunted down and destroyed, I would always have to live with the fear that they would be trying to find me.

The living Screechers I was less concerned about. Without a dead Screecher to guide them, and to give them the final drink of blood they needed to become immortal, they would soon decay so much that they would be beyond any hope of transformation. Their bodies would eventually be discovered in cellars, and attics, and under railroad arches, so extensively decayed that nobody would ever realize that they had once been vampires.

Louise flew home five days later. She was still advised by my doctors not to kiss me, and it occurred to me that I might never kiss her again.

Napa, 1957

I returned to the States on November 22, leaving Heathrow Airport in a silvery-grey fog. With George Goodhew and Warrant Officer Tim Headley I had tracked down only two more *strigoi mortii* – one close to Oxford and the other in Swindon – but I was pretty sure that we had now caught all of them. There had been six or seven more outbreaks of 'Korean Flu' in the London suburbs, but as far as I could tell these were the last desperate feeding frenzies of the few live Screechers who were left. After Guy Fawkes' Day, on November 5, there were no more reported killings.

Charles Frith came to the airport himself to see me off. He wore a grey suit and tan leather gloves. 'I want you to know that we deeply appreciate what you've managed to do for us, Captain. It's a great pity that ah. We can never give you the public credit you so richly deserve.'

George had been carrying my Kit for me and when I reached the gate he handed it over. 'Let's hope you won't be needing this again.'

'Thanks, George. Let's hope so.'

I returned to New Milford but when I arrived the house was empty. Louise was in Boston, visiting her sister. I was pretty sure that she had timed the trip deliberately, so that she wouldn't have to welcome me home, but I didn't have any proof of it.

I had been back less than a day when I was visited by the two counterintelligence officers from Fort Holabird who had first briefed me on my mission to London – the one with the sandy hair and the one with the Clark Kent spectacles.

They came into the house with their caps tucked under their arms.

'We've received a very positive report back from MI6,' said the sandy-haired officer. 'This little operation has done great things for our relationship with British intelligence.'

'Well, I'm glad to hear that I wasn't half-cremated for nothing.'

'You won't be staying here for very much longer?'

'I need to pack some things, make some arrangements. Talk to my wife.'

The officer in the heavy-rimmed eyeglasses looked around the room and said, 'Expect you'll be sorry to leave. But we've fixed you and your wife up with a very pleasant home in Louisville.'

'Louisville, Kentucky?'

'That's the one. A four-bedroom house with an orchard in back. And we can handle all the moving for you.'

'Why the hell would I want to live in Louisville, Kentucky?'

'Because . . . it's a very friendly city. And it's very central. And that's where they invented the Hot Brown sandwich. And . . . who's going to think of looking for you there, of all places?'

Louise refused to come with me. I can't say that I blamed her, but she put me into an impossible position. If I stayed in New Milford with her, there was always the possibility that one of the *strigoi mortii* would find me, and kill me, and kill her, too, and I couldn't expose her to a danger like that, especially since I wasn't even allowed to tell her what the danger was.

We said a very polite goodbye, almost as if we scarcely knew each other. I took my Kit and a single suitcase and climbed into my car. There was a fresh breeze blowing and the street was filled with whirling storms of red and yellow leaves.

Louise came out of the house and I wound down the car window. 'I'll call when I get there,' I told her.

She nodded, but said nothing.

'You know that I haven't stopped loving you, don't you?'

'Love doesn't mean anything without trust, Jim.'

'I'm sorry. I never wanted to have a double life. I just wanted to spend all of my time with you.'

'You can't, though, can you?'

'No,' I admitted.

I sat there for a little while longer. Louise started to shiver, so I started up the engine and said, 'I'll be seeing you, sweet-heart.'

'No you won't.'

At Christmas I flew out to San Diego to see my father. Earlier that year he had sold the house in Mill Valley and moved south to Rancho Santa Fe, a small retirement community in the hills near Escondido. It was very quiet here, and the weather was always warm, and there was a strong fragrance of euca-lyptus in the air.

He lived in a small Spanish-style cottage with a walled garden filled with flowers. He was white-haired now, but the sunshine and the gentle lifestyle had been kind to him. We sat on the red-tiled veranda on Christmas morning, drinking champagne and orange juice.

'You don't want to get the sun on those burns of yours,' he cautioned me.

'They're healing, Dad. Don't worry about it.'

'Still can't tell me what happened?'

'Secret stuff. Sorry.'

'Goddamned oppressive interfering government. If a son can't even tell his own father how he ended up with burns all over his mush . . .'

'Just like you never told me the truth about what happened to Mom.'

He looked at me over his half-glasses. 'You know about that?'

I nodded. 'Let's just put it this way . . . what I was doing in England, that was connected with that. And a debt got repaid. That's all I can tell you.'

'I see. Well, as a matter of fact, I don't see.'

He sipped his champagne and orange juice for a while. Then without another word he got up from his chair and went into the living room. It was cool in there, with a draft that stirred the zigzag-patterned drapes. Most of the ornaments and pictures were familiar to me from the house in Mill Valley, although there were quite a few photographs that I didn't recognize.

Dad sat down at the piano and started to play.

'"*Who made doina?*
The small mouth of a baby

201

Left asleep by his mother
Who found him singing the doina."

Remember that one? Your mother loved that one.'

On top of the piano stood a framed photograph of a handsome-looking woman in a smartly pressed US Army uniform. One hand was raised to shield her eyes from the sun. The other was holding the collar of a glossy-looking bloodhound.

'Who's this?' I asked my father.

He carried on playing – very softly, his wrinkled hands barely touching the keys, as if he were remembering the music in his mind, rather than listening to it. 'That? That's Margot Kettner. Friend of your mom's, during the war.'

'That's a bloodhound. A man-trailer.'

'Really? I wouldn't know. All I know is, Margot Kettner and your mom, they were very close.'

'I never heard her mention any Margot Kettner.'

'More than likely you weren't listening.'

I put the photograph back on top of the piano. 'No, Dad, you're right. I probably wasn't. You know me.'

A Postcard from England, 1961

I settled down in Kenwood Hill, Louisville, under the name William Crowe. They gave me a new social-security number and a new bank account and even a new passport. I started up a freelance business consultancy, pretty much along the lines of the work I had been doing before I was sent to England.

I made friends, I joined a couple of local charities, I played golf at Quail Chase. I dated a few women, and with one of them (a vivacious redhead called Mandy Ridgway) I had a long and serious relationship that almost went as far as marriage. Somehow, though, I could never bring myself to make the commitment. Every time I thought about marriage I thought about my Kit, lying on the top shelf of my bedroom closet, and the possibility that I might be called on to use it again.

'There's something you're not telling me,' said Mandy, one September evening in 1961, as we sat in Stan's Fish Sandwich on Lexington Road, eating rolled oysters.

'What do you mean?'

'It's always like there's something on your mind. Something private. Something that's worrying you.'

'Such as what?'

'You tell me. But wherever we go, you're always looking around you, like you're checking everybody out. Look – you're doing it now. You're not looking at me, you're looking over my shoulder.'

'Sorry. It's a bad habit, that's all. Guess I'm just nosey.'

She reached across the table and held my hand. 'There's something else, too. A couple of times lately you've been talking in your sleep.'

'Oh, really? Don't tell me I've been calling out another woman's name.'

'Not unless "Duca" is a woman.'

The next morning, I opened up my mailbox and found a plain yellow envelope in it, postmarked Washington, DC. Inside was a compliments slip from MI6 in London, and a picture postcard of Nelson's Column in Trafalgar Square, with an improbably blue sky.

The postcard was dated June 12, 1961, so it had taken nearly three months to reach me. Presumably it had been vetted by MI6 and then by US counterintelligence before it had been decided that it was harmless, and that they could send it on.

The writing was loopy, in smudged purple ink. *'Dear Jim, Even after all this time I still think of you. I am so sorry for the way things turned out. Poor Bullet died late last year. I would love to know how you are. Yours, Jill.'*

I felt as if I had been punched in the stomach, very hard. I sat down at the kitchen table just as Mandy came in, tightening the belt of her robe. 'Jim? Are you OK?'

'Sure. I'm fine.'

'I was thinking maybe we could go to Shakertown today. You've never been, have you? It's really fascinating. Actually,

I have an unnatural craving for a slice of their lemon pie. I hope I'm not pregnant.'

'Not today, Mandy, OK? Something just came up.'

She came over and sat on my lap and kissed my ear. 'I certainly hope so,' she said, suggestively.

It was Jill herself who opened the front door. Her hair was different, flicked up like a tulip, and she was wearing a tight white sweater and a russet-coloured tweed skirt. She looked even more beautiful than I had remembered her – dark-skinned, with those dark feline eyes, and those full, suggestive lips.

'*Jim!*' she said, in total shock, and clapped her hand to her mouth.

'Hey, I got your postcard,' I told her, holding it up. 'I thought of writing back – but then I thought – nah, I'll come over to see you instead.'

She rushed out of the doorway and threw her arms around me and kissed me. I felt like I was in one of those ridiculously romantic TV commercials. But she felt so good, and she smelled so good, and she seemed to be so delighted to see me, that I really didn't care.

'Oh God,' she said. 'I thought I was never going to see you again.'

'Oh, yeah? I hope you didn't think you could keep me away that easy.'

'Why don't you come inside? Mummy and Daddy are both out for the day. When did you arrive?'

I followed her into the house. Outside the living-room window, a gardener was raking up beech leaves from the lawn and burning them on a bonfire. There was a melancholy smell of smoke in the air.

'Would you like a cup of tea? Or a drink, perhaps?'

I took hold of her hands and looked at her. I couldn't believe how gorgeous she was. What's more, I couldn't believe how excited she was to see me, after more than four years. After all, I was forty-three now, while she couldn't have been much older than thirty-one.

'I could murder a beer, if you have any beer.'

'I think Daddy's got some Mackeson's.'

We sat together on one of the flowery-covered couches.

'Are you still married?' she asked me. 'You're not wearing a wedding ring.'

I told her about Louise, and she nodded seriously. 'I'm so sorry,' she said. 'But maybe it was all for the best.'

'Maybe. What about you? Nobody swept you off your feet yet?'

'Not the way that you did.'

'I'm flattered.'

'I'm not flattering you, I'm telling you the truth. I've never been able to get you out of my mind.'

I sipped my stout. There was something in her intonation that made me think: *This isn't just about sexual attraction. This is something more.*

'I suppose there was some unfinished business between us,' I said, warily. 'A few loose ends that needed to be tied up.'

'I know what happened to Duca,' she said.

'So they told you.'

She reached out and gently stroked the twisted burns on the left side of my neck. 'You were very brave,' she said. 'There aren't many men who would have the courage to face up to a creature like that.'

I didn't say anything, but watched her eyes.

'You're different from other men. That's why I couldn't forget you. That night we slept together . . . I *felt* it. And then, when I saw you and Duca together . . . '

'What happened, Jill? What happened that day in the surgery? What did Duca do to you?'

She turned her face away, in profile. 'Nothing. He didn't do anything. *It* didn't do anything.'

'But afterward, you were dizzy, and you were sick. Duca must have done something. Did it cut you? Did it scratch you? Did it inject you with any of its blood?'

'I was frightened, that's all. I was suffering from shock. I didn't have any experience of Screechers, not like you. I simply couldn't take any more.'

'OK,' I reassured her. 'I'm sorry. I didn't mean to give you the third degree. It was just that I was worried about you.'

'I know,' she said. 'But you didn't have to worry. And you don't have to worry now, ever again.'

* * *

I stayed in England for another five weeks. Jill and I saw each other nearly every day. We went walking in the parks, we visited the National Gallery, we sat in pubs talking to each other as if it would take a whole lifetime of talking for us to catch up.

We made love, in my hotel room, with the grey afternoon light falling through the net curtains, and the sheets twisted beneath us. Afterward she would lie next to me and stroke my back with her fingertips, so lightly that my nerve endings tingled. I could have stared at her all day, with her broad, angular shoulders, and her huge rounded breasts, and her nipples that crinkled like raisins.

One morning, though, I realized that this couldn't continue. It was a dream, not reality, and I couldn't ask her to spend the rest of her life in a dream.

'I have to go back to the States,' I said.

'That's all right. I'll come with you.'

'You can't. I'm sorry.'

'But why not? I want to stay with you for ever!'

'You can't, Jill. It's too dangerous. You shouldn't even be here with me now.'

'But you destroyed all the Screechers, didn't you?'

'Maybe I did. Maybe I didn't. One thing's for sure – I didn't manage to dispose of Duca's body. Not only that, Duca went into the harbour, and Screechers are always revived by water. The Belgian resistance made that mistake during World War Two. They shot Screechers and threw them into the River Scheldt. They might just as well have given them the kiss of life.'

Jill sat up, naked, and put her arms around me. 'I'm not frightened. I want to come with you.'

I looked at her closely. She was absolutely flawless, and I was in love with her.

'All right,' I said, at last. 'So long as you know what the risks are.'

The Face In The Mirror

We were married at Kenwood Heights Christian Church on Saturday, April 28, 1962. It was a bright, warm day, and pink cherry blossom blew over us as we left the church.

I saw a man in a long dark coat standing on the opposite side of the street as we climbed into the wedding car. His face was white and he looked strangely two-dimensional, more like a black-and-white photograph than a real person. I looked at him and he looked back at me, but there was no way of telling if he was a Screecher or nothing more than a curious passer-by. But who wears a winter overcoat, on an April afternoon, in Louisville?

The years came and went, and we lived the kind of life that most everybody lives in Louisville – playing golf, eating out at Mike Linnig's Place, going to Churchill Downs in May and betting against the crowd. I was William Crowe and Jill was Jill Crowe and we were happy. We bought a black Labrador and called him Ricochet.

In March, 1965, Jill gave birth to Mark. He was a quiet, introspective boy who always preferred playing on his own, but he was very clever, and by the time he was eleven years old he could play the piano as well as his grandfather.

I'll never forget, though, that summer morning in 1977 when he came into my study and stood there for a long time, saying nothing, and the way that the sun shone red through his ears reminded me of Ann De Wouters' little boy, kneeling in front of the window in Antwerp, all those years before.

He looked so much like Jill – dark-haired and almost too pretty, for a boy.

'What am I?' he asked me. Not '*who* am I?' but '*what* am I?'

I looked up from the papers on my desk and smiled at him in amusement. 'You're a twelve-year-old boy. Haven't you looked in the mirror lately?'

'No, but what am I?'

I leaned back in my chair. 'You're an American. But you're part Burmese, and part Romanian, and part Irish.'

'I feel as if I'm something else.'

'Something else like what?'

'I don't know. That's why I'm asking you.'

'Well, tell me what it's like, this feeling.'

He frowned. 'It's like being alone. It's like being different. It's like being inside somebody else's head.'

I ruffled his hair. 'You're growing up, that's all. You're a boy now, but there's a young man inside you, trying to get out.'

But I remembered his words three years later. It was just past 11:00 in the evening. I was sitting in the armchair in the corner of our bedroom, trying to finish the cryptic crossword that I had started earlier that day, and cooling off after my shower. Jill was sitting in front of her dressing table brushing her hair.

'Do you know what I'd like to do for my birthday this year?' she asked me. 'I'd like to go to Mexico.'

'You know I hate Mexican food. All those beans. All those burritos.'

'Molly and David went to Mexico and they loved it.'

'OK,' I said, dropping my newspaper on the floor and standing up behind her. 'If you want to go to Mexico, we'll go to goddamned Mexico.'

I kissed her on top of her head. But it was then that I thought: she's going to be forty-nine years old next birthday. Forty-nine years old and she doesn't have a single grey hair or a single line on her forehead. In fact, she looks exactly the same as she did when I flew back to England in 1961, eighteen years ago.

'What's the matter?' she said, looking at me in her dressing table mirror. 'You look like something's bothering you.'

'Nothing, no.' But then I thought: her figure is just the same, too. She has no cellulite on her thighs, her stomach is flat, her breasts are still big and firm. I had seen men turning around to look at her in the street, and I had always taken it for granted that they were looking at her because she was so attractive. But supposing they were wondering what a woman who had the face and the figure of a thirty-one-year-old was doing with a grey-haired man of sixty-one?

For the next few days, I couldn't stop thinking about it. I hated myself for being so disloyal, but the thought wouldn't leave me alone.

'Something's wrong, isn't it?' she asked me, over breakfast. 'You don't have money worries you're not telling me about, do you?'

'No, no. Everything's fine.'

'But you've hardly spoken to me for the past two days, and you keep staring at me in this really strange way. It's almost like you've forgotten who I am.'

I haven't forgotten who you are, I thought. *Maybe I never knew who you were to begin with.*

I went upstairs, opened up my bedroom closet, and took down my Kit. I looked at it for a long time before I opened it up. I loved Jill so much and this was an act of betrayal, no matter what I found out. But I had to know for sure, or else I was going to spend the rest of my life wondering what I was sharing my bed with.

She was still sitting at the kitchen table when I came down, holding a cup of coffee in both hands, watching television. The sun was shining on her hair and on her pink satin robe. She looked so beautiful that I almost went straight back upstairs, without doing what I had come down to do.

'Bill?' she said. She always called me 'Bill' in case she accidentally slipped up and called me 'Jim' in front of our friends. 'Come and take a look at this.'

'Hold on,' I told her. I stood to one side of the kitchen door and held up the pure silver mirror that I had taken out of my Kit. My hand was trembling so much that at first I couldn't focus properly. But then I steadied it against the door frame, and angled it so that I could see Jill's profile.

It took only a split-second glance to tell me what I needed to know. The woman sitting at the kitchen table had hair that was streaked with grey. There were wrinkles around her eyes, and her hands were patterned with liver spots.

I came into the kitchen and sat down next to her. 'This is hilarious,' she said. 'This woman thinks that her husband is

209

having an affair with another woman, but all the time—'

She stopped, and stared at me. 'Jim?' she said. 'Jim, what's happened? You look terrible.'

'I had to find out sooner or later, didn't I?' I told her. My throat was constricted, and I found it very difficult to speak.

'I don't know what you're talking about. You had to find out *what*?'

'Come on, Jill, how much longer did you think you could keep it from me? You're going to be fifty in a couple of years. What happens when you get to sixty, and you still look just as young as you do now?'

She lowered her coffee cup. 'I couldn't tell you. I tried to, lots of times. But I love you, Jim. I knew what you would do if I told you.'

'What did Duca do to you?' I asked her.

Her eyes filled with tears. 'Can't we just go on like we are? Can't we just pretend?'

'Tell me what Duca did to you.'

'Jim – think about Mark. Please. Think about us. We can still be happy, can't we?'

I stood up and went to the window. Next door, Fred Nordstrom was lathering his new green Buick Electra. He saw me and waved his soapy sponge.

Jill said, 'It asked me to lie on the couch. It stood next to me, and at first I didn't think it was going to do anything. It just talked to me, very quietly. I don't even remember what it said.'

'Then what?'

'Jim, please! There was nothing I could do to stop it!'

I turned around. 'I know,' I told her. 'It was all my fault, not yours. I shouldn't have expected you to do it.'

I tore off a sheet of kitchen tissue and handed it to her, so that she could wipe her eyes.

'I felt as if I didn't have any willpower at all. I was lying there and I simply couldn't move. I wasn't unconscious or anything. I simply couldn't make my muscles work.'

'It's a form of hypnosis,' I said. 'Some Screechers use it to stop their victims from resisting them. If you practise it for as long as Duca must have been practising it, I guess you can make a person do whatever you want.'

'It opened up its pants. It was hard, and I was sure that it was going to rape me. I tried to call you, but I couldn't make my voice work.'

I closed my eyes for a moment. I was dreading to hear what she was going to say next.

'Duca picked up a scalpel. He showed it to me, held it right in front of my face, and it was smiling. Then it sliced the end of its penis, right across. All this blood came spurting out. Duca held its penis over my lips so that the blood dripped into my mouth.'

She wiped her mouth with the back of her hand, as if she could still taste it. 'That was when it heard you upstairs, and it stopped.'

I pulled out one of the kitchen chairs and sat down next to her. I didn't take her hand. 'Why didn't you tell me at the time?'

'I don't know. I was very confused. I was ashamed, too. I thought it was disgusting, what Duca had done to me. But I hadn't resisted it, had I? I didn't want you to think that I might have encouraged it.'

'But you began to change?'

Jill nodded. 'I tried so hard to fight it. I needed to drink blood so badly, I felt as if my throat was on fire. I could feel what was happening inside my own body, too. I hated myself. I hated the way I was starting to smell. I hated the way I looked. I pretended that I was sick so that I could stay in my room. You don't know how much willpower it took not to kill my own parents.

'Then Duca came for me. It said that it had to get away from England, because you were coming after it. It wanted to go to America, because it had a score to settle. I don't know what score. It never said.'

'So you went with it?'

'It promised me blood, Jim. I was worse than a drug addict, how could I say no?'

'So you and Duca . . . you killed somebody, and drank their blood?'

'No. It was going to kill a young woman who was waiting at a bus stop, but I wouldn't let it. I was burning for blood but I couldn't let it take an innocent woman's life, not for me. I drank some of Duca's blood instead, and that's why I am what I am. I'm never going to grow any older, Jim.'

'You're not immortal, Jill. You're dead. The only difference is, you're dead but you won't lie down.'

'Don't you think I know that? I love you, Jim, but I'm going to have to watch you grow older right in front of my eyes! One day I'm going to have to bury you!'

I took a deep breath. This was a nightmare. Jill didn't look any different. I couldn't stop myself from loving her. But she wasn't 'her' any more. She was 'it'. She was a thing, rather than a person.

'Jim,' she pleaded. 'Please try to forgive me. You could be the same. You could live for ever, too.'

'You want *me* to become a Screecher? Are you out of your mind?'

'So what are you going to do? Cut off my head, chop me into bits, and bury my body?'

'I don't know. I don't know what the hell I'm going to do.'

'Jim, please!'

'You're a *strigoaica*, Jill. How can I pretend that you're human?'

'Because you love me. Because I love you.'

I pushed my chair back and stood up. 'If you're a *strigoaica*, you need to drink human blood at least once a month, don't you, or you'll start to lose those perfect looks?'

'Jim—'

'Come on, Jill. Whose blood have you been drinking?'

'Nobody that matters, I promise you.'

'Nobody that matters? What the hell do you mean, "nobody that matters"?'

'Derelicts, down-and-outs, mostly from southern Indiana. People that nobody's going to miss. And nobody *has* missed them, Jim. Ever. Did you ever see a story in the papers about them? Did you ever see them mentioned on TV?'

'Christ, Jill, we're talking about twelve people a year for eighteen years! That's a massacre!'

'I have to, Jim! I can't stop! But *strigoaica* . . . we're not like *strigoi*. We don't have the same need to spread the infection. We just want to be normal. We just want to be loved.'

I looked at her, and she looked so desperate and so miserable. Who would have thought that I could love a Screecher? Me, of all people, the bane of Screechers everywhere.

'I'm going out,' I told her. 'I need some time to think.'

The Sacred Seal

I took Ricochet for a walk around the Scenic Loop at Cherokee Park. It was a warm, gusty afternoon, and kites of all shapes and sizes were flying from Hill One. They reminded me of that Japanese print of people being caught in a sudden gale, with papers flying in the air, and their whole lives suddenly being turned into chaos, as mine had been.

Jill was a *strigoaica*. I wondered if I had ever suspected it before, and deliberately ignored it. But it really didn't matter. What did matter was that I was morally obliged to do something. She would have to kill more people to satisfy her endless thirst for blood, and even if they were derelicts or drunks or down-and-outs that nobody else would miss, they were human lives, and I couldn't allow her to take them.

But I loved her. I had loved her from the moment I had first seen her, in St Augustine's Avenue, in Croydon, on that hot summer day in 1957. So how could I drive nails into her eyes, and cut off her head, and dismember her? I couldn't even ask anybody else to do it.

I sat down on a bench and Ricochet came up and laid his head on my knees, as if he understood what I was going through. He was so much like Bullet, except for a tiny tan-coloured smudge between his eyes.

'Goddamnit, Ric,' I told him. 'If it hadn't been for Duca—'

It was then that I thought: *Duca was caught by my mother, but she didn't kill it. She had sealed it into a casket, and if that plane hadn't crashed, Duca might still be preserved today. Not destroyed, not dismembered, but rendered harmless.*

Maybe I could do the same to Jill. Seal her away, so that she wouldn't kill anybody else. Then maybe I could find a way to bring her back to life, as a human being. But how was I going to do it? Only my mother had known how.

I stood up. The kites were whirling in the wind. 'Come on, Ric,' I told him. 'I think I need to go to San Diego.'

Who Made Doina?

I flew to San Diego the next day. I told Jill that I wanted to talk to my father. After all, he was eighty-three now, and suffering from a heart condition. I didn't tell her that I was going to look for something that my mother may have left behind – a note, a book, a diary entry – anything that might have told me how to seal away a *strigoaica*.

Before I left, she took hold of my hand and tried to kiss me.

'I'm so sorry,' she said.

'You can't blame yourself. You didn't know what you were getting into, and I used you. I'm the one who should be saying sorry.'

In the hallway, with the light shining on us like two blood-shot eyes, we held each other close. God almighty, she didn't feel any different. She didn't feel dead. She was warm and soft and my heart felt as if it were crumbling apart.

'Jill,' I said, stroking her hair.

'Come back soon,' she said, and she tried to kiss me. But I couldn't help thinking of all the people she had cut open, and whose blood she had drunk, warm and sickly, straight from their pumping hearts.

'Sure,' I said, and left her.

I paid off the cab and stood outside my father's house with my overnight bag. It was a warm, fragrant afternoon, and the sunlight was very bright. I was beginning to feel very tired, so that everything looked almost too vivid to be true, as if I had been smoking pot.

I was about to open the gate which led into my father's garden when I heard a woman singing. I stopped, and listened, and gradually I felt a terrible coldness soak through me. It was a sweet, high voice. A voice I hadn't heard in a very long time.

'Who made doina?
The small mouth of a baby
Left asleep by his mother
Who found him singing the doina.'

I opened the gate. My father was sitting on the veranda, with a glass of white wine. On the other side of the yard, my mother was cutting roses.

She stopped singing, and dropped all the roses on to the terracotta tiles. Her hair was dark and she looked exactly the same as the last time that I had seen her.

'*James*,' she said.

She picked up the photograph from the top of the piano, and smiled at it sadly. 'Poor Margot. When the plane crashed, I tried to get her out, but her leg was caught under the seat. Of course *I* got out. I couldn't die, even if I was trapped in that plane for the next hundred years.'

My father stood on the opposite side of the room, saying nothing.

'Don't blame your father,' said my mother. 'Love can make us blind to other people's suffering. Love can make us very selfish, and cruel.'

I shook my head. 'So it was you that Duca was after, when it tried to sail to America. Duca knew that it wasn't your body in that airplane.'

My mother nodded. 'It may be looking for me still.'

'And if it finds you?'

'If it survived, and it manages to find any of us, then I'm afraid we have a very horrible experience waiting for us.'

I didn't know what else to say. My mother came up to me and held out her hands, but I couldn't take them.

'I have your watch,' I told her. 'I'll make sure you get it back.'

So now you know the truth. Now you know what really happened during that summer of 1957, in South London, and now you know what happened afterward.

Now you know that when your great-grandfather first went

215

to Romania, and fell in love with your great-grandmother, and decided to marry her, he was quite aware of what she was, and he was also aware of the price that other people would have to pay to keep her perfect for all eternity.

Now you know what blood runs in my veins, and why I was capable of being so heartless in my pursuit of Screechers, and so cruel when I finally caught up with them. I have Screecher blood in me too, as your father does, and you do.

In spite of our cruelty, though, we're deeply sentimental, which is why your great-grandfather could never destroy my mother, or seal her away; and which is why I could never bring myself to destroy your grandmother, although she still lies in the cellar, in a lead casket, bound by the seals and rituals which my mother was taught in her childhood.

I don't know for sure if Duca is still walking this earth, looking for me, and looking for your grandmother. But vampires never forgive, and they never forget, and you should keep your eyes open for men and women with pale faces, and you should tightly close all of your windows at night.

I am old now, James, and I cannot protect you any longer. One day soon you will inherit my house and you will also inherit the casket that lies in the cellar. I could never bring myself to destroy the woman I loved, and I am sorry that I have left you such a legacy. But whatever you decide to do, always remember that I loved you.